Eternal

ALSO BY
Gillian Shields

Immortal

Betrayal

GILLIAN SHIELDS

Eternal

KATHERINE TEGEN BOOKS
An Imprint of HarperCollins Publishers

Katherine Tegen Books is an imprint of HarperCollins Publishers.

Eternal

Library of Congress Cataloging-in-Publication Data
Shields, Gillian.
Eternal / by Gillian Shields.—1st ed.
p.   cm.
Summary: When Sarah, Evie, and Helen see that the horrors
surrounding Wyldcliffe Abbey School are not over, Sarah tries to
continue working in the background, being strong and good for others,
but finds herself thrust into prominence as evil surfaces again.
ISBN 978-0-06-200039-2
[1. Boarding schools—Fiction. 2. Supernatural—Fiction.
3. Friendship—Fiction. 4. Witches—Fiction. 5. Love—Fiction.
6. Schools—Fiction. 7. England—Fiction.] I. Title.
PZ7.S55478Ete 2011   2010027773
[Fic]—dc22

Typography by Amy Ryan
11 12 13 14 15 LP/RRDB   10 9 8 7 6 5 4 3 2 1

First Edition

for Sarah Massini

It is the eternal struggle between these two principles—right and wrong.

—*Abraham Lincoln*

And many of them that sleep in the dust of the earth shall awake...

—*Daniel 12:2*

Prologue

I am not like Evie. I don't belong in some great romance. I'm just the best friend in the background. Always there, always reliable, down-to-earth. Good old Sarah. That's how it's always been. Until now.

Now I have to make the hardest decision of my life. To go on or to go back.

I am standing on the hillside above Wyldcliffe. The sun is setting over the wide, wild land. I love this place. I love the wind on my face, and the high call of the birds, and the deep life and history of these ancient hills. The rocks that lie like bones underneath the heather and gorse speak to me of power and strength and eternity.

When all this began, I thought I could be like those rocks: a backbone of strength for everyone else. "Good old Sarah, she can cope with anything." I have discovered, though, that I am weak. It turns out that I don't just want to tend and nurture the needs of others. I have feelings too—and failings. I love. I hate. I feel anger. And what I feel frightens me. It might stop me from doing what I have to do.

The sun has almost gone now. Night begins to spread over the moors. Out there, in the land that I love, Evie is lost. She has been taken by the enemy and is a prisoner in the still and secret earth. Only I can save her. It is my turn to act.

Where is my courage now? Where is my strength? What shall I do?

There are no answers. The day is over. I have to choose. I begin to walk down the hill, under the dark sky, and into the valley that is called Death.

One

I hadn't been expecting this. In all the chaos and uncertainty of the last few months I had learned to accept many strange things, and I guess I had thought that nothing would ever surprise me again.

But this was something else.

Velvet Romaine.

I'd heard of her, of course. Everyone's heard of Velvet Romaine. The lurid details of her first sixteen years have been splashed across every tabloid newspaper. It's just that I didn't expect her to turn up at Wyldcliffe Abbey School for Young Ladies. Wyldcliffe isn't the kind of school that attracts the daughters of rock stars. The daughters of duchesses, maybe, but not a flashy wild-child rebel like Velvet. But there she was, when I arrived at the school on the first day of the summer term, and she was making a sensation. Her huge limo had pulled up outside the school's imposing Gothic building, and as she stepped out she was surrounded by a crowd of excited students and a gaggle of paparazzi. The photographers snapped away eagerly and Velvet stood there lapping up the attention, dressed as though she was ready for a hot date in some sleazy nightclub.

But I don't want to sound judgmental. Hey, this is me, Sarah Fitzalan, the earth mother type, got a kind word for everyone, always looking for the positive, always ready to defend the underdog. That's what they say, anyway.

I had been so desperate to get back to school. Not that I'm some academic genius or anything. It wasn't my studies that were pulling me back to the remote valley where Wyldcliffe lies hidden. It wasn't the spell of the wild moors either, where the gorse and cowslips would be in bloom. The awakening earth called to me, but I turned my face from the hills and thought of nothing but seeing Evie and Helen again.

You know how people say about their friends, oh, we're so close we could be sisters? Well, Evie and Helen and I really are sisters. Not related by blood, but by deeper ties. Mystic, elemental forces bind us together, in this life and the next. Sounds stupid, but I've always believed there are things in life that we don't understand, that maybe we can't see, but they exist all the same. The feel of a place, an atmosphere, premonitions, and prophecies—I think all that means something. I believe that the soul is eternal and that the spirits of the dead can speak to us. And so when Evie first arrived at Wyldcliffe as a lonely scholarship student and started seeing visions of a girl from the past, I didn't call her crazy. I believed her. I accepted what was going on, and everything that followed.

How the girl was Lady Agnes Templeton, Evie's distant ancestor. How, more than a hundred years ago, Agnes had discovered the secrets of the Mystic Way and had become a servant of the sacred fire. How Agnes's former admirer, Sebastian Fairfax, was the same person as the mysterious young man that Evie was secretly seeing. How Sebastian had become trapped in a futile quest for immortality. How we had discovered our own elemental powers—water for Evie, air for Helen, earth for me—and used them to save Sebastian's soul. And how, finally, Sebastian had passed from this life and left Evie grieving for an impossible love.

All things considered, we had a lot to talk about. We had faced death together. Evie had lost her first love and Helen had lost her mother, and I had been desperately sad for them both. As usual I had put all my energy into trying to understand and sympathize with and care for my friends, but to tell the truth, when I'd said good-bye to them at the end of term and gone home for the holidays, I had felt lost and uprooted without them. It was as if I didn't exist without Evie and Helen and their problems, as though I were just wandering about on the edge of the story of my life. Sarah the kind one, the supportive one— but if there was no one to support, what was I supposed to do?

And then the dreams had started.

It was the same thing, night after night. I was in an underground cave. Torches were burning in the shadows. Someone was near me. His eyes met mine. It was someone who knew me, right the way through. Someone I had no secrets from. Someone who loved me. Not for being good or strong, but just for being me, all of me, good and bad. I reached up to kiss him, my heart and lips yearning. And then I was chilled by an indescribable feeling of horror. The face turned into a wizened mask. There was a knife. I was in pain. Thick smoke swirled around me. There was chanting and singing and the sound of drums; drumming, drumming, drumming in my head until I thought I would go insane.

Perhaps it was simply a reaction to everything I had been through with Evie and Helen, but I believed it was an omen, a sign of more danger to come. Whatever the truth of it, dreams and darkness were pulling me back to Wyldcliffe, and I was longing to see my friends. So I really wasn't too pleased when the circus surrounding Velvet Romaine seemed to be bringing the whole place to a grinding halt.

There she was, posing next to her over-the-top car as the photographers screamed, "Velvet! This way! Give us a smile!" She wasn't smiling, though. She looked furious. Her hair was jet-black, cut into a Louise Brooks–style bob, and she exuded the same kind of dangerous sexiness as the classic screen star. Her short skirt showed off slim legs, torn fishnet stockings, and expensive-looking black lace-up boots. All the other Wyldcliffe girls, who were staring with disbelief, were wearing the old-fashioned red and gray school uniform. I wondered what Velvet would look like when the Wyldcliffe teachers, or mistresses, made her get rid of her designer clothes and her heavy eyeliner and goth lipstick. But right now she was making the most of her grand entrance as she pouted for the photographers, sultry and rebellious. Whatever Wyldcliffe's past secrets were, it had never seen anything like this before.

As I watched Velvet, she reminded me of a cornered animal putting up a defiant last stand, ready to lash out at anything and anyone who got in her way.

"Is that really her?" a girl from my class, Camilla Willoughby-Stuart, whispered excitedly at my side. "Velvet Romaine?"

"It looks like it."

"What is she doing here? Doesn't she live in L.A. or somewhere like that? She'll be bored to death at Wyldcliffe. I mean, she goes to these amazing parties with actors and musicians and rock stars. I've read about her in all the magazines. Didn't she go to rehab when she was only thirteen? And last year she ran off with some guy twice her age. . . ."

Other stories about Velvet Romaine flashed into my mind. Despite her money and glamour, she'd already met with tragedy in her short life. I recalled that she'd been in a car crash where her younger sister had been killed, and then there had been some incident about a fire at her last boarding school—I couldn't quite remember what had happened. I usually read magazines about horse riding, not celebrity gossip. But Camilla seemed to know all about her.

"Ooh, it must have been awful for Velvet at L'École des

Montagnes," she rattled on. "It's a fantastic school in the Swiss Alps—all the European royals go there—but her best friend was scarred for life after that fire they had. No wonder she didn't want to stay there. But why come to Wyldcliffe? It's far too quiet for someone like Velvet Romaine!"

"Perhaps that's why her parents want her to come here," I said. "You know—order, purpose, discipline, and all the rest. Old-fashioned values."

Camilla grimaced. "She's going to hate it. Have you seen her clothes? She looks so amazing. I wish my mom would let me have some boots like that. . . ."

As Camilla chattered away, a woman with a plain face and scraped-back hairstyle opened the school's massive oak door and came out to stand on the step next to Velvet. It was Miss Scratton, our history teacher. She addressed the photographers coldly.

"This is private property. If you don't leave immediately, I shall call the police. Please respect the fact that this is a school and a place of learning." She turned to Velvet. "I am Miss Scratton, the new High Mistress of Wyldcliffe. I want to welcome you to the Abbey, but let's go somewhere more private. Girls, what are you all doing hanging about here with your mouths open like goldfish?

Most undignified. I'm sure you all have plenty to do to unpack and settle down before classes start tomorrow." The gaping students reluctantly moved away, and Miss Scratton beckoned me over. "Sarah, could you please stay a moment?" She smiled faintly. "You are just the person I was looking for. You can help show Velvet around."

Velvet flicked a snooty stare at me, as though I were some kind of servant. My heart sank. Normally I was only too happy to help new students, but she was giving off such a hostile attitude, like she could read my thoughts and didn't think much of them. If Miss Scratton wanted me to be friendly with Velvet Romaine, I would try my best, but I was desperate to see my real friends as soon as I could. I looked around uneasily. "Um . . . I was looking for—"

"For Evie and Helen?" Again there was a faint gleam of sympathy in Miss Scratton's sharp black eyes. "They haven't arrived yet. I believe they are traveling to Wyldcliffe together on the train. You'll see them soon enough. Come, both of you. Follow me!"

There was more clamor and flurry from the photographers as we followed Miss Scratton through the heavy door. She closed it firmly behind us, and I found myself in the familiar entrance hall. The somber black-and-white tiles, the grand marble staircase, and the stone hearth were exactly as they had always been, but then I gasped in surprise. For a moment I thought that Evie was staring at me across the hallway like a ghost. The face of a girl with starry gray eyes and long red hair seemed to float in front of my eyes in the gloomy light.

"I see you're admiring the portrait of Lady Agnes, Sarah," Miss Scratton said. "I had it moved here during the vacation. It looks very well in the entrance hall, don't you think?"

For a moment I couldn't speak, but Velvet glanced at the painting and said insolently, "She looks as crazy as the rest of this place. Who is she anyway?"

"Lady Agnes was the daughter of Lord Charles Templeton, who built the present house in the nineteenth century," Miss Scratton replied in calm, measured tones. "She was an extraordinarily gifted young woman who sadly died young. I feel it is only right that we should remember her." Then she swept across the hallway and down a windowless corridor, paneled in dark wood. Our feet echoed on the polished floor as we followed her. Velvet slouched along behind Miss Scratton, and I tried to look as though I hadn't a care in the world. But seeing Agnes's picture unexpectedly like that had unnerved me.

To me, she wasn't just someone from history to

remember and wonder about. To me, she was real. Agnes was Evie's link with the past, but she was also our Mystic Sister of the fire element. And her sea-gray eyes had seemed to hold a clear warning for me that, despite the victories of the term before, our struggles weren't yet over.

Two

I didn't want to come here. I've been expelled from six schools, and you'll probably end up expelling me too." Velvet looked belligerent as she faced Miss Scratton over the mahogany desk in the High Mistress's book-lined study. I wondered if her aggressive attitude was a cover for feeling lost and isolated, but she actually seemed pretty at ease as she leaned back in her chair and crossed her long legs. Her voice was attractively low and husky, and sounded more American than English.

"Yes, your parents have explained about your interrupted schooling, Velvet," replied Miss Scratton. "Let's hope that the routine and traditions of Wyldcliffe will provide you with some much-needed security. If you have any problems settling in, you can come to me or to Sarah.

She will be in your dorm and has been at Wyldcliffe for nearly five years. Sarah's mother was a pupil here, as was her grandmother, Lady Fitzalan, so she knows all the ways of the school."

Velvet's sulky face registered a flicker of interest and surprise as she heard my grandmother's name. "Is everyone here, like, titled? It's all a bit snobby, isn't it?"

"We are fortunate to attract the daughters of some of our oldest families. But we believe that everyone is capable of developing the attributes of a lady: selflessness, loyalty, and honor. We are interested in each individual student, not in her pedigree."

"Well, mine sucks," mocked Velvet. "Dad was brought up on the wrong side of the tracks, and Mom had me when she was sixteen. But they've got something your stuck-up ladies haven't got—talent."

"Then let's hope you've inherited some of it. There are lots of opportunities for music at Wyldcliffe—"

"You don't get it, do you? My dad's Rick Romaine—the biggest rock star on the planet. I made a hit record with him when I was twelve years old. I'm not going to join some crappy school choir. I'm not going to do anything I don't want to do, and you can't make me."

Miss Scratton held Velvet's gaze for a moment, then

sighed. "We are simply trying to help you and your parents, Velvet. No other reputable school would take you. This might be your last chance."

"Yeah, whatever. Thanks a bunch and all that, but the sooner I'm out of this dump the better."

"We shall see," replied Miss Scratton calmly. "Sarah, would you please take Velvet and show her the school? Then take her to the dorm. She will need to change into the school uniform before the bell goes for dinner tonight."

Velvet looked mutinous again, so I hurried her out of Miss Scratton's study before she could launch into another argument. As soon as I had got her away from the High Mistress, Velvet dropped the attitude and turned to me with a smile full of lazy charm, but I felt somehow that this was just another pose she was trying out.

"Sorry about dissing your beloved school," she said with a laugh, "but I have to start as I intend to go on."

"What do you mean?"

"If I behave badly enough, I reckon it'll be a month at most before they chuck me out. Then I can get back home to L.A. God, I don't know how you can stand it here. It feels so dead," she said, glancing around at the antique prints and paintings that hung on the walls. As we walked along, I opened various doors to show her the magnificent formal library and the high-ceilinged classrooms. "Yeah, it's all very fancy," Velvet admitted. "But it doesn't mean that I'll stay. I've been to loads of schools, and this is definitely the weirdest. No boys, no male teachers, no TV allowed, practically no contact with the outside world, stuck in the middle of the hideous countryside. My parents must have chosen this particular hellhole as a joke."

"Perhaps they thought it would help you."

"Well, I don't need this kind of help." For a moment her mouth trembled and she looked upset, but then she pulled herself together and said, "Okay, what else have you got to show me? Cold showers? Dungeons?"

"Come outside and you'll see." I led the way to the grounds. Most of the girls were up in the dorms, unpacking, but a few had escaped outside to the gardens. It was a beautiful April afternoon, and everything looked green and fresh. Little groups of students were sitting under the trees or strolling about on the lawns that swept down from the main buildings to a wide, glassy lake. Mirrored in its depths were the famous ruins of the Abbey's ancient chapel. Beyond the lake and the wooded grounds, the moors rose up to the distant horizon. It was an impressive sight. Even Velvet couldn't play bored about this.

"Actually, this is kind of cool," she said, heading for

the chapel. "It looks like Sleeping Beauty's castle or something. What goes on in the ruins?"

"Nothing much, generally. But we have the Memorial Procession there every year on the anniversary of Lady Agnes's death."

"So this Lady Agnes really is a big deal round here? I like that. I'm into ghosts."

"She's not a ghost," I said shortly, but Velvet wasn't listening. She had gone ahead to explore the ruins. The walls of the Abbey's chapel were only half-standing, and the remains of the great east window hung like a tattered cobweb against the sky. Broken pillars indicated where a row of arched columns had once marked the chapel's aisles. Now grass grew in between the weathered stones, and the roof was open to the sky. Velvet stood on the green mound where the chapel's altar had been and flung her arms up to the sky in a dramatic pose. "This would be a great place for some fun. You know, a voodoo ritual, or some black magic stuff. My dad's into all that."

I vaguely remembered that there had been a scandal a few years back about her father's stage shows and his so-called occult performances, with some parents trying to ban them and get warnings put on his records. Velvet threw her head back and began to sway from side to side, dancing rhythmically with no hint of self-consciousness. Then she began to chant, in a low, wailing voice, as though appealing to unseen forces.

"Stop it!"

She broke off and stared at me. "Hey, I was only kidding around. What's up, Sarah, are you scared of the dark side? I'm not. I'm not scared of anything. In fact, I quite fancy all that pagan stuff. I can see myself as a priestess, can't you?"

I tried to speak lightly, to let the moment pass. "I can see you getting a demerit if you don't get changed into your uniform before the bell goes for supper. Let's go up to the dorm."

"But I haven't seen everything yet," she complained. "What other cool stuff is there? Miss Scratton said you had to show me everything."

"I'm afraid the ruins are the highlight of the tour. There's an open-air swimming pool behind the trees over there that we use in the summer term," I said, pointing it out.

"Doesn't sound too bad."

"I wouldn't get overexcited, the water's usually pretty cold. And the sports fields are down the path next to that big oak tree, you know, hockey and lacrosse. The stables are up near the main house."

"Jesus, I loathe team games. Stables, please. But I haven't finished with those ruins. They might come in useful one of these nights."

"Useful for what?"

"Oh, I don't know, some kind of pagan party," Velvet replied carelessly. "That would be cool. Midnight magic—what do you think? It would liven the place up."

I led the way to the stables, feeling uncomfortable. It was so bizarre to hear Velvet joke around about rituals and magic when such things were real for me and my friends, and not only real but threatening and deadly. There were two Wyldcliffes. One was the world of the exclusive school with its exams and traditions, where people were concerned with academic success and preparing for college, getting onto the sports teams, and being invited to society parties during the holidays. But the other Wyldcliffe was a battleground between the dark and the light, where ancient forces and deeper powers were at work.

On that bright spring afternoon it was hard to believe that only a few weeks earlier we had released Sebastian's soul into eternity, and seen Mrs. Hartle—the previous High Mistress and Helen's mother—cross over into the shadows as a vengeful spirit. She had chosen to dedicate her warped existence to serving the corrupt king of the Unconquered lords, the terrible powers who had cheated death and found unholy immortality in the shadow world. And now who knew whether she would leave us alone, or whether she was planning some fresh attack? And what had happened to the remains of Mrs. Hartle's coven of Dark Sisters? Had they abandoned their pursuit of elemental power, or were they waiting to group together again, even stronger and more dangerous than before? As I walked with Velvet in the bright spring gardens, my heart sounded in my chest like a war drum, and I sensed eyes hidden in the hills, watching me like carrion crows. Drumming—there was drumming in my head and I felt afraid.

My Wyldcliffe, my *real* Wyldcliffe, was not just about the day-to-day dramas of being at boarding school, so Velvet's self-indulgent nonsense was not what I needed to hear right then. I needed to see Helen and Evie and plan our next move. I decided I would show Velvet the stables, take her to the dorm, and then leave her to unpack so that I would be ready as soon as my friends arrived. I didn't think that Velvet Romaine really needed me to babysit her.

Arriving at the stables calmed me down. I have always loved horses; they are in my family's blood. My father trains racehorses, sometimes for himself, sometimes for other wealthy owners. Now the earthy smell of the stables—a mix of straw and feed and the sharp, sweet tang of the horses' coats—soothed me. It spoke to me of a time when the earth was greener and we lived in harmony with both horses and the land. I walked over to the loose box where my horse Starlight was waiting and kissed his soft muzzle. A groom from home had driven him up to Wyldcliffe in the trailer the day before, together with my other pony—funny, fat, cheerful little Bonny. I was getting a bit too tall for Bonny really, but I had brought her for Evie, who had learned to ride on Bonny's broad back and was not comfortable with any of the other horses.

"Is he yours?" asked Velvet, patting Starlight's arched neck. "Nice."

"Yes. Do you ride?"

"You could say that. We lived in Argentina for a while and I hung out with the polo crowd. That was fun. Wow, who owns this beauty?" She walked over to the other side of the stable yard to admire a magnificent white mare that was tethered in a wide stall. Velvet whistled through her teeth and expertly made a fuss of the beautiful creature. I could see that she was used to being around horses. "Now you would be worth riding, sweetheart," Velvet crooned. She turned to me inquiringly. "Who does she belong to?"

"Seraph is Miss Scratton's horse, and she doesn't let anyone else ride her."

"So what? I can always find a way round that."

"Seriously, Velvet, you mustn't do anything silly."

"Why not?" she demanded. "What can they do to me? Expel me? That's exactly what I want. Anyway, I'm a pretty good rider. I wouldn't come to any harm."

"I was thinking of the horse," I replied coolly.

Velvet stared at me for a moment, then laughed. "I like you, Sarah. You're different. You seem really—I don't know—really *good*, but I'm not so sure that you're as angelic as you make out."

I blushed. Evie had always called me "good." Sweet and good and wholesome, like the fruit of the harvest, she said. But sometimes, being good was an effort. Being good meant putting others first, standing aside. Letting go of things you wanted for yourself. I shook my head and moved away, not wanting Velvet to see that her words had had an effect on me. I pushed open the door of the little tack room in the corner of the yard, talking about the first thing that came into my head. "If you want to sign up for riding lessons with Mrs. Parker, you write your name in the book in here—oh—"

My voice faltered. Two people in the shadows of the tack room broke away from each other with a guilty start. One of them was a tall boy with hair the color of ripe corn—Josh Parker. And the other one was Evie.

22

Three

O h—Sarah! I was just going to look for you."

Evie stepped forward and threw her arms around me, but for an instant I felt a cold sluice of disappointment that Evie had arrived at school and sought out Josh before she had found me. And what had they been doing, huddled together in this hidden corner? Had she forgotten Sebastian already? The next moment I blamed myself for being so unkind. I was being totally oversensitive. I had no right to judge Evie. Nothing mattered except our friendship. I hugged her back.

"I'm so glad you're here, Evie. Where's Helen? Miss Scratton told me you were arriving together."

"We did, about ten minutes ago. Helen said she was feeling suffocated after being stuck for hours in the train and then the taxi. She's gone for a walk down to the village to get some fresh air before unpacking."

"Should she really have gone on her own?"

"Of course, why not? Our year is allowed to leave the school grounds on a Sunday."

That wasn't quite what I had meant. I was thinking of the hidden dangers that could be lurking all around Wyldcliffe.

"Evie, I'd better go," Josh said. "I've got tons to do to get all the horses settled in for the night. See you later, Sarah," he added casually, pushing past me on his way out. I experienced the familiar ache as his body brushed against mine. He paused at the door and nodded to Velvet, who was staring at him appreciatively, then spoke to Evie again. "So, tomorrow after school?" Josh's voice was warm and eager, as though full of secret happiness. I had never seen anyone so clearly and hopelessly in love—but not with me. Of course not. "Say, five o'clock, Evie?"

Evie looked slightly self-conscious, but she smiled back at him. "Yeah, sure. See you tomorrow."

He left, and there was an awkward silence. My Wyldcliffe training in perfect social manners came to the rescue. "Evie, this is a new girl, Velvet Romaine. I've been showing her around. She's going to be in our class. Velvet, this is my best friend Evie Johnson."

"Hi there," Velvet drawled. "Where did you find *him*? I thought this place was strictly all-female."

"Josh isn't a student here," Evie explained. "He works in the stables sometimes, and helps his mother give the riding lessons."

Josh wasn't just Evie's riding instructor. He was crazy about her, just as I had been crazy about him for so long. He had lived in Wyldcliffe all his life and knew some of its secrets, and had learned about Evie's connection with Sebastian and the coven. But Josh hadn't been frightened off by what seemed like an impossible situation. He had stayed loyal to Evie through everything and was here for her now, reassuringly devoted and grounded and sane. Not only that, he was pretty good-looking, which Velvet couldn't fail to notice.

"He can give me a lesson anytime." Velvet glanced provocatively from under her glossy fringe. "Or maybe I could teach him a thing or two."

Evie's smile faded, and she looked annoyed. "So are you *the* Velvet Romaine? The one in all the magazines?"

"The one with the famous parents and the dysfunctional childhood and drug problems and the unsuitable boyfriends? Yeah, that one." Velvet's dark eyes flashed with resentment.

"I'm sorry—I didn't mean to—," Evie began.

"It doesn't matter. I'm used to it. Like they say, I don't give a damn."

I stepped in hastily. "I'd better take you to the dorm, Velvet, so you can change into your uniform. And then can we talk before supper, Evie? We could walk down to meet Helen coming back from the village. Have you heard that Miss Scratton is the new High Mistress? Did you know?"

"Mmm . . . yes, some of the other girls were talking about it. . . ." Evie tore her gaze away from Velvet and turned to me. "See you at the front door in a few minutes? I'll wait for you there."

"Okay, great. Come on, Velvet, we'll have to be quick."

We left the stable yard and entered the main school by one of the many side doors. I hurried down an echoing corridor, and soon we arrived back at the black-and-white-tiled entrance hall. The grand marble staircase swept up to the higher floors, and I led the way.

"The second floor is where the mistresses live and have their common room," I told Velvet. "If you need to see the housekeeper, or go to the infirmary, that's on the second floor too. The dorms are all up on the third floor."

"I hate dorms. I hate having to share a room."

As we climbed the winding steps, I wondered how on

earth Velvet would settle at Wyldcliffe. So many people had been hurt by the place: Agnes, Laura, Helen, Evie— even poor little Harriet, who had been controlled and made use of by Mrs. Hartle the term before. They were like birds flying through a storm, unable to escape the spell of this strange valley. And now a thought cut through me: It would be my turn soon.

"So your mom came to school here?" Velvet asked. "And your gran?"

"Both my grandmothers, actually," I replied with a rueful smile. "And my great-grandmother before that. I'm afraid I'm Wyldcliffe through and through."

"So your family must be kind of posh, what with your grandmother being Lady Thingamajig and all that."

"People will be much more impressed that your dad's a rock star and your mother's a famous model than they are by anyone in my family. Everyone says that Amber Romaine is one of the most beautiful people on the planet, don't they?"

"Yeah, they do, especially Amber," Velvet replied sourly. "She's her own biggest fan."

I was a bit surprised to hear Velvet talk like that about her mother. I didn't want to pry, but for an instant, Velvet had dropped the mask of her cynical pose and I had caught a glimpse of her unhappiness. "So, don't you two get on or something?" I asked.

Velvet shrugged. "It's not exactly a secret that we clash. Why do you think she's packed me off to so many boarding schools? She got on better with my sister, Jasmine. But she's dead." Velvet glared at me, challenging me to respond. But there was nothing much I could say, beyond the old clichés.

"I heard about it—I'm really sorry."

"Yeah. Anyway, Amber and I are probably too alike. And having a teenage daughter around isn't really on her agenda. Makes her look old, I guess. We're always fighting. Every time we have a fight, Dad tries to make up for it by buying both of us masses of stuff. Funny, though, all his money can't actually stop her from hating me."

I was kind of shocked. I love my mother dearly, and even though there are some things I can't share with her— secret hopes and dreams—she is always there in the background, always loving and supportive. When I am with my friends at school I don't talk about her much, as I am acutely conscious that Evie's mother is dead and Helen's mother, Mrs. Hartle, has brought her nothing but misery. And here was Velvet now, angry with her mother, talking of hatred.

"She can't hate you, she's your mother—"

"Whatever." Velvet switched back to her earlier flippant manner. "So tell me about these snobby grandmothers of yours."

"They aren't snobby," I said, thrown back on the defensive. "My dad's mother just happens to be Lady Fitzalan, but she's totally down-to-earth. She's a typical Englishwoman, mad about horses and dogs and her garden, that's all." Then I laughed reluctantly. "Okay, my other grandmother, on the Talbot-Travers side of our family, was pretty stuck-up. But her own mother, my great-grandmother, wasn't born into privilege. She was called Maria, and she was an orphaned Gypsy child who was adopted by wealthy people."

"Really? A Gypsy? That's really cool." At least this was one thing that Velvet and I could agree on. "So you've got Gypsy blood?" She scrutinized my features as though sizing them up for some kind of modeling assignment. "Yeah, I can see that now—you've got the dark, curly hair and that kind of natural, outdoor look—"

"Mmm . . . maybe," I murmured in reply. But the connection I felt with Maria went deeper than any superficial chance of hair color or looks.

I had often thought about my great-grandmother and felt her presence in my life. I was drawn to any scrap of information I could find out about Maria and her Romany family. Perhaps it seems odd, but I felt some kind of spiritual bond with them. Maria had been sent by her adoptive parents to Wyldcliffe long ago, and sometimes I felt as though she was watching over me at school, as though we actually knew each other and had some secret understanding. Sounds impossible, I know. But when I had met Cal, a young Traveler, the term before, it seemed that the Romany world was opening up to me at last. For a short time I had begun to believe that the secret loneliness that had always brooded under my oh-so-calm exterior might be healed. Of course, I knew that I was lucky, really. I had a great family and home. I had my horses and friends. I loved the land around me and the earth under my feet, and I would be faithful to my gifts of the Mystic Way. But I secretly wanted more. I wanted to have someone special, who really understood everything about me. Was I being greedy?

As Velvet followed me up the steps to the third floor, I thought of my dream, of those eyes looking into mine, full of warmth. I remembered the way Cal had talked to me, as if I really mattered. I remembered his watchful eyes and his quick, rare laugh. I remembered the feeling of connection between us. But Cal's family had moved on, away from Wyldcliffe, and I had been left behind. Cal had told me that he would see me again and had promised to write, but I hadn't heard anything. He didn't even have a cell phone, so there was no way I could get in touch with him. He would be far away by now.

My heart suddenly felt so weary. I had thought that I could trust Cal, but it seemed that he had forgotten me. And now that I was back at school, the old nagging disappointment that Josh regarded me as nothing more than a friend—a really nice girl, good old Sarah—was creeping over me again. But I forced myself to walk briskly down the door-lined corridor, telling myself off for being weak and self-indulgent. After all, I had something more important than a schoolgirl romance. I had friends, true deep friends: my sisters, Evie, Helen, and Agnes. That was what was important to me, not falling in love. That's what I told myself, and tried to believe.

I opened a door that led into a plain, bare room. It was smaller than some of the Wyldcliffe dorms, with only three narrow beds, but it was furnished in the same austere style as the rest. "Your bed is at the end, under the window, next to mine. Look, the porter has brought your bags up already. Ruby Rogerson has the other bed. She's a nice girl. Very quiet, brilliant at math. Caroline Woodford used to be in this dorm, but her parents have moved to Australia and she's gone with them."

Velvet stared around the stark white room and exclaimed in disgust, "My God, it's like a prison! No, it's worse. At least in prison you're allowed to put up pictures on the walls. At my other boarding schools we could decorate our dorms. This is so—so cold and weird. It's like they expect us to be like nuns or something."

"This is Wyldcliffe. They do things differently here."

Velvet sank down onto her bed, and for a moment I sensed that her despair was genuine. It wasn't about sharing a room, or not being allowed to put up some Metallica poster; it was about being left here all alone by her parents. For all her celebrity connections, she had been dumped at Wyldcliffe by her mother, who was too beautiful and busy to care for a difficult teenage daughter. I went over to Velvet and gently touched her on the shoulder.

"You said I was good," I murmured. "I'm not really, not so much. But I do want to help you if I can. Remember that."

Velvet pulled away impatiently. "I'm perfectly okay." She began grabbing stuff out of her Louis Vuitton suitcases, scattering clothes all over her bed. "If I'm going to wear this repulsive uniform, I'd better get on with it. Aren't you going to meet your friend, the one with the gorgeous red hair? I got the feeling she didn't like me very much."

"Evie's had a hard time lately," I began, automatically protective. "She's been through a lot. She lived with her grandmother, but she died and so Evie had to come here, and it's not been easy—"

"Yeah, whatever. She just doesn't want me messing with her stable boy property. I can see why he's keen on her, though; she's stunning, like a kind of Victorian mermaid. Hey—she looks a bit like Lady Agatha in that freaky old painting the principal was on about."

"Lady Agnes . . . um . . . do you think so? Gosh, look at the time, it's getting late."

"It's okay, go downstairs." Velvet busied herself with her clothes. "I'll be fine."

"Will you find your way to the dining hall?"

"I found my way round Manhattan last New Year's Eve when I was stoned out of my mind, so I think I can manage." She stopped tugging at her cases for a minute and looked up at me. "Look, Sarah, you don't have to be good and nice and pretend that you like me or want to look after me. I don't need you and I don't need anyone else. I just want to get out of here, and I usually get what I want, whatever it takes. Don't get in my way."

I felt strangely exposed and foolish as I stood there, as if she knew more about me than could be possible and that her warning went deeper than her words. It seemed to me that Velvet had a bitter anger inside her that would poison anyone who got too close, and I found myself wishing that she hadn't come to Wyldcliffe. There was nothing I could do about her, though, or her problems. I had other things to worry about.

Leaving Velvet in the dorm, I hurried down the marble stairs. Evie would be waiting for me by now. But when I got to the entrance hall, there was no sign of her. I opened the front door and stood for a moment on the worn stone step, looking down the drive. The late afternoon sun was fading in a hazy glow of gold. Blackbirds were beginning their evening song. The hills that ranged around the ancient Abbey seemed so peaceful, but they had been forged by gigantic upheavals: glaciers and landfalls and earthquakes. What new shocks and upheavals might be waiting for us in this apparently peaceful landscape? Again, I felt exposed and vulnerable, as though I were in full view of the enemy. I tried to shake off my mood and turned my thoughts back to Maria. She must have stood on this same step and seen the same views when she had been a Wyldcliffe student. I wondered what she had thought of the school, and who her friends had been, and whether she had ever mourned for her Gypsy mother. What had she known and felt and seen at Wyldcliffe that could help me now?

"Maria?" I reached out for her in my thoughts. "Maria, can you hear me? Are we still in danger? What should I do?" The wind stirred the leaves in the branches of the great oak trees that grew on either side of the drive, but no answers came to me. I stifled my disappointment and glanced at my watch. The next moment Evie walked up to the front steps from the direction of the stables.

"Hey," she said quietly. She smiled at me, but her eyes seemed to hold tears. I smiled back. I wanted to help her, now that she was back at the place where Sebastian had lived and died. Just being here must be an effort for Evie, I thought, and I wished I knew how to comfort her.

She doesn't want your comfort, she wants Josh, said a nasty little voice in my head, but I ignored it. I linked arms with Evie, and we set off walking down the drive. "Tell me all about it, if it helps," I said.

Evie squeezed my arm gratefully. "Thanks, Sarah. You're so good. I don't know what I'd do without you."

Good Sarah. Kind Sarah. That's what I had to be— today, tomorrow, forever.

Four

We slipped through the gates at the end of the drive, into the lane that led to the village. In the other direction a path wound its way up to the moors, and to the places that had burned themselves into our memories—Uppercliffe Farm, where Agnes had hidden her little daughter from the eyes of the world, and Fairfax Hall, Sebastian's childhood home.

I heard Evie catch her breath. "It's so odd," she said in a low voice. "This place is full of such beauty and yet such pain. I keep thinking, I first met Sebastian here, I first saw Agnes there, we first made our Circle there . . . but now that's all over."

"Is it?"

She looked at me with a faintly stubborn expression.

"It has to be. I've been thinking about it a lot during the holidays. Sebastian wanted me to move on, and I have to do that, for his sake as well as my own. I have to try and live like he wanted me to—I have to try to be happy, so that his death was worthwhile. It was his gift to me as well as mine to him. I have to try and live now as though meeting Sebastian never happened."

It sounded like something she had told herself over and over.

"But what about the Mystic Way? What about your powers?" Evie's own mystic element was water, and the term before, she had used the Talisman, the necklace that was her precious heirloom, to share Agnes's powers of fire. "You can't pretend that wasn't real. You're still part of that."

"No, I don't mean it wasn't real," Evie replied, shaking her head. "Loving Sebastian was the most real thing I ever experienced. But I can't live in the past. It's over now. And I think perhaps our powers were lent to us to save him, just for that time and for that specific purpose. To save one immortal soul. That was worth doing, wasn't it?" Her eyes shone with tears, but she held them back. "I'm so grateful that we could be part of the Mystic Way to help Sebastian, and so grateful for everything you and Helen did for me, but . . . well . . ." Her voice faltered, and she swallowed hard.

"Well . . . what? What is it, Evie?"

Her expression hardened. "Sebastian is dead, Sarah. I don't want to rake everything up again. I just can't. I don't think I even want to talk about it anymore. We have to move forward."

"And is Josh part of moving forward?" I asked casually, but I felt a kick of jealousy in the pit of my stomach as I spoke the words. I drew my arm out of Evie's.

"I don't know," she answered. "I told Josh last term I wasn't ready for another relationship. Oh, I hate that word! It sounds so pompous." She reached down and picked a handful of daisies from the long grass at the side of the lane and began to knot them together in a chain. "I just don't know. I really like Josh. He's warm and kind . . . and full of life. He makes me feel like the sun is shining." She suddenly threw the flowers to the ground. "We're just friends. That's enough for the moment, isn't it? I don't want to worry and analyze everything. I just want to be happy."

"Don't we all," I said, unable to keep a note of bitterness from my voice.

"God, that sounded really superficial and selfish, didn't

it? I don't mean it like that. It's just that everything has been so tough." Evie gave a long sigh. "When Frankie got sick and I had to come here, my life changed. I still miss her terribly. And then losing Sebastian . . . Thank God I've got you and Helen."

"And Josh."

"Yeah, and Josh too." Evie looked at me anxiously. "You don't mind, do you, Sarah, me being friends with Josh?"

"Mind? Why should I mind?" I forced myself to smile. "It's great that you've got someone to talk to, honestly. But you must realize that Josh wants to be more than your friend. You might end up hurting him."

Again, the slightly stubborn look came over her face. "Every connection—friendship, love, whatever—can be painful. It's all a huge risk. Life is a risk. Josh is prepared to take the risk. Don't you see, Sarah, that we have to be ready for anything? We have to be big enough for whatever happens next. And does it really matter that things are sometimes painful, if you're really feeling and—and *doing*—and experiencing life? Sebastian told me to live, good and bad, joy and sorrow. That's all I'm trying to do."

I didn't reply. That was my problem, I thought dully. I hadn't done or experienced anything, not really. I had been too timid, afraid of hurting people, afraid of getting

39

hurt. And all that had left me with was this anxious, aching emptiness. At least Evie was alive, like a bright flame.

We walked the rest of the way in silence and soon reached the village with its rows of cottages and blackened stone church. The village store was closed, and there was no one about except a solitary old man walking his dog.

"Where do you think Helen will be?"

"Where else?" I led the way to the churchyard. Slanting rows of headstones and black yew trees gave the place a gloomy air, despite the bright bunches of flowers that had been left here and there on the graves. We spotted Helen sitting alone by an old-fashioned tomb that was overshadowed by a large statue of an angel. This was the earthly resting place of Lady Agnes Templeton. The local people whispered various superstitions about this spot. There were rumors that her ghost sometimes walked up to the door of the church and mysteriously passed inside, and that touching her tomb could heal the sick. They even claimed that one day Agnes would return to Wyldcliffe in its hour of greatest need. Most of it was just gossip and hysteria, but even Miss Scratton had said that her grave was a place of protection for us. I could understand why Helen wanted to sit here peacefully before facing the new term, trying to draw strength from the past. She had never fitted in at Wyldcliffe, and most of the students gave her a hard time.

Helen was sitting on the ground, with her arms clasped around her knees. Her fair hair tumbled around her face and hid her expression. For a moment I thought she was crying, but she jumped up and smiled determinedly when I called her name, and offered me her cool cheek to kiss.

"How are you, Helen?" I asked.

"Oh . . . I don't know . . . fine, I suppose," she answered, but she didn't meet my eye. "I was just thinking about Agnes. Whether we would ever see her again."

The three of us stood in front of the tomb without saying anything; then we linked hands and paid silent tribute to our secret sister. The stone angel held an inscription that had been weathered by time and wind and rain. It read LADY AGNES TEMPLETON, BELOVED OF THE LORD. For an instant it seemed to me that the angel faded and Agnes stood there in its place, looking down at us with love and serenity in her mild eyes. Then she vanished too and instead a figure dressed in black snarled at us, snapping with hatred. The next second everything was just as it had been: the quiet graveyard, the moss-covered tomb, and my friends lost in their thoughts. I stepped back and wrenched my hands from theirs. They didn't seem to have seen anything.

"Let's get back to school," I said hurriedly. "We shouldn't be out late. They'll soon be ringing the bell for supper."

"Is it that time already?" asked Evie in surprise.

Helen glanced at me searchingly, then sighed. "Yeah, let's go back. Might as well face it."

I hurried them along, marching briskly back down the lane and toward the school gates.

"So, did you see your father in the holidays, Helen?" asked Evie.

"Yes."

"How was it?"

"Mmm . . . strange."

"Strange how?" I asked.

"Well . . ." Helen frowned. "I thought it was going to be wonderful, but it wasn't like that. Because I've only just met Tony, I don't really feel any connection with him yet. But the connection must be there all the same. I mean, he is actually my father. I still can't really take it in."

"I guess it will take time," I said reassuringly.

Helen looked troubled, then said in a rush, "It's weird to think of him being in love with my mother. He showed me photos of when they were young, before she left him when she found out that she was expecting me. He talked about how beautiful she was, full of spirit and adventure."

42

She hunched her shoulders miserably. "I never knew that side of her."

It must have been so hard for Helen, I thought, being brought up in an orphanage, not knowing either of her parents. And then Mrs. Hartle had sought her out and brought her to Wyldcliffe, yet she had forbidden Helen to tell anyone that she was the High Mistress's daughter. And when Helen had refused to use her elemental powers to join Mrs. Hartle's coven, her mother had rejected her utterly. Only after the High Mistress's death last term had Miss Scratton been able to track down Helen's father.

"What's your dad like?" asked Evie. "Is he married?"

"Yes. His wife, Rachel, is very nice. She's a doctor. They have two little boys."

"So they are your brothers? Helen, that's so great!" I exclaimed. I would have loved to have a brother. My mother had told me that she had lost a baby boy the year after I was born and had not been able to have any more children after that, so Helen's news touched me deeply. It was strange, I thought, how we were all only daughters, Helen and Evie and Agnes and myself. But now Helen's life could be about to change completely. "You'll have a real family now. That's wonderful."

Helen's smile was like a wintry ghost. "Yes, of course."

"So what's wrong?" We had nearly reached the school.

"Oh, I don't know, it's so hard to explain. I don't want to be ungrateful, but they are already a family—Tony and Rachel and the boys. They're so happy with one another. They don't need me. I know they tried hard to welcome me, make me feel at home. But that was just it, we were all *trying* to belong to one another and somehow, that made it worse. Tony is my father, but he's actually a stranger. I don't think I'll ever fit in with them." Her voice sank to a whisper. "I don't think I'll ever belong anywhere."

"You belong with us," I said firmly, "doesn't she, Evie?" At that moment I vowed that I would look after them both, whatever happened. My heart was telling me that Evie was wrong. The Mystic Way hadn't finished with us yet. The signs were all around us. My dreams, the sound of drums, a brief glimpse of a snarling face—this valley was still full of danger for me and my sisters. I had to forget Josh, I had to forget Cal and anything that wasn't connected with our survival. "We all belong together," I repeated. "We're sisters. Remember?"

"Sisters," whispered Evie, and Helen murmured, "Thank you, Sarah."

From now on, I promised myself, I was only going to be what they needed me to be: strong, supportive, and calm, like the quiet hills. Every other secret longing and desire I would lock in an invisible box and bury out of sight.

I took my place next to Helen and Evie at the long wooden dining table. The vaulted, chilly room was filling up with girls. Although they were different ages and sizes, they all had the same Wyldcliffe uniform and the same superficial air of serene, privileged confidence. A few moments later a bell rang and the mistresses began to walk into the dining hall, wearing black academic gowns that made them look like a flock of crows. The students rose respectfully to their feet, all two hundred girls. Yet I thought it seemed that the dining room wasn't quite as full as usual. I also realized that I couldn't see Velvet anywhere, but before I had time to wonder where she was, Miss Scratton began to speak.

"It gives me great pleasure to welcome you back to Wyldcliffe as the new High Mistress of our school. The summer term is traditionally a happy time, and I intend to make it so for you this year, particularly after the sad events of last term. I also aim to maintain the high academic standards set by Mrs. Hartle, whose loss I am sure we all still feel." Miss Scratton paused and looked shrewdly at the sea of faces in front of her, then continued.

"At Wyldcliffe we are very aware of the past. Tradition has almost been our motto. As a historian, I am naturally in favor of valuing the lessons of the past. However, we must look to the future. In other words, we must modernize."

A murmur of surprise ran around the room. It was as though she had said, "We must burn down the school." A few of the teachers on the platform next to her looked sour with disapproval.

"I have arranged for our rather meager stock of computers to be upgraded and new books to be ordered for the library," Miss Scratton went on. "The unused rooms in the red corridor, beyond the library, have been converted into common rooms for students to use in the evenings. They have been equipped with radio and television, games and magazines. Of course, these new facilities must be used sensibly and only when all prep and study has been done. In addition, I am determined to open Wyldcliffe's doors to the local community. For too long we have been regarded as exclusive and excluding, and this must change. I have arranged for a group of children from the village elementary school to come once a week to use our swimming pool and tennis courts. I hope this will be the beginning of many such schemes. There will also be a program of activities this term that will take us out of the school walls and into the wider world. This will culminate in a summer celebration. For the younger girls there will be a garden party and swimming races. For you older students I have arranged a dance at the boys' school St. Martin's Academy, which as you know is located some twenty miles away in the town of Wyldford Cross. If this event is a success, we will invite the gentlemen of St. Martin's to a Christmas ball here at the Abbey. Ladies, we must let the light into Wyldcliffe."

There was absolute silence. Then enthusiastic applause and cheering broke out from the students. I felt pretty surprised myself. Wyldcliffe hadn't changed for generations, but if anyone could drag it into the twenty-first century, it would be Miss Scratton. This dry, severe teacher was more than she seemed. She had helped us in our battle with the coven, and revealed herself as a visionary Guardian, who had been intertwined over the years with Wyldcliffe's long history. Now she smiled and acknowledged the applause, then held up her hands for quiet. As she did so, someone entered the dining room. It was Velvet.

She was wearing the regulation school uniform, but she managed to make it look incredibly sexy. Perhaps it was the fact that she had hitched up her skirt and loosened her collar, or perhaps it was the five-inch black spiked heels she was wearing, or perhaps it was simply the confidence with which she made her entrance—whatever it was, she looked stunning, and she knew it. Everyone fell silent and stared, except Helen, who gave a tiny gasp of breath and clutched her arm as though she had been stung. I turned and gave her a questioning look, but she shook her head warningly as Miss Scratton spoke again.

"Good evening, Velvet," she said. "As I have not yet said grace, you are not officially late, but try to be a little less tardy in the future. Please take your place next to Celeste van Pallandt." She indicated an empty place next to Celeste, who didn't look very thrilled to have Velvet as a neighbor. Celeste was used to queening it over the rest of us as one of Wyldcliffe's most glamorous students, and it looked as though she had finally been upstaged. My heart sank. Girls competing about looks and clothes and money—I hated all that. I wished I could be out riding, galloping over the moors with the wind in my hair and hoofbeats echoing in my heart. Then my head was filled with the sound of insistent, tormenting drumming that almost made me cry aloud. I saw the dull red light of the torches, I smelled the acrid smoke, I felt a blade against my throat and saw the eyes hovering over me turn savage—

I gripped the back of my chair and forced myself to

wipe the images from my mind. Helen was plucking at my sleeve.

"Can you both meet me tonight?" she whispered. "In the usual place? We can't talk here. I wasn't going to tell you, but—there's something . . . well, I just need you."

"Of course," I whispered back. "Evie?"

She hesitated for a fraction of a second, then nodded. Miss Clarke, the untidy, harassed-looking Latin teacher, frowned in our direction, and we had to be attentive again.

"And now let us say grace and give thanks for the good things put before us," Miss Scratton was saying. *"Benedic, Domine, nos et dona tua . . ."*

As the students joined in with the archaic words, I secretly made a prayer of my own. "Please watch over my sisters, Great Creator, and don't let the shadows of Wyld-cliffe touch them." Miss Scratton had spoken about letting in the light, but as I looked up through the row of long windows I saw that the bright spring day was over. Night, and darkness, brooded over the Abbey once more.

Five

MARIA MELVILLE'S WYLDCLIFFE JOURNAL

APRIL 3, 1919

There is a terrible darkness here in Wyldcliffe, and I am frightened, really frightened, for the first time in my life. Miss Scarsdale has asked me to write everything down while I am laid up with my broken ankle. She has given me this book for the purpose and says that when I have finished, the nightmares will stop. Thank heavens for Miss Scarsdale. Without her, I think I would have gone crazy.

It is hard to know where to begin, but I must do my best.

My name is Maria Adamina Melville, and I am fifteen years old. I am a pupil at Wyldcliffe Abbey School.

At first I was excited to come here, although I was sad to leave my home, Grensham Court. Grensham is the nicest house in the whole of Kent, or at least I think so, and Mother and Father are the best parents in the world. I am truly grateful for them and everything they have taught me. For as long as I can remember they have been my dearest friends and companions. I miss them so much.

It is best not to think about home. Father wanted me to come here, and so I have to be brave like a soldier. Peter Charney in our village did not come back from the Great War, and he was only seventeen. I must be brave like he was. Mother also said it would be good for me to come to school and make friends of my own age. Instead of doing lessons with dear old Miss Frenchman, my governess, I would be taught by some of the finest women teachers in the country, and perhaps even go on to study at university. Mother said that the world has changed now, after this dreadful war, and that women can do all sorts of things, not just wait for a husband. We are even allowed to vote now, thanks to Mrs. Pankhurst and her brave supporters. Wyldcliffe is the best girls' school in all England. Here I can learn mathematics and Latin and science, just like a boy. But I cannot make any friends. That is what Mother did not know.

On that first day when Mother brought me here, the High Mistress, Miss Featherstone, showed us around the school. Miss F. was all smiles and bows and nods, but I didn't like her. She didn't smile with her eyes, only her lips. Miss Featherstone made a big fuss of Mother because she and Father are rich, but it seemed to me that the High Mistress was secretly angry about something. Daphne Pettwood and her cronies told me later what that was.

"You're only here because your parents paid the school to take you," Daphne sneered.

"But we all have to pay fees to come to boarding school, don't we?" I didn't understand what she meant.

Daphne laughed. "Yes, but your parents had to pay an awful lot more. Five thousand pounds is what I heard they had to give to make Miss Featherstone agree to have you. She didn't want you here."

I felt dizzy. Even to rich people, five thousand pounds is a fortune. "Don't be silly, Daphne. That can't be true."

"I heard ten thousand," said her friend Florence Darby.

"I heard twenty," added Winifred Hoxton spitefully.

"Stop it! What do you mean?"

Daphne pushed her face close to mine. She was almost shaking with rage and excitement. "Your parents had to give money to the school—a big fat donation—just so that you would be allowed to come. Wyldcliffe doesn't usually accept people like you."

"People like what?" Now my voice was shaking too.

"Gypsies. That's all you are—a dirty Gypsy."

"Dirty Gypsy!"

"Thieving Gypsy!"

"You don't belong at Wyldcliffe, and you never will," Daphne whispered savagely. "Really, I don't know why your parents bothered to spend their money on you. My mother told me all about it. She told me that they're not even your real parents. I don't know why they don't send you back to the disgusting Gypsy camp where they found you."

"Send you back, send you back!" Winifred and Florence mocked, pushing and jostling me. They shrieked with laughter at my distress, congratulating Daphne for putting me in my place, and at last they all flounced away. And they were supposed to be intelligent young women— the cream of polite society! I was trembling with shock and rage and injustice. I didn't want to cry, but I couldn't help it. That's when Miss Scarsdale found me and told me to take no notice of such ignorance and petty-mindedness. If it hadn't been for her, I would have run away right then. I *wanted to run and never stop until I found my way home to Grensham.*

My bruised wrist aches from writing this, but the weight in my heart is far worse. I wish I could forget everything that I have seen in the wild hills of this strange place, but when I close my eyes I see it all again. I feel as though I am still in the dark, and the monsters are reaching out to destroy me.

Six

When I opened my eyes, it was dark. I had slept dreamlessly for a couple of hours, and now the miniature alarm clock I kept under my pillow had woken me. The numbers on its tiny face glowed luminous green, and I saw that it was just before midnight. I sat up cautiously. Velvet, who had sighed and complained and flopped around on her narrow bed for ages before finally falling asleep, was lying on her back with her arm flung up over her pillow. A thin gleam of moonlight passed over the window, and I saw that she looked younger and prettier without her makeup, as if she were dreaming innocently. She sighed and turned over as I got out of bed, but she didn't wake up. I was safe. Ruby was deeply asleep as usual, snoring slightly. I put on my robe and crept out of the room, carefully feeling my way.

I knew exactly where I was heading. There was a hidden staircase in the corridor outside Evie and Helen's dorm, concealed by a curtained door. It led up to the abandoned attic on the third floor, and down to the disused servants' quarters and old kitchens way below us. Evie had used these secret stairs many times to sneak out and meet Sebastian at night, and lately we had discovered Agnes's private study in the old attic. That was our special meeting place. I reached the curtained alcove, quietly opened the door, stepped through, and shut it behind me. The air was stale and musty in this closed-up wing of the old building, but I didn't care. I began to climb the narrow stairs. A faint light wavered ahead, and I guessed that the others were already there.

"It's me—Sarah," I called softly, and soon I had reached the dusty wooden landing that led to a warren of attic rooms. Helen and Evie were standing outside the door of one of them. Behind that door was a rich store of potions and ingredients, books and learning, which had been used by Agnes in her work of healing and her study of the Mystic Way.

"What's the matter?" I whispered. "Why haven't you opened the door?"

Helen turned to me, looking sickly pale in the harsh rays of Evie's flashlight. "We can't open it. We've already tried. It's locked from the inside, like it was when we first discovered it."

"Can't you pass through the door, Helen?" I asked in surprise. Locks and bolts were usually no barrier to Helen, our sister of air, who could travel distances by the power of her thought. Dancing on the wind, she called it. She had first opened Lady Agnes's study for us by vanishing like a silver mist in front of our eyes and stepping invisibly through the air to the other side of the door, where she had unfastened the inner bolts.

"No, I've tried twice," Helen replied. "Both times I get turned back. Some stronger force stops me getting through. That's never happened before."

"What do you think it is?" I asked. "Could it be the coven?"

"But the coven was broken and scattered the night that Mrs. Hartle died," said Evie. "Isn't everything safe now that Miss Scratton is in charge? It's like I said before—perhaps we don't really need our powers now. Perhaps it's all over for us."

I recognized the hope in her voice, and the fear in her eyes. Poor Evie, she had already been through so much.

It was as though one minute she could convince herself that she was strong, and the next she simply wanted to run from the past. If at that moment I could have made everything how she wanted it to be, I would have done it. I would even have made it so that she could enjoy the warmth of Josh's smile and the comfort of his arms.

"I can't believe it's going to be so simple, Evie," I said gently. "Don't you think that the coven will band together again? Those women hate us. Why would they just leave us alone? And Mrs. Hartle's body might be dead, but her spirit isn't. We saw her go with her Unconquered master into the shadows."

"Yes, but we don't know that she can enter this world again," Evie replied. "Anyway, it was Sebastian's powers that she wanted, and now Sebastian is . . ." She stopped, then began again with an effort. "Sebastian has gone. He's at peace. Surely the coven has no reason to pursue us anymore?"

"Then why do I have this feeling that we are still being watched?" I asked.

Evie shuddered. "I hope that you're wrong, Sarah. I really do."

"I don't think she is," said Helen in a low voice. "Something, or someone, is trying to reach us. Trying to reach me, at least. I didn't want to tell you, Evie. I wanted this term to be a new start. You deserve that, after everything that happened. But Sarah's right. It's not over yet."

"Why not?" Evie asked, looking scared. "What's going on?"

"I need to show you something." Helen fumbled with the sleeve of her nightgown and rolled up the material to expose her slim white arm. There was a mark on her skin, a circle with a pattern across it shaped like a bird, or a pair of wings. Or even, perhaps, the crossed blades of two sharp daggers. "Look," she said. "It won't wash off. The mark is burned into my skin, like some kind of tattoo."

"How on earth did that happen?" I gasped.

Helen covered her arm again. "It first appeared in the holidays." She stared ahead, remembering. "I was staying with Tony—my father—and I woke up in the middle of the night, feeling confused. I was sleeping in the spare room in their apartment in London, of course, but at first I didn't recognize it. I thought I was back in the children's home and that I was locked in as a punishment, like I had been so many times. I needed to feel the air on my face, so I got out of bed and opened the window. There were bars on the window—the apartment was high up and Rachel had told me they were to protect the children, but I forgot all about that now. I thought I was in some kind of prison, and I just had to get out. I placed my hand on the bars and imagined them moving and dissolving and—well—they did. But perhaps it was only a dream." She pushed her fair hair out of her eyes and frowned.

"Anyway, I managed to squeeze through the bars until I was standing outside on the window ledge. It was a long way down to the ground. In my mind I was back in the children's home and had crept up onto the roof, and I was looking down, wanting to stop hurting—to stop existing even—daring myself to jump. And then I saw my mother standing below me. She looked like a bright angel. I wanted to throw myself into her arms and be wrapped up in her love. I wanted that so badly."

"Oh, Helen—"

She waved away my sympathy and carried on. "But that image was broken up like interference on an old TV set. Everything changed. I was seeing another scene. It seemed far away. My mother was young and pretty like she had been in those photos of my dad's. But she was holding a baby and crying. She was crying about me. I saw her taking me to the home with just a few little dresses and keepsakes. One of them was a small gold brooch, which she pinned to my shawl. Then she left. After that I saw someone come in—I'm not sure who, a nurse maybe, I couldn't see her face properly. Anyway, this nurse came in and picked me up. She saw the brooch and unfastened it and put it in her pocket." Helen looked up hesitantly. "That brooch was the same shape as the mark on my arm."

"Go on," I said. "What happened next?"

"There was more interference and flashing lights. I was back standing on the ledge with the road spread out below. My mother was waiting for me. 'Come to me, Helen,' she was saying. 'All you have to do is jump. I'll catch you.' She was smiling, but when I looked again, her face changed to a . . . to a horrible mask . . . like a shrunken white skull. 'Come to me, come to me, my daughter,' she said, again and again. 'No, never, never,' I screamed, and there was this terrible noise. It was drums beating wildly, on and on, as though the sound itself could destroy me."

"Drums?" I whispered. "But I—"

"That was only a dream, Helen," said Evie. "You mustn't let it get to you."

"Yes, but when I woke up a pain was burning in my arm. And this mark has been there ever since." She touched her arm again, rubbing the place where the mark was hidden by her nightshirt. "It had stopped hurting, but the pain started again when Miss Scratton was speaking before supper. That's why I decided I had to tell you."

Dreams. Faces like masks. The sound of drums. It was the same as I had seen and heard. For a moment I couldn't speak. "So what—what do you think the mark means?" I stammered. "What do you think is happening?"

"I think my mother is trying to contact me from the shadows and drag me into her world," Helen replied. "She won't let me alone until I am her creature. That night last term, out on the moors, she said I would acknowledge her as both mother and High Mistress before she was through."

"But she's not the High Mistress anymore," argued Evie. "She's dead. She's gone, Helen. Wasn't all that stuff about seeing her just a bad dream?"

"So how do you explain the mark?" asked Helen.

"Well, I guess it could be a good sign," Evie suggested. "A protection of some kind." Helen looked unconvinced, and Evie turned to me pleadingly. "What do you think, Sarah?"

I didn't know what to think. "I suppose it could be a good omen," I said cautiously. "Let's hope it is. But why would Agnes's study be sealed against us? Who—or what—is behind that?"

Evie answered hurriedly. "What if it's Agnes herself?

Maybe this is her way of telling us that our time with the Mystic Way is finished. And if the mark on Helen's arm is for protection, maybe Agnes is telling us there is nothing more we need to do."

"And what if the mark is hostile and it's Mrs. Hartle or the coven stopping us going through the door?" I asked.

Evie looked self-conscious and replied in a strained, artificial voice. "Of course," she said, "there's the possibility that the mark could be some kind of psychosomatic phenomenon—"

"How sane and rational!" Helen's pale eyes flashed with quiet anger. "Yes, it could be that. I could have imagined the whole thing. Everyone says I'm half-crazy anyway. Is that what you think too, Evie?"

There was a silence. It was the nearest we had ever come to a quarrel. I had to sort it out, be the peacemaker.

"Evie doesn't think that, Helen. She's just tired and upset. It's all been so difficult for her, we have to remember that."

"I know—," began Helen.

"Do you? Do either of you really know what is feels like to be me?" Evie said with a sob in her voice. "I am so tired of hiding in the shadows, of dealing with death and sorrow and ancient wrongs and powers. Sebastian wanted me to move on, to live in the light, and that's what I'm try-ing to do. I just don't think I can cope with any more of this."

"Don't you think I've had stuff to cope with too?" replied Helen wildly. "I'd been tormented by my mother long before you even came to Wyldcliffe, Evie. You and Sarah both take the fact that you have your families for granted. And you had Sebastian, if only for a short time. You were loved! No one . . . *no one* . . . has ever loved me."

Helen's face was tight with pain, and she leaned against the wall in despair. I wanted so much to reach out to her, but she seemed to radiate a cold, invisible barrier. Evie was crying quietly, wrapped up in her own unhappiness.

This couldn't happen. We had to stay together. "Stop it, both of you," I begged. "Please, we mustn't fight. Evie, don't let this happen!" She took a deep breath and scrubbed the tears from her eyes, then pulled herself together before making a stilted apology.

"I'm sorry, Helen, I didn't mean to upset you."

"We love you, Helen," I added. I gave her a hug, but she didn't respond. "And don't you remember what Miss Scratton said? That one day you will meet someone who will love you—"

"Beyond the confines of this world," finished Helen

in a shaky voice. "Yeah, I remember. But I don't see how that can ever happen. Anyway, it doesn't matter about me. Please forget what I said. The mark is my problem, not yours. And I do want you to be happy, Evie. I want you to find the peace you're looking for, I really do."

The moment of anger was over. We were sisters again, but for how long?

Seven

Evie sighed. "It's not just your problem, Helen. Sarah was right. We're in this together. So what are we going to do?"

Helen shook her head hopelessly. "I don't know. I've run out of ideas. And I feel that I'm running out of time."

"Don't worry," Evie murmured. "Everything will be okay." But I felt she was speaking with her lips, not from her heart. The bonds between the three of us suddenly seemed so fragile. We stood there, waiting silently in the dark, and it seemed that it was left to me to come up with some kind of plan.

"We could walk away," I said slowly, "and pretend none of it ever happened—Sebastian and Agnes and the coven. But there's the mark on Helen's arm. It appeared after her dream, or vision, about Mrs. Hartle, which can't be a coincidence. And I've had—"

I paused. For some reason I didn't want to tell them about my dreams. They had been menacing, with their drums and grotesque images, but I couldn't forget the look in those eyes. There had been someone looking at me, someone who knew me, right the way through. Someone who loved me, and I had longed for his kiss. . . . It was too personal, too private for even my dearest friends to know about.

"Well, like I told you, I feel something is watching us," I went on. "And now something is stopping us getting into Agnes's study. Don't forget that the Book is locked away in there. Why are we being prevented from getting hold of it?"

"The Book," said Helen, looking with up with interest. "There might be something in it about this mark on my arm. It might tell us more. I need to know what this thing is."

The Book of the Mystic Way, describing ancient secrets and spells, had been discovered by Sebastian. It had survived the years since then and was a priceless treasure. The other relic of the Mystic Way that had come down through the years was Evie's Talisman, bequeathed to her by Agnes. The Talisman was a finely wrought charm of silver, with a glittering crystal at its center, and it was hanging safely on a chain around Evie's neck. The Book, however, was hidden in Agnes's old writing desk, on the other side of the sealed door.

I glanced at my watch and shivered with cold. We had been up in the lightless attic for over an hour. Every minute that we spent out of our beds in the middle of the night was putting us at risk of being caught by one of the mistresses. If Miss Scratton found us breaking the school rules, I was sure she would understand and forgive us. But there were others—the plump, gushing geography mistress Miss Dalrymple, for instance—who were secret members of the coven and would love to discover our meeting place.

"Look, we'd better not stay up here much longer," I said. "Why doesn't Helen try one last time to pass through the door and retrieve the Book? At least then we could see if it would tell us anything about the sign on her arm."

"All right," said Helen.

"And, Evie?" I asked. "Are you willing for Helen to make one more attempt?"

"If we must," she said. Then she shook herself and spoke more enthusiastically. "Yes, of course. Let's try."

"We should make the Circle," I said. "That will strengthen our efforts."

I bent down and drew a Circle in the dust on the floor. Standing up again, I whispered, "Lord of Creation, we draw this Circle, round and whole like your sacred earth. Let it protect us. Let it be a holy place, where we seek only truth."

We all stepped inside the Circle and held hands.

"We are sisters of the Mystic Way," said Helen. "We put our gifts in the service of the Light."

Together we began to chant the familiar words, "The air of our breath, the water of our veins, the earth of our bodies, the fire of our desires . . ." As the chanting quieted our minds, we went deep into ourselves, reaching out to the mysteries. Then Evie finished the incantation, saying, "Water . . . Fire . . . Earth . . . Air . . . we ask the mystic elements to work through us for the common good."

When the opening invocation was over, Helen closed her eyes and began to murmur secret words, swaying slightly from side to side. The air stirred in the stuffy attic, and Helen's hair whipped around her face. She seemed to burn with silver light, until she was so bright I could hardly look at her. The next moment she vanished. Evie clutched my hand tightly and whispered, "Oh,

Sarah, I hope she'll be all right."

I strained to listen for any sound to indicate that Helen had made it to the other side of the door and was drawing back the bolts to let us in. There was nothing—just a dreadful, cold silence. All the things that could go wrong began to race through my head. I didn't really know how this gift of Helen's worked. We had simply accepted it when she had first revealed her ability to dissolve into the air and reappear somewhere else. It was just one more of the marvels we had stumbled across. But now I wondered anxiously what was happening. What if she got trapped in the in-between state? What if the spirit of Mrs. Hartle was able to enter that hidden place and ensnare her? I stared down at the circle in the dust and repeated, "Protect her, protect her, protect her . . ."

An eternity later, Helen crashed into us, coughing and gasping. There was blood on her face, streaming from a gash over her eye. "I couldn't . . . I couldn't find my way. Something was pushing me. . . ." We waited for her to get her breath. "I went into the tunnel of wind, as usual, but I couldn't control it. I fell out at the other end, far up on the hills, near those huge stones on Blackdown Ridge."

"And you're bleeding—"

"Oh that, yes. I fell against one of the stones."

"But how did you end up on the Ridge?" asked Evie anxiously.

"Someone sent me," Helen replied, sounding dazed. "And then I was blasted back here."

"At least you came back safely," I said.

"Am I safe?" Helen's yellow-green eyes looked strange in the dim light. "I heard something out there on the moor. It sounded like—I don't know, voices, far away. And then—"

"What?"

"Someone calling my name." Her head drooped. "Perhaps it was only in my mind. Crazy, like they say. I'm sorry. I can't open the door."

"Has anyone got any other ideas?" I asked. "Evie?"

"There's one thing I could try." She drew the Talisman from around her neck. It glinted in the torchlight, swinging on its silver chain. Lady Agnes had locked her powers and her love for Sebastian in its glittering heart. Evie held the necklace up and said, "Agnes, my sister and ancestor, I invoke your strength and wisdom. Help us now. If it is your will, open the door to us."

I knew somehow that nothing would happen. Perhaps Evie didn't really want it to. Perhaps Lady Agnes really was no longer able or willing to help us. Or maybe this simply wasn't the right moment. We have to wait for the signs and be ready for the way to be shown to us. There is a time for everything. I truly believe that.

Evie lowered her arm and slowly let out her breath. "I'm sorry. I seem to have lost my way."

"But last term you did so much, with fire as well as water," Helen said. "You were in control of the Talisman."

"Last term was different!" Evie's anger flashed out; then she controlled herself, taking a deep breath. "Last term Sebastian was in Wyldcliffe. Just knowing that gave me strength. I'm sorry. I'm not ready for this." She hid the Talisman away again. "Why don't you try, Sarah?"

I had no idea what I could do. My powers of earth were slow and deep; the movements of the seasons; the mysteries of plants and herbs; the way of animals; earth and bone and blood and clay; the innermost secrets of the heart. I walked up to the door and examined it. It was made of smooth wood, but here and there, knots and grooves showed in the grain. I tried to let the wood speak to me, to hear the sigh and sway of the living tree that it had come from.

Let me pass, I thought, as I stretched my hands out and placed them on the door.

It began to shake. A fine spray of dust began to spurt

from the crack where the door fitted into its surround. The dust grew faster and thicker like a tiny avalanche, until it was pouring onto the floor in soft heaps. A tearing, splintering noise came from under my hands and at last I staggered back, falling against Evie and Helen.

The surface of the wood had erupted into raw, fresh markings. They formed a pattern of letters that read:

LISTEN TO THE DRUMS

And below that, scored across the panels of the old door like an angry snake, there blazed the letter *S*.

We stared in silence as the door of the hidden study swung open to reveal its treasures. An antique writing desk. Purple and scarlet drapes. Parchments and manuscripts and cobwebbed jars of spices and herbs. Carved boxes and leather trunks, stuffed with curious objects. All relics of Lady Agnes and her deep studies.

Helen reached down cautiously and ran her fingers through the dust that had piled up on either side of the door. "Look," she said. "It's not dust. It's earth, Sarah. It's a sign. For you."

Eight

MARIA MELVILLE'S WYLDCLIFFE JOURNAL
APRIL 5, 1919

Miss Scarsdale says that what I saw was a sign, from the past to the future. I don't really understand what she means. I only know how I felt when the drums began.

I can't write about that, not yet.

I am sitting up in bed in the infirmary, waiting for my ankle to heal. My other cuts and bruises are getting better, but it will be days, perhaps weeks, before I can walk or ride again. Miss Scarsdale has told Miss Feather-stone that she has given me books to study while I am an invalid, but really she wants me to carry on as I have begun, and write everything down that has happened to me since I arrived at Wyldcliffe.

I will try. I will do my best. I am sorry if I cannot tell my tale well, but this is my story.

Before I came to Wyldcliffe, Mother and Father protected me from every hurt, but they have always told me the truth, even when I was very young. Mother's favorite line from the Gospel is "The truth will set you free," and I have tried to live by that too. So when Daphne tried to shock me with her unkind gossip about my birth, what she said wasn't actually a surprise. I have always known that Mother and Father, Katherine and William Melville, aren't my blood parents. As far back as I can remember, I knew that my real mother had died when I was a baby. Her name was Adamina, like mine. It means "daughter of the earth," and Adamina was a Gypsy. "One of the Roma, a proud and ancient people," Mother always said when she talked of her. "Don't ever forget that, Maria darling. Be proud of who you are."

And I am, I really am. Stupid, ignorant girls like Daphne and Winifred cannot destroy that pride.

When Mother and Father first got married they wanted to have a big family and dreamed of having lots of children to live with them at Grensham. But no baby came along, and when Mother was nearly thirty the doctor told her she couldn't have a child. She and Father tried not to be sad, and because they loved each other so much they were determined to make a happy, useful life together, even without children. So they looked after their land and the tenants on the estate. Mother ran a school, and Father built a village institute and started a health clinic, with a doctor for the local people. But still Mother said that they sometimes felt empty.

It must have been hard for them, having so much, but not the one thing they truly wanted.

Life at Grensham carried on as it always had, following the seasons of the earth and the church and the quiet country life. Father had always let the Gypsies camp on his land every year, which some of the neighboring landowners didn't like. There was trouble sometimes, but Father said it was an ancient right and the old ways of the land had to be respected. The Gypsy people came at harvest time and helped to bring in the crops, and Father was grateful and paid them fairly. They loved Mother especially and one year did her the honor of giving her a beautiful embroidered Romany dress in return for the help she gave to the women and their children. But one year there was dreadful trouble. Adamina was the most beautiful of all the young Gypsy wives, and she was expecting a baby. Her husband, Stefan, was accused of stealing from a local farmer and was sent to prison by the magistrate. The shock and upset made the baby come early, and Adamina died after the birth, with the baby in her arms. That baby was me.

I feel so sad when I think about her, my real mother, but my sadness seems far away in the past, like a beautiful piece of music that soothes as well as hurts.

After Adamina died, Mother helped to look after me, and soon she loved me as if I were her own baby. The Gypsies did not know what to do with me, as I belonged to the whole tribe, and yet to no one, as my father Stefan was still in prison. He had not yet claimed me by tying a red lace around my neck, according to the custom. Father knew that Stefan would never steal, and he went to great lengths to clear his name and get him freed. When Stefan came out of prison, he was heartbroken over Adamina's death and said he was going to travel far away to forget his grief and never come back to Grensham. It was a place of death and ill omen for his people now. But out of gratitude for the kindness he had received there from Mother and Father, he gave them the red lace and told them to claim Adamina's child as their own. It was what they both had dreamed of ever since they had first seen me.

And so that's how this "dirty Gypsy" came to be

adopted by a rich English couple. They have loved me so dearly and given me everything, even this fine education at Wyldcliffe. They did not imagine that the young ladies here would bully and despise me and drive me to seek more dangerous companions. . . .

I must rest now.

After the first couple of weeks I stopped trying to make friends with the stuck-up madams at Wyldcliffe, but in my heart I desperately wanted someone to love. Instead of trying to persuade Daphne and Winifred to like me, I looked for friends in other places. One comfort was darling Cracker, a beautiful, sturdy hill pony that Father had given me to ride. I was so glad Cracker was here with me. Sometimes I crept to the stables and wrapped my arms around his neck and breathed in his strong, warm scent. That felt like a little bit of love in this bleak place. Though perhaps if I had not had Cracker with me, none of this would have happened.

I was allowed to get up early and ride him down to the village and along the banks of the little river, as long as the groom came with me. On Sunday afternoons, a small group of girls who had brought horses from home were given permission to ride over the lower slopes of the moors with the grooms. These were precious hours of freedom. And on my fifteenth birthday, a few weeks after I had arrived, I had an even greater treat. Miss Scarsdale rode out with me on her beautiful white mare, and we took the path right over the moor that leads to the standing stones on the top of Blackdown Ridge. She said the stones were brought there hundreds and hundreds of years ago by people who worshipped them as part of their gods. The great stones were eerie, standing on the horizon all black and cold against the sky. Miss Scarsdale knows so much about geology and archaeology and history, and so many other things. She makes me realize how much I have to learn. I loved being out on the open moor and hearing the bleat of the lambs and the cries of the birds. I saw a curlew and a lapwing. We also rode past the entrance to some caves. Miss S. told me that they spread under the hills like a honeycomb.

I dreamed about the caves again last night. I woke up sobbing and gasping and had to call the nurse. I am ashamed of being so weak and childish, but I can't stop myself. I must be strong! I must be a soldier. . . .

But I was writing about trying to make friends. Sometimes I kept a piece of cake from supper and offered to share it with the maids in the servants' hall. I have always been great friends with the village girls at home who help Mother in the house, but these servants were different, sullen and suspicious. No doubt they are given a hard time by Miss Featherstone and are unhappy with their lot. Whatever the reason, they looked at me differently because I was a young lady, and the young ladies at the school looked at me differently because I was a Gypsy. So I was alone. Alone. It is a dreadful word. It makes my heart ache just to write it.

But when the Brothers came to Wyldcliffe, I was no longer alone.

Nine

I felt terribly alone. The sign, the dust, the earth. The first letter of my name. Now it felt as though I had been pushed into the spotlight, and I wasn't sure that I liked it. That night my dreams were troubled again, and I woke with my heart racing and my head throbbing. Perhaps, after all, I was better suited to being the one in the background.

Listen to the drums. What did the message mean? And who had sent it? I had heard drums in my dream—I had listened to their insistent rhythms. What more could I do to obey this strange instruction?

I got out of bed quickly, trying to shake off my unease. The morning bell hadn't rung yet, and my dorm mates were still asleep. I dressed without disturbing them and hurried down to the stables. All around me, life was renewing itself. Flowers were in bloom, trees were in blossom, and lambs were growing long-legged and fat next to their mothers on the sloping hills. But in my mind I was still crouching in the dark, gazing at that splintered door and trying to understand.

During the first hour of the early morning, before anyone else was about, I hid in a corner of Starlight's stable and searched the pages of the leather-bound Book that we had brought from Agnes's secret room. It was a curious object, and full of ancient lore and wisdom, though some of the pages were written in Eastern languages that I didn't understand. The Book also had a will of its own. Sometimes pages would stick together, concealing their contents from the reader, or the writing would melt away and go blank, or change from English to Latin, or into unknown symbols.

I searched through it patiently, looking for guidance, but found nothing. The only entry that seemed at all related to the mark on Helen's arm was a small footnote that read:

As to those who call themselves Witche Finders and do search a Woman's body for Blemishes, if any such Markes

are founde, that poor Soule is declared a servant of the Evil
One and is set apart and destroyed. This may be Igno-
rance and Superstition and yet there remains a Questione.
From where do such signs come? Many Scholars declare
they are a Sign of great Destiny, with Death in their wake.

Set apart and destroyed. Was Helen marked out
for some dreadful fate? And was there any connection
between her vision and my dreams, and the bizarre message emblazoned on the door of Agnes's secret study? We
had been back at Wyldcliffe for less than twenty-four
hours, and already I felt that a great snare had been laid
around us, and that our enemies were waiting for us to
fall into some kind of trap. We had to stick together to
survive; that much I knew.

I began to search the pages of the Book again, desperately looking for anything that would make sense of
the message about the drums, but by now the school was
waking up. I heard a cat mewing, a gardener's rake rattling
across the terrace, and two girls chattering in the yard as
they came to see their ponies before breakfast. Soon Josh
would arrive, and I didn't really want to bump into him.
I hastily closed the Book and scratched under the straw
in the corner of the stable. Long ago I had found a loose

brick that could be pulled away to unearth a shallow hiding place. When I had first arrived at Wyldcliffe I had hidden sweets and childish diaries there. Now I laid the Book in the narrow enclosure, and went to face the day.

On that first morning of the term, the general mood in the school was one of lighthearted optimism. When it was time for break, the students sat out on the wide terrace that overlooked the lake, enjoying the fresh scents of grass and blossom and talking excitedly about the changes that Miss Scratton had introduced.

"Did she really say we were going to have new computers?"

"And a dance!"

"My friend's brother goes to St. Martin's—the guys there are so hot! I can't believe it. . . ."

The exceptions to the general wave of approval were the die-hard snobs like Celeste van Pallandt and her uptight friend India Hoxton. They took a different approach.

"My mother says that the standards at Wyldcliffe have really been slipping recently," Celeste announced to anyone who would listen. "All that tacky publicity about Mrs. Hartle going off her head last term, and now these changes."

"They're hardly improvements, are they?" agreed India. "I mean, who wants a whole pack of village kids using our tennis courts and swimming pool? I'm seriously thinking of transferring to Chalfont Manor next term."

"Now that really would be an improvement," commented Evie, and a few other girls laughed. Celeste was in danger of losing her grip over the students in our form. It was Velvet who was the big excitement now. Everyone wanted to sit next to her and make friends with her and ask questions about her famous family. Velvet reveled in the flattery and told wilder and wilder stories about various musicians and actors she knew, and parties in L.A. that had been laced with drugs and alcohol and limitless amounts of money.

Superficially, it seemed that the usual Wyldcliffe student merry-go-round would launch itself again—petty squabbles and power struggles over who was going to be queen bee, who had the most money, the best holidays, the coolest friends; and it looked as though Velvet would win easily. Celeste might mutter like some outdated old dowager that "the Romaine girl really is most awfully common," but nobody cared. For once Wyldcliffe was eager to move out of the past century and embrace the modern world.

For me, though, as I watched those giggling, gossiping girls, I couldn't help feeling that they were like children playing on a beach, innocently unaware that a tidal wave was coming to sweep them all away. The new term that should have been full of hope—a new start for Evie and all of us—had been secretly overshadowed by the brand on Helen's arm, and the sound of distant drums.

When classes had ended for the day, we went to see Miss Scratton in the High Mistress's book-lined study and told her what had happened the night before.

"Are you sure?" she asked, sitting at her desk and watching us intently. "Are you sure it was the letter *S?*"

"Quite sure," Helen said. "*S* for Sarah."

"Or Sebastian," Miss Scratton replied.

"But Sebastian's story is over," said Evie with an effort. "That's what we—what we achieved last term. Why would he be mixed up in this?"

Miss Scratton frowned. "It depends who sent the message. Is it a warning or a trap? We can't be sure. We might be tempted to assume that the message is friendly, perhaps a sign from Agnes, as you were permitted to open her door, Sarah. And you came away with a great prize, the Book itself."

"Yes," I said. I had retrieved the Book from the stables and hidden it in my sports bag only a few minutes earlier, and now I took it out and handed it to the High Mistress. She laid it on her desk, lightly tracing the outline of the embossed silver letters on the cover: *The Mysticke Way.* As she touched the Book, other letters formed, silvery and uncertain. They glimmered in front of my eyes, and I saw the words THE PATH OF HEALING melt and dissolve into another phrase: THE PATH TO HELL. When Miss Scratton took her hands away, the milky, flickering words faded and vanished.

She looked up at us, her eyes narrowed. "This Book has brought either hell or healing to the many souls who have come into contact with it. Both madness and wisdom lie in its pages. Perhaps we might believe that we are far above any temptation to use it for evil, but we must be careful."

"What about the writing on the door?" I asked. It said 'Listen to the drums.' Do you know what the message means, Miss Scratton?" I asked. "Can the Book help us?"

"If the message is important, it will be made clear in time," Miss Scratton replied. "There is a time for all things. They cannot be forced." She looked at me and gave me a tired smile. "Dear Sarah, you are always eager to do the right thing. But sometimes we have to wait until the right path is revealed to us. Patience is a neglected virtue."

"But what about this?" Helen pulled up her sleeve and showed Miss Scratton the livid mark on her arm. "I can't just wait to find out about this. Sarah told me what the Book said. People thought marks like this were evil. An omen of death."

The High Mistress seemed to suppress an exclamation, but she merely said, "Cover it up and show no one else. Some force is reaching out for you."

"Is it—my mother?"

"Celia Hartle's spirit has not left this valley," Miss Scratton answered gravely. "The remnants of the coven have been gathering, and rumors of her new and deadlier powers are being spread by her faithful favorites."

For many months Miss Scratton had masqueraded as a member of the coven in order to track their plans. I hoped fervently that they had no suspicion that she was in fact acting against them and helping us.

"But the coven is finished, isn't it?" said Evie. "Their dreams of immortality died along with Mrs. Hartle."

"Sadly, there is no limit on evil. It is like foul water that will mold itself to any new shape that it finds. The hatred of evil for innocence is eternal and unchanging. The Dark Sisters are fewer than they were, as any waverers were frightened off by Mrs. Hartle's apparent death. But she is not truly dead, Evie. She has rejected that great mystery with all her twisted force. And those of her followers who remain—and even I do not know all their identities—are unyielding in their loyalty."

"Do they still think you are one of them?" I asked.

"They do not trust me entirely, and my plans for the school have horrified the members of the coven who work here. Secrecy and rigid rules suited their purposes. I have had to convince them that in opening up the doors of Wyldcliffe we will deflect some of the talk and suspicion that had begun to hover over the school like clouds. Already some parents have withdrawn their daughters this term, and more will go if the school does not change." She sighed. "In other circumstances, I could have wished to stay here. To be the High Mistress, guiding so many young hearts and minds, would be a worthwhile task." She fell silent, as if brooding on a deep, insoluble problem, then spoke again. "In the meantime, the Dark Sisters have one aim, and that is to serve Celia Hartle's corrupted spirit. And in turn she has one simple aim—revenge. She hates you for depriving her of Sebastian's strength and powers and soul. Sadly, I fear she hates Helen most of all."

"I hate her too," Helen said in a whisper. "Was it her stopping me passing through the air? It is the only freedom I've had all these years—I won't let her take that from me. I won't!"

Miss Scratton glanced at Helen with cool pity. "Remember that forgiveness is stronger than hatred, Helen. It could well have been her. But there are other hidden forces at work in Wyldcliffe. As I told you before, deep in the tangle of caves and tunnels under the hills there is a crack, a fractured time shift between this world and the shadows and the unseen lands of the past. You have reached out to mysteries, and this makes you vulnerable to many influences, both good and bad. However, for the moment, I think we can assume that if Celia Hartle is roaming the edges of this world once again, the daughter who dared to defy her will be uppermost in her thoughts. I am sorry, Helen. This is a great burden to you. I wish I could do more."

"But there must be something we can do!" I said. "Isn't there any way of protecting Helen from her?"

Miss Scratton lowered her voice. "I have already told you too much in revealing that I am a Guardian and in speaking of these matters. That is why I may not be allowed . . . I wish . . . but I will not leave you powerless or unprotected. Tomorrow night—" Miss Scratton broke off, listening.

There was a sharp knock on the door. Miss Scratton hastily thrust the Book back into my gym bag and pushed it into my hands.

"Enter!" she called. Then she continued in a cold, loud voice. "Helen Black, your work last term was disgraceful. I would expect better from a ten-year-old. All three of you need to improve . . . ah, Miss Dalrymple, do come in, I have nearly finished." She turned back to us with a severe expression. "You seem determined to be a bad influence on one another's studies. I do not wish to see you sitting next to one another in class from now on. And you will each bring me your notes on the French Revolution first thing tomorrow morning. You are dismissed."

We filed out silently. Miss Scratton's pretended anger was convincing, but I wondered if it would fool Miss Dalrymple. We knew that she had been one of Celia Hartle's inner circle, although she smiled at us hypocritically as we walked past her into the corridor. Then she closed the study door firmly in our faces and shut herself up with Miss Scratton. I looked at the others. They both seemed depressed, occupied with their thoughts.

"What do you think Miss Scratton was going to say about tomorrow night?" I whispered. "How can we find out? We need to—"

"Do you mind if we don't talk about it now?" asked Evie wearily. "My head is killing me. I'm sure Miss Scratton will tell us whatever we need to know later. Until then, why don't we just forget it?"

"Evie, we can't just ignore—"

"Do you really think Miss Scratton wants us to do

those notes on the French Revolution?" she interrupted. Her face was pale and its expression distant.

"I don't know, maybe we should," I said doubtfully. "Miss Dalrymple heard her tell us to do them. We should act like Miss Scratton is nothing more—or less—to us than the High Mistress."

"Bother. I wanted to . . . oh well. I'm going to the library to get started straightaway."

"We could do it together," I offered.

"No. It's okay." Evie walked away in the direction of the library. Helen watched her go, then shrugged and walked off too, heading out to the grounds. What was happening to us? I wanted to pull us all together to fight our enemies, but it was like trying to catch smoke.

I sighed and turned to my only comfort—my horses. I would go down to the stables before starting the notes Miss Scratton had asked for. When I reached the cobbled yard five minutes later, my heart tightened in my chest. Josh was taking a break from his work, sitting on a bale of hay with his long legs stretched out in front of him. He looked up and smiled. "Hey! Sarah!"

I smiled back. For one moment I thought that he actually wanted to see me. For one moment, that was all.

"Have you seen Evie anywhere?" Josh jumped up and

walked over to me eagerly. "She promised to meet me after class. She must be free by now."

My stupid smile froze. How could I have been so naive? A sick tremor of rejection churned in my stomach. I was such a fool. Josh didn't want me. And he wasn't the only one. Helen was withdrawing into herself again, and Evie—my best, my dearest friend—had made it perfectly clear that she wanted to get away from me. I had imagined myself to be the faithful anchor of our little world, but it looked as though I had been deluding myself. In that moment, I felt totally humiliated and useless.

"Sarah? I was asking about Evie? Do you know where she is?"

"Um . . . Miss Scratton has given us some extra work. Evie went off to the library to do it. I don't know how long she'll be."

Josh frowned. "That's a pain. I have to get home now to help my mother, then get down to some studying. Did I tell you I'm going to try to get into vet school next year?"

"Oh . . . no . . . that's great, Josh."

His smile shone out again. "Yeah. I'm still going to keep up my riding, though, but I think a career looking after horses properly would be better than mucking out stables for the likes of Celeste, don't you?"

I laughed feebly. "Oh, definitely." I just wanted to get away. This was even more painful than I had expected. I felt plain and dumpy and totally uninteresting to anyone. Despite my good intentions, my raw longings for attention and sympathy came flooding back. But I was just kidding myself. My dream of love had been exactly that—a dream, a total fantasy.

"I was telling Evie about it yesterday," Josh went on. "She's been encouraging me to apply to college. We've been in touch all through the holidays, but it's so good to see her again."

So they'd been writing and phoning each other. Another thing that Evie hadn't told me.

"I wish she'd been able to meet me tonight. I really wanted to show her some stuff before I left. I think she's going to be amazed by it." Josh hesitated, looking at me as if he was making up his mind about something. "I wanted to give it to her myself, but it's more important that she sees it. Hang on." He dived into the tack room and came out a few moments later holding what looked like a small bundle of papers stuffed in an envelope, and a tightly folded note.

"Can you give her this? Don't let anyone else see it, except Helen, of course. It's some incredible news. Well, I'll let Evie tell you about it." He handed me the bundle and the note. "And tell her I'll see her tomorrow, okay? You won't forget? Thanks, Sarah, you're so good."

Good old Sarah. Always reliable, always there. Josh swung away with his graceful, confident stride. I waited until he had gone, fighting temptation. As soon as he was out of sight I gave in weakly and unfolded the note. *Dear Evie, I've been thinking about you all day. Meet me by the gates before breakfast tomorrow. I can't wait to hear what you think of this. . . .*

Bang, boom, bang . . . My heart thudded, wounded by jealousy and despair. Why was I bothering? I had tried to be strong and good, but no one wanted anything that I had to offer. I looked up, and the evening sun dazzled my eyes. *Bang, boom . . .* Hope drained away. The hills seemed full of watchers. The drums were coming closer, but I still didn't know what they meant.

I turned away from where Josh had been standing and leaned my head against Starlight's neck. No one could help me. Nobody wanted me.

My heart ached for everything that I might have had if Cal had not moved on. I wished with all my soul that I could ride away from Wyldcliffe and follow Cal and his Gypsy brothers over the horizon, into a different life.

Ten

It was when we walked to the village church one Sunday that I first saw the Gypsy Brothers. We were walking as usual in a "crocodile"—a long row of neat girls dressed in Sunday-best coats and hats. I was walking next to Violet Deane from the lower form. No one ever walks with her, as she stutters. Poor Violet, I don't mind her slow speech. As we walked together I told her the names of all the plants and trees that I could see. Some I already knew from home, others Miss Scarsdale had shown me.

"Maria Melville, we do not need you to make a commentary on the local wildlife," Miss Featherstone scolded. She told me to walk in silence like the others, but just then a murmur ran along the line of girls like a flame running through dry grass.

"Look! Look over there in the field! They've come back. We saw them last year, don't you remember?"

"Oh, look at their little carts! Aren't they sweet?"

But there were other whispers too.

"That man is staring at us."

"How black his eyes are!"

"What a ruffian he looks—it shouldn't be allowed."

Now Miss Featherstone was really angry. "Young ladies, you will not notice, you will look straight ahead, and you will remain silent!"

But we couldn't help noticing. A Gypsy camp had sprung up overnight on the edge of the village. It was like something from a fairy tale. There were brightly colored wooden houses on wheels and a smoking campfire and horses and dogs. And the people! I thought my heart would burst with excitement. There were people like me with dark hair and skin. Their eyes seemed full of sharp wisdom, as if they could see far away and yet right inside my heart. I stood staring, and a boy of about sixteen grinned at me. I smiled back. This was my family—my real family, like Adamina and Stefan.

"Maria Melville, stop gaping like a street urchin,"

Miss Featherstone snapped at me. "Take two bad conduct marks."

After that we marched in silence into the stone church, which was too cold and empty for my God to inhabit. Later Miss Featherstone told us that we were forbidden to visit the village because of the "undesirable strangers in our midst." But I knew that this was a rule I would break. I had to see them again, especially the boy with the black hair and laughing eyes.

Mother had given me a purse of pocket money to take to school for treating my friends to cakes and ices. Poor dear Mother, she didn't know that no one at Wyldcliffe would condescend to take tea with a Gypsy brat. But the money came in useful. All through the following week I bribed the groom to let me ride to the village every morning before breakfast, despite Miss F.'s edict. Joseph knew it was against the rules now for me to go to the village, but he was torn by the money, and he didn't mean me any harm. He would ride out of the school grounds with me just after daybreak, and then hang back by the entrance to church, muttering and praying to himself as I went on to meet with the Gypsies.

The boy, Zak, was my first friend. He was dark-eyed and fearless, poised between boy and man, and he welcomed me with frank curiosity. I showed him the little photograph I have of my blood parents, Adamina and Stefan, and he accepted me straightaway. He said that Wyldcliffe was one of his family's regular stopping places, where they could rest and wait until the better weather had settled. Then they would travel on the open road again, following the traditional routes. While they stayed in Wyldcliffe the men did odd jobs in the village, and the women sold lace and baskets where they could. The older people in the camp were wary of me at first, but once they believed my story they accepted me as one of their own. Zak's father gave me a carved whistle, and his mother taught me some of her secrets for foretelling the weather. And every morning Zak and I raced our ponies over the sweet turf of the moors and laughed until I could hardly breathe. I thought I knew a lot about the countryside, but he showed me where the earliest flowers were raising their heads, and where the mother birds had laid their eggs, and where the badgers made holes for their young. Then I had to hurry back to school before I got into trouble with Miss Featherstone.

Once, as we lay on the grass under the bright new sun, Zak leaned over and kissed me.

Perhaps I should cross that part out of my tale, but

I am not ashamed of it. His lips tasted of sweet apples, and there was a look in his eyes as he held me that turned my heart over. The next moment he laughed again and pulled me to my feet. But I thought often of that kiss, and the smell of his skin and the touch of his dark hair on my cheek. I still think of him. I always shall.

The Gypsy men kept themselves a little apart from the women and the children in the camp. They were proud and handsome and marvelous riders. They talked amongst themselves in harsh voices, sometimes in English and sometimes in their own language. Zak told me that they called one another "Brother" and would do anything to protect one another's honor and safety. One day soon, Zak said, on his next birthday, he would be a Brother too.

There was another man living in the camp. He was very good-looking, with long black hair like the Gypsies, but his skin was fair and his eyes were as blue as the sapphires in Mother's ring. He spoke softly, just like Father does. The other men called him Fairfax, and Zak told me that he was gaje. That means that Fairfax was not one of the Roma. But Zak said that Fairfax often traveled with his family for a while; then he would go away and no one would know where he had gone. He was a great conjuror and helped the Gypsies earn money when they visited towns and fairs.

When Fairfax was in a good mood, he showed me some of his conjuring tricks. He made coins and playing cards disappear and drew an egg from my ear. At least he seemed to. Once he broke a little mirror into pieces, then spoke some strange words, and when he showed me the mirror again it was smooth and unbroken. He made me laugh with his tricks, but his blue eyes looked sad. Zak whispered in my ear that Fairfax had killed someone and was under a curse that meant he could never grow old. I didn't believe him. Fairfax couldn't have been a murderer. He was too sad and beautiful for that. Besides, I wasn't afraid of him, and I am sure I would have been if he had really been a criminal. I wasn't afraid of any of the Brothers. Perhaps it would have been better if I had been.

The nurse is coming into the room.

I must hide this.

Eleven

Darling Sarah,
Hide this when you get it. I couldn't bear anyone to
read it except you, my Gypsy girl. I can only speak in
this way to you and to no one else. I don't open my
heart easily.

It is three weeks since I left Wyldcliffe with my
family, and every day has been filled with thoughts of
the time we spent together. It was far too short, but the
memories will always be precious. I remember our rides
on the moors and evening sun on your hair. I wanted
so much to hold you in my arms, and to ask you to run
away with me, but I knew that would be impossible.
Fate has declared that we must be apart. Instead I only
have your memory for consolation, but I will return one
day, so that we can be together again. Then you will

have a thousand kisses from me, my angel. . . .
Yours for all eternity, Cal

I never got that letter. It existed only as a fantasy in my head. Even if Cal had written to me, he wouldn't have used such words. They were the clichés I had read a hundred times in library books, and had nothing to do with the rough-haired, fiercely independent boy that I had met. Cal had been terse and guarded and unexpected, but I had sensed his warm nature underneath his caution of strangers and his hard way of life. And he had liked me, I was sure of that. On the night of Mrs. Hartle's death on the moors, when we were all standing about in shock, it had seemed the most natural thing in the world for me to lean against Cal for comfort, and to feel his arm round my shoulders. Afterward we had often ridden out together, and he had given me small tokens and gifts—a flower, a feather, a carved whistle—but he had never kissed me. My body was aching with secret desires, and I knew it wasn't really about Josh.

As I watched Josh walk away from the stables, happy in the knowledge that he would see Evie in the morning, I forced myself to acknowledge that my feelings for Josh had been nothing but a crush that would fade as easily as it had blossomed. Officially, of course, I had already completely forgiven Evie for being the one to attract Josh instead of me.

What was it I had said? *My heart isn't broken, only bruised.*

It wasn't just my heart that had been bruised, though; it had been my pride. If Cal had stayed, maybe things would have been different, but he was gone and he hadn't written and I felt abandoned. My pride had turned sour, like milk standing in the sun.

I gave Starlight a last, lonely hug and wandered out of the stable yard and into the walled kitchen garden nearby. Hardly any students went there, apart from the few of us who were keen on growing flowers and fruit on our own little patches of ground. This place had given me such pleasure once, but it seemed dead and overgrown now. There was no one there, and I sat disconsolately on a low stone bench, alone with my uncomfortable thoughts.

Oh, I had always been so honest and frank, but I hadn't been truly honest with Evie, or even with myself. Now I had to admit to my shame that although I loved her like a sister, I also secretly resented her. What do they call it? Sibling rivalry?

I loved Evie for her beauty and grace and courage, for her talents and the mysterious depths of her personality. She seemed to me to be like some kind of mermaid princess, with her sea-gray eyes and her slim figure and her long red hair. Sebastian had loved her almost to madness, and now, as easily and naturally as breathing, Josh was ready to love her too. And what was I in comparison? Apple-cheeked Sarah, everybody's friend and nobody's soul mate, my fingers grubby from digging herbs and plants in my garden, or from grooming horses and playing with the stable cat. There was nothing mysterious about me. Nothing to attract that look of love that I had dreamed about so many times.

There is a temptation to tear this part out of my story and present myself in a better light, but I won't. The Mystic Way is a path of healing, and telling the truth about one's malady is the first step to being cured.

Sitting on that stone bench in the empty, chilly garden, my self-pity threatened to overwhelm me. But the promises I had made to myself dragged me back to the present like a heavy chain.

I stood up and pushed Josh's envelope into my pocket. It was no use brooding over pathetic dreams of love and romance, I told myself, when my sisters were in danger. Miss Scratton had said there would be something we could do to protect ourselves. At least I could find out what that was and do it, whatever it was, whatever it cost. It would be a way for me to hide my ugly feelings and be useful to the others, to prove that I loved them and to earn their love in return. . . .

I would be good.

I would be strong.

I would be Sarah.

I found Evie in the music room, where she was sorting out scores for choir practice—one of the jobs she had to do as a scholarship student.

"Hey," I said. "Have you got a minute?"

"I'm kind of busy," she mumbled, not looking up from the sheets of music spread out on the top of the grand piano.

"I saw Josh. He asked me to give you something."

Now I had her attention. "Josh? What did he say? Is he still waiting for me?" Her cheeks flushed slightly, and there was eagerness in her voice.

"No, he had to go home. But he wanted me to give you this."

I handed over the little package, and she opened the note quickly. I was going to walk away and leave her there to enjoy her love letter, but she gave a low gasp.

"Sarah, wait, it's something about Agnes. Oh my God!"

"What? What is it?"

"Josh has found a connection between his family and Agnes . . . listen . . ."

She smoothed the note out and started to read aloud in a hurried whisper.

"'Dear Evie'... um ... then it says, 'I've found something out about Agnes. I can't wait to hear what you think of it. You remember I showed you the photo my family has of Martha—Agnes's old nurse? She lived at Uppercliffe Farm and secretly looked after Agnes and her daughter, Effie (your great-great-grandmother, of course), when they came back from London. I told you my mother's family was related to Martha's. They lived at Uppercliffe before the farm was abandoned after the First World War. The three brothers in the family were all killed, and there was no one to carry on. Anyway, I asked Mom to dig out any more photos she had of the old days, and she gave me a whole bunch of mementos that had come from the farm, old photos and letters, all sorts. Mom isn't really interested in the past—much too practical, and she'd never really bothered to take much notice of this stuff, but I think it's amazing. And it might be important—for us. I must see you tomorrow—'"

Evie broke off. She looked scared, but I was burning with curiosity. "So what is it?" I said. "What has he found?"

She slowly undid the bundle of papers. There were more sepia-tinted photographs printed on stiff card, of long-dead people connected to both Martha and Josh.

The photos showed strong, upright farmers and their stoutly handsome wives, dressed in their awkward Sunday best and staring rigidly ahead into the camera. But one photo was of a young girl of about eight years old, with fine features, silky curls, and haunting eyes.

"Look, Sarah, this has to be Effie!" Martha's family had adopted her as one of their own after Agnes died, so Agnes's parents, Lord and Lady Templeton of Wyldcliffe Abbey, never knew anything about her. Evie gazed in fascination at the faded image of her great-great grandmother.

"There are some other things," I said. "What are they?"

Tucked under the photographs was a fine sheet of paper, almost as thin as tissue. Evie unfolded it and said, "It's Agnes's handwriting . . . it's a letter."

She sat down at one of the desks in the music room, and I could see that she was trembling.

"Aren't you going to read it?" I asked.

"Yes . . . no . . . I . . . oh, Sarah," she whispered. "It brings it all back! This brings Agnes so close . . . and Sebastian . . . I don't know if I can take it."

"But Josh thinks it's something you'd want to know. If it had been something bad, he would have warned you, wouldn't he?"

"Yes, I guess you're right. I'm sorry, I'm being stupid." She raised her beautiful gray eyes pleadingly. "Will you read it, Sarah?"

She passed the fragile piece of paper to me, and I began to read the letter aloud.

"*London, ninth November 1884. My dear Martha, How good of you to write to me here in my humble lodgings! It was kind of you indeed to send me your heartfelt consolations after my poor Francis's death. He was a tender and faithful husband, despite his poor health and ill fortune. My grief for him is tempered by the knowledge that he is released from his earthly sufferings, and I am comforted by the "sure and certain hope" that we shall be reunited in the next life. And he has left me with the most precious gift, my bairn as you call her, dearest darling little Effie. She is such a bonny baby, and I long for you to see her and pet her as you once petted me. Your letters are like treasures that I pore over again and again, my faithful friend. You are my only link with my old life at Wyldcliffe. I long to get away from this smoky, foggy city, and I dream of returning to my dear valley's clear air and familiar scenes. If only my parents at the Abbey could see my baby and welcome her too.*

"*There is something I need to speak of, Martha—*'

"Are you okay, Evie?" I asked, breaking off from the letter. She was gripping her hands together as though dreading what might come next.

"Yes—carry on—we have to know—"

"'There is something I need to speak of, Martha. When, almost two years ago at the start of this strange journey, I healed the blindness caused by the cataract in your eyes, you did not know then that it was the sacred fire of the Mystic Way that gave me the power to help you. Now you know all my secrets, and although you were first afraid that such dealings were ungodly, you understand now that all I could do was sanctioned by nature and the Great Creator. After long study, I know more of these mysteries and their workings. I must tell you about something that I did not know when I cured your failing sight.

"'In reaching out to heal you, a spark of the sacred fire passed from me to you. It will do you no harm, but will warm and radiate the people around you—passed in its turn by your love to your dear family, those living now and those to come. It is a great mystery, but I repeat—it will do them no harm. The spark may lie hidden for generations, then blaze out like the sun, linking that person back to me and my path of healing. Fire is the divine force that sears to cleanse and cure, that touches all our passions and drives our loves. I hope that you will not be afraid but welcome this news as a gift. Your family may not be rich in coins, but touched by the secret flame, they will always be rich in love. I see your descendants striding tall and courageous over the moors, tending the land and their flocks, golden-haired like the ripe corn, as true and strong as the oak trees that grow on the grounds of my old home! May they be blessed.

"'I hesitate to ask, but is there any news of my dear friend at Fairfax Hall? I pray for him every day, as I do for you.'

"'In hopes that I will see you again soon, I am your ever-grateful friend, Agnes Templeton Howard.'"

I folded the letter up and gave it back to Evie.

"It's Josh, isn't it?" I said. "He's the one touched by the fire. A spark of healing."

"Do you really think so?" Her voice was barely audible, and she didn't look at me. "I want so much to be healed. I feel that I'll never be the same again."

"But what you said before about hope—not being afraid to live, embracing the good and bad—"

"It's easy to say," she replied with the ghost of an unsteady smile. "Not quite so easy to do."

I thought I heard a noise in the corridor. I turned quickly to see who it was and noticed a shadow in the doorway. Someone was there, hovering by the door.

"Who's there?" I called. I heard a cough, and then a slight figure entered the room. It was the music master, Mr. Brooke. He was a nervous, pale young man with a hesitant manner and a permanent cold. He was one of the few male teachers who had been allowed at Wyldcliffe and was obviously not considered a threat—it was impossible to imagine any student ever having a crush on him.

"Have you finished sorting out those copies, Miss Johnson?" he asked in his high, reedy voice. "You should have done it by now. The bell will be ringing soon for supper."

"Sorry, Mr. Brooke," Evie murmured as she quickly gathered the music together, hiding the letter and photos under one of the scores. "You go to supper, Sarah, I'll be okay." She turned her back and bent over her work. Mr. Brooke frowned at me, and I had no option but to leave her to get on with her chores.

The letter confirmed what I had really already known—that Josh was fated to bring Evie back from the barren places she had wandered in, back into the warmth and the light.

But who would ever heal me?

Twelve

The next morning after breakfast, I went with Helen and Evie to knock on the door of the High Mistress's study.

"Enter."

Miss Scratton was once again in deep conference with Miss Dalrymple, looking through some papers. There was tension in Miss Scratton's thinly pressed lips, and she didn't look up as we trooped into the room. Miss Dalrymple eyed us greedily, however, as though weighing up our suitability for some secret task. Knowing that this fat, fake, smiling teacher was in fact one of the Dark Sisters made me so angry, but we were helpless to act against her. The police would have laughed at any claims we could make. That Miss Dalrymple belonged to a black magic cult? That a year ago Helen had seen Laura van Pallandt, Celeste's cousin, being sacrificed and murdered by Mrs. Hartle? Only we knew that Mrs. Hartle had stolen some of Laura's life force in a sick ceremony, sucking her soul away. But she got greedy and went too far and Laura had died. No one would believe us, though. We had no evidence. It was an accident, they would say, the poor girl had drowned in the lake. A terrible, tragic accident.

No, there was no way we could run to the authorities. It was only in the midnight world of shadows that we could confront Miss Dalrymple and the rest of the coven. I forced myself to smile back and promised my anger that one day Rowena Dalrymple would pay for the wrongs that she and her kind had done.

"Good morning, ladies," she simpered. "I hope you have completed the task our dear High Mistress has set you. You should be setting an example for the other students, not falling behind. I'm sure you don't want to let yourselves down in any way." She smiled as if to encourage our efforts, but her eyes were heavy and blank like two wet pebbles.

"Here are the notes you asked for, Miss Scratton," I said, handing them over.

"And mine." Evie laid hers down on the desk, and so did Helen.

"I shall be reading them carefully to make sure they are satisfactory," Miss Scratton replied icily. "You may go." We turned to leave; then she called us back. "Wait. It would be useful for you to read this account of the Reign of Terror. Chapter eighteen. We shall be discussing the topic in my next class."

I took the book she was holding out, and then she dismissed us. Miss Dalrymple's heavy stare followed us as we walked out of the paneled room and into the corridor. As soon as we were out of earshot of the High Mistress's study, I pulled the others into an empty classroom.

"Chapter eighteen! Let's look and see if there's any message for us."

A thin piece of paper had been tucked discreetly into the book at the beginning of the chapter. I snatched it eagerly and recognized Miss Scratton's neat handwriting: *Meet me tonight at midnight at the ruins. Bring the two gifts. Do not be seen too much together. Let it be understood that you have quarreled. If you are being watched, it will be better for the watchers to think that you are no longer united in strength and purpose. DESTROY THIS NOTE.*

"Tonight then," said Helen. "With the gifts. The Book and the Talisman. Is that all right, Evie?"

Helen and I both looked at Evie questioningly. Would

she be willing to plunge into the dark once again?

"Why not?" Evie replied. "If you go, I go. We are bound together in sisterhood, each to each. Isn't that how it works?" But she didn't sound natural; it was as if she was quoting from an old book.

"Are you sure?" I said.

"Of course. We haven't really quarreled, have we? Why would we ever do that?"

Because you don't really want to be part of this any longer. Because you're scared and confused. Because you want to bury your love for Sebastian in Josh's arms. Because I'm angry and jealous and can't admit it. Because you can't look me in the eye anymore.

I didn't say any of that, of course. "We'll never quarrel" was what I really said. I didn't mean to be a hypocrite. At that moment I desperately wanted it to be true.

"But you heard what Miss Scratton said," Helen reminded us. "We have to stay away from one another. Until midnight."

She walked away quickly, as though she was glad of an excuse to be alone. Evie mooched away in the opposite direction. I tore the note into a hundred tiny fragments, then went outside and dropped them like seeds at the back of a bed of spring flowers, praying that something good would grow from Miss Scratton's plans.

* * *

There was no moon. Thick clouds had drifted in from the west and blotted out the stars. That was a good sign, I thought. There would be less chance of being seen.

I reached the stable yard. It looked so different at night, closed up and secretive. Trying not to make a sound, I raised the latch on Starlight's stall and crept inside. My darling horse raised his head sleepily.

"Shhh . . . ," I murmured. I lifted the loose brick in the corner and found the Book, then made my way across the empty courtyard and down to the lake, keeping to the trees and the shadows. I didn't dare turn on my flashlight, but I felt sure-footed in the dark, and soon the ruins rose up in front of me. How still and silent they were, how old they felt; a mysterious link with a forgotten way of life. And yet the earth under my feet was far, far older, and so were the hills and the hidden stars. Our human gains and losses seemed very small and fragile in comparison.

I was the first one there. I waited under a broken archway that was deep in shadow. Mist hovered over the lake and crept along the ground. A few moments later I saw Helen and Evie flitting over the damp grass. I gave a low whistle and they joined me in my hiding place. As we waited a star emerged from behind the clouds and looked down on us like a cold, staring eye. I shivered, and wished that Miss Scratton would arrive. The bell of the village church began to toll midnight and then died away.

A figure wrapped in a long cloak began to pace across the empty spaces of the ruins, looking down on the ground, shrouded by a hood. Whoever it was didn't seem to have the same air or gait as Miss Scratton. I held my breath. The unknown person was getting closer, apparently searching for something, or someone.

A fox barked in the distant fields. The figure looked up with a sudden jerk, changed direction, and hurried away. Then I heard Miss Scratton's voice in my ear. "Don't move. Wait."

The hurrying figure had disappeared into the thick shrubs. The sound of rustling footsteps faded into silence. I turned in relief to Miss Scratton and whispered, "Who was that?"

"One of the coven, no doubt. We have to work quickly."

"But what are we going to do?" asked Evie.

"We are going to attempt to perform a powerful spell of protection that may help to ward off Mrs. Hartle's spirit. You are all vulnerable to attack, so at least this may be a way of creating a protective circle around you."

"You mean she won't be able to get at us?" asked Helen doubtfully. "Could anything really keep her away?"

"We must hope so. Evie, do you have the Talisman?"

Evie took the necklace off and handed it to Miss Scratton, who shook her head. "No, it is yours. You must use it."

"But I don't know whether I can anymore. . . ."

"Then we shall find out. Now, Sarah, did you bring the Book?" I brought it out from under my jacket. "Excellent. This was once a holy place, the heart of Wyldcliffe, and its blessings may aid us." She looked at us solemnly. "Let us begin. Do not be afraid of what you see. They are simply dreams and visions. Remember that: Do not be afraid."

I can't reveal all the secrets of the ceremony that followed. But first we placed the Book on the earthen altar, opened its pages, and read its instructions: "To Guarde against an Evil Spirit . . ." The heavy black letters had a menacing look. What if we didn't succeed?

We made the Circle, then linked hands. "I stand here as Guardian and protector of these your servants," Miss Scratton intoned. "Accept my presence, Lord of Creation. May it be pleasing to you. Let us do your work in secret."

All at once, the walls of the chapel sprang up whole, as they had once been hundreds of years before. But they were silvery and insubstantial, like the milky lettering that had appeared under Miss Scratton's long fingers when she had handled the Book. I seemed to see them and yet not see them, with the lake and the trees and the shrubs still faintly outlined beyond the walls, like the ghostly negative of a photograph.

We all stared at our teacher questioningly.

"What . . . how . . . ?"

"For a brief moment we are protected from spying eyes. This much I can do. The rest is up to you."

We fell to work, following the instructions of the book, tracing complex patterns on the ground and speaking the incantations: "For the protection of our sisters . . . to guard against the wolf, the raven, and the nameless dead . . . to bind the spirit to the grave . . . to bind the enemy in the wilderness . . ."

We summoned the powers of the earth, air, and water. The wind sang outside the glassy walls, and the lake murmured in its bed, and the earth rumbled beneath our feet. I seemed to see shadowy rows of women kneeling in the dim corners of the chapel and whispering ancient prayers.

"Evie, now you must ask Agnes for her aid," urged Miss Scratton. "Call upon the sacred flame. But do not fear anything you might see."

With trembling hands, Evie raised the Talisman on high.

"Agnes?" she called. "Please help us. We need you." A flash of lightning tore across the black sky. My eyes were blinded for a moment; then I saw the outline of a girl dressed in white. She was standing under the ruined east window with her hands stretched out toward us. Agnes had heard and answered our plea.

"We make a Circle against the demon and the goblin," we chanted. "We shield our sisters against hatred and revenge, in day and night, in sun and storm."

A streak of fire shot around the edges of the Circle like a whip crack of electricity. Then Agnes spoke, her voice far away and faint. "It is done, my sisters. Do not release the spell. Let it protect you now and tomorrow and for all time."

"Now and for eternity."

The spell was made. The flames died away, and Agnes was no longer with us. Miss Scratton spoke. "Well done." But just as we were about to break the Circle, everything changed. A violent wind sprang through the chapel ruins, tearing at our clothes and hair, snatching our breath away. We were plunged into complete blackness. Strange sighing voices sobbed and howled in the air. "Hold hands," commanded Miss Scratton. "Don't let go! Don't be afraid!"

I seemed to see the rows of shadowy women again,

but now I could see their faces under their veils; pale holy faces, intense with prayer and fear. They rose like frightened birds as a band of men, armed with swords and clubs, burst into the chapel. The thud of violent blows and screams and the shattering of glass pierced my mind. Then the shadows wavered and changed, and now I saw a crowd of black-robed women carrying a muffled, heavy burden. They stumbled and jolted, and I saw what they carried. I swayed in horror. It was poor dead Laura, her lips blue and her wide eyes staring and empty. Her body was being dragged in secret to the lake by the Dark Sisters. I wanted to scream, but Miss Scratton gripped my hand and whispered, "Hold on! Don't look!"

The dreadful image dissolved and the air swirled. I saw Agnes again. Now she was in front of me, now behind; now she was running past, her rich auburn hair streaming down her back. The next moment someone was running over the grass with her: a dazzlingly handsome young man with black hair and blue eyes. He radiated confidence and energy, as though nothing could ever hold him back or diminish his bright youth.

"Sebastian! Sebastian!" Evie cried in agony. But neither Agnes nor Sebastian could see or hear us. The images flashed from one scene to another. The two friends were reading under a broken archway. They were carrying a picnic basket to the lake. Now they were laughing, now quarreling—arguing violently. Then, most dreadful of all, Sebastian was stumbling toward the chapel's grassy altar, carrying Agnes's lifeless body in his arms. He was weeping and cursing himself. I stood and watched him in speechless horror, but Evie tried to wrench her hand out of mine and run to him.

"NO!" shouted Miss Scratton. "Do not break the Circle!"

Sebastian stumbled nearer and nearer to us, until I could have touched him, and then as abruptly as it had begun the wind dropped and the wailing voices were stilled, and the shadows of Sebastian Fairfax and Lady Agnes Templeton were no longer visible to our sight.

"It is over."

Miss Scratton stepped out of the Circle. The glimmering chapel walls melted away, and the ruins took on their familiar shape. We were back in reality, whatever that meant now.

Evie was crying, sobbing in desperation. I had never seen her break down like that before. I should have rushed over to comfort her, but for an instant something held me back. I am ashamed to confess it, but I actually envied her for having had something that was so precious that losing it was such agony. As she covered her face with her hands, I picked up the Book from where it lay on the cold earth. The words that Agnes had written in her journal came back to me: *If it were up to me, I would fling this book into the lake and let it sink into those deep waters, never to be seen again.* I didn't want to accept it, but deep down I understood now why Evie wanted nothing more to do with the Mystic Way. Loving Sebastian had left her with memories almost too painful to bear.

Thirteen

The memories of what I have to describe next are almost too painful to bear. I would never have imagined the places that my innocent rebellion would lead me. But that was later. At first I was happy, because of Zak.

At school I pretended to be the perfect student, though I couldn't help smiling to myself when I thought about my hours of freedom at the Gypsy camp. Sometimes I saw Miss S. looking at me, and I wondered if she guessed.

I had imagined that my secret life with Zak and his family would carry on just the same, carefree and happy, but one morning I rode up to the camp and found everything in confusion. Women were crying and wailing and the men looked angry and the children looked scared. I jumped off Cracker and ran up to Zak. "What's wrong? What has happened?"

Zak looked different, as though he had become a man in a single night. "My father is missing. He went out hunting late last night and has not come back."

"Perhaps he is just sleeping out on the hills."

"No! Old Rebekah has spoken. She says he has been taken by the evil spirits who dwell in the caves."

"Don't be so foolish!" I exclaimed.

"You call the Romany ways foolish?" Zak glared at me. "Everyone knows that Rebekah has the Sight. If she says a thing, it is true. The men are going out to look for him."

"But where will you look? The moors are vast. Where will you start?"

"My uncles saw my father late last night up near the entrance to the caves by the White Tor. He said he was looking for a fledging linnet as a gift for my mother and would stay a little longer on the hills. He must have strayed too close to the caves and angered the spirits that live there. That is where we will go to search for him. Underground."

"Let me come with you," I begged. I didn't believe in

the spirits story, of course. I thought that his father must be lying hurt on the moors after an accident.

"This is not for girls, Maria. Besides, we hunt at night. My father was taken at night, so he will be found at night." Zak shook his head to fight back his tears. "If my father does not come back, I will have to be the head of our family before my time, and look after my mother and sisters."

"I am sure you will find him, Zak. But I wish you would tell the doctor or the village constable. They would help you to search."

Zak laughed a hard, unhappy laugh. "They would be only too glad that one of our kind is lost." I had never heard him speak so bitterly before.

"But what if your father has fallen and has broken his leg?" I asked. "You will need a doctor to help him."

"Your ways are not our ways."

"But I am like you! I am one of the Roma."

"Then accept what the Elders have decided," he said with a scowl. "We will hunt for my father tonight, and it is only the Brothers who will go. The women will stay at home and keep the fire burning. That will keep his soul alive."

Fairfax passed by us and stopped to speak to me.

"Don't worry. We won't rest until we find him."

"Are you going with the Brothers? But you are not even Roma! It's not fair!"

"But I am older and stronger than you are, little Maria." Fairfax gave me a tired smile. "And I have some powers of my own."

"I am not little," I snapped. "I am nearly sixteen. I am not a child!"

I turned away and mounted Cracker, then galloped back to school, crying all the way. I wanted so much to help, but it seemed that Zak had turned against me. I was good enough to be his carefree companion, to be given secret kisses, but not good enough to ride with the Brothers. I wanted to prove that I was really part of the Gypsy family and just as strong as a boy.

If I had known what I would see, would I still have gone?

I do not know. I will never know.

I turned to Joseph again for help. Another shilling bought what I needed from him. He agreed to leave Cracker saddled and ready in the little paddock by the school gates that night. After lights-out, I told Winifred that I was not well and was going to see the nurse. Then I crept softly down the marble stairs and fled through a side door and into the moonlit grounds. My heart was beating so fast, I thought it would burst. Joseph had done what I had asked and had left a heap of boys' clothing next to my pony. I pulled them on, muffling my figure with a thick jacket and scarf, then led Cracker out of the gates and down the lane to the village. I didn't ride straight up to the Gypsy camp. My plan was to hide in the shadows of the trees by the river. Then I would join the men as they rode past in the darkness, hoping that they would not notice one more young lad joining in the hunt. With my hair pushed into a cap, I prayed that I would not be recognized.

My plan worked at first. After a few minutes I saw the riders file out of the camp to the river, on their way to the open moors. Zak was riding at the front, solemn and fierce, next to his uncles. I hung back until they had all gone by; then I urged my pony forward and joined their company. Once we reached the moors, the signal was given and the horses galloped away into the night.

Although I was sorry for Zak and wanted so much to find his father, I could not help rejoicing in that ride. The stars and the hoofbeats and the wind on my face! And the men cried out in low, strong voices; a chant that sounded wild and sad at the same time. They halted now and then to wait for an answering call from Zak's father, but we heard nothing.

We reached the ridge with the stars shining high above us, and rode up to the standing stones. They looked like a holy temple in the moonlight. The men fell silent and we came to a stop. One of them dismounted and buried a bundle at the foot of the tallest stone. It was food and drink and gold coins. "Spirit of the hills, take this offering in return for our Brother," he said. "Open the secret ways to us. Release his body and soul."

Then the man sprang back up onto his horse and we galloped away again. Soon the land became marshy and wet and the horses had to pick a path carefully for fear of falling into the bog. But at last we passed that danger and climbed up to the White Tor, the great outcrop of limestone where the caves led under the hills.

The mouth of the biggest cave looked so black, as though a hole had been cut out of the earth. It felt like the entrance to another world. Everyone dismounted, and the horses whinnied in alarm as they were tethered outside the cave mouth. I shivered and began to think that perhaps this was not such a splendid adventure after all.

"Our Brother has been taken under the earth. We must follow him into Death."

It was too late to turn back. I pulled my cap farther over my eyes and looked down at the ground as we moved forward, hoping that no one would speak to me and guess who I was. But someone jostled me and stepped on my foot. I looked up guiltily and saw Zak staring at me in recognition.

"You'll get into such trouble!" he hissed at me.

"I just wanted to be with you," I whispered back. "Please, Zak, don't tell."

I think in truth he was glad I was there, because he didn't give me away. He grasped my hand for a moment, and then we followed the men into the cave, walking silently like in a dream.

I can't write about it anymore. That is enough, for now.

Fourteen

We had done enough for one night. After we managed somehow to get back into the school, I fell into a deep, exhausted sleep. My dream came again.

I was back in the underground cave. Torches were burning. I could smell the resin and sap of broken branches, a sweet smell above the fumes of smoke. "Where are you?" I called out, and then, "I am ready." The face in the mask was there again, but I wasn't afraid now. I was wearing a crown of leaves, like a queen. A pair of eyes met mine, full of love, then the drums began and the blade struck.

When I woke, I felt strangely calm, as though I had slept for hours.

Listen to the drums. This dream had been different, as though something good and hopeful had been just out of reach. I felt an unexpected surge of strength and energy run through me. Getting out of bed, I went over to the window to look out at the grounds. The sun was already warming the smooth lawns. It was going to be a beautiful day. But the sight of the empty ruins brought back the events of the night before with a sickening crash. A wave of guilt poured over me as I remembered what had happened.

Evie's storm of tears over the vision of Sebastian had eventually subsided, and Miss Scratton had explained that what we had seen had simply been an illusion, memories of times gone by.

"After we made the protective spell, the images of some of the evil done in that place appeared to us. They weren't real, Evie, only memories."

"But I saw him! I could have reached out to him, stopped the quarrel with Agnes, saved her . . . and him . . ."

"These things have already happened. You in particular, with your gifts of water, are susceptible to the river of time, and seeing past shapes and stories. But they have already happened. There was nothing you could have done to prevent what has already been fixed. It is over. Sebastian and Agnes are both at peace."

"So why can we contact Agnes?" Evie asked passionately. "She came when I called her. Why can't I contact Sebastian again?"

"The Talisman is your link to Agnes," Miss Scratton

said. "But you have no way of reaching out to Sebastian again, Evie. The dead can return, but we cannot summon them at will. Let him be."

"That's what I wanted! I wanted him to be free of all this! And I wanted to be free too. I can't bear to go through all this again!"

"Then let us hope that our work will hold fast and that the spirit that was Celia Hartle will not come near you."

"Do you really think what we have done tonight will be enough?" I asked.

"I cannot say," Miss Scratton replied at last. "I hope so, but for the moment it might be wise for you to stay away from one another. That way, you cannot be attacked together, and any watchers that she might send will have to spread themselves more thinly to keep you in their sights. And the coven still watches me with a suspicious eye, so do not seek me out, unless in great need. Agreed?"

"Agreed."

"It may also be advisable," Miss Scratton added, "for you not to leave the school grounds."

Evie stared at her. "So we're prisoners?"

"No, I merely advise caution."

"So we're 'free' and 'protected' and the people we love are 'at peace,' but we have to creep around in hiding? We're free to live and look to the future but we have to keep raking over the past? Well, that's not the kind of freedom I want. I can't carry on like this, I can't!" She clutched at the Talisman around her neck as though she were being suffocated.

Miss Scratton looked steadily at Evie. "We are none of us free to command life to be exactly as we would wish. We are only free to make the choices that seem good to us. Be sure of what you choose."

"Oh, I am sure," said Evie. "I'm sorry. I can't do this anymore."

"You can't back out now," I said sharply.

"Can't I? Just watch me."

"That's right, run away, why don't you?" I said, suddenly furious. "At least you've got your precious Josh to comfort you. Why don't you run off to him and his healing hands and leave the rest of us to face the danger?"

"It's not that—," Evie protested, but I wouldn't listen.

"And what about poor Helen?" I demanded. "Don't you care about her? She's been marked out and we need to protect her. Have you thought about that? We won't even have the Talisman to help her if you abandon our sisterhood."

"Take it! Take it!" Evie threw the necklace at my feet,

trembling with passion like a bright flame. "Here, you can have the Talisman. I don't want it anymore! Isn't that what you want? S for Sarah. That's what the sign on the door said, didn't it? Well, take the Talisman! It's your turn now."

She had left us there, in the shattered ruins. Our circle had been truly broken.

I left the window and quickly felt under my pillow. The Talisman was still there. I felt it heavy and cool in my fingers. Despite my awful quarrel with Evie, I couldn't help feeling a flicker of excitement as I held the necklace in my hand. S for Sarah. Perhaps this was meant to happen? I put on my robe, slipping the Talisman into my pocket, and headed for the door.

As soon as I reached the bathroom at the end of the passage, I went in and locked the door behind me. There was a small mirror over the basin. Wyldcliffe didn't believe in encouraging personal vanity. We weren't allowed to wear makeup or jewelry, although perhaps Miss Scratton was going to change all that too. But the mirror was big enough for me to see myself as I fumblingly fastened the Talisman around my neck.

What had I expected? That it would transform me into the princess, the special one? The Talisman hung cold and quiet against my nightdress. With my untidy hair and sleep-heavy eyes, I looked about ten years old, like a kid dressing up in her mother's finery. Stubbornly, I placed my hand over the crystal and whispered, "Agnes . . . Agnes . . ." Nothing happened.

Why should it? I was not Evie, and the Talisman wasn't mine. I wasn't connected with Agnes. This wasn't for me.

Everything is connected, a voice seemed to say in my head. An image flashed into my mind of a girl with dark, curly hair streaming out in the wind as she rode a stocky pony over the moors. I clutched the necklace tighter and said aloud, "Maria . . . this is Sarah."

The Talisman blazed with light for an instant, and I pulled my hand away in shock. The skin on the palm of my hand was red and burning. What was happening? Was Maria linked with Agnes? But she couldn't have been—she had been a pupil at Wyldcliffe, and it was only after Agnes's death that the Abbey had become a school. So why had her name caused the Talisman to flare out like that?

Someone knocked on the bathroom door.

"Coming!" I shouted, snatching the necklace off and pushing it into my pocket. *The Path to Hell*, the Book had warned. I longed to know more about Maria, but the

Talisman was not really mine. I had no right to probe its secrets simply for curiosity's sake, and although Evie had used the precious heirloom, it had been at great cost. Was I really ready to pay that price? Besides, I reasoned, if the spirit of Celia Hartle had been contained by our spell, and if Miss Scratton was in charge, why did I need to dig deeper into mysteries that should be left alone?

And so for the moment, I hid the Talisman at the bottom of my bedside drawers, muffled in a thick scarf, and made no more attempts to use it. *Let it lie there*, I thought, *let it be quiet.*

For the moment.

Helen and Evie and I avoided one another over the following days, as Miss Scratton had counseled. Helen would smile vaguely in my direction as we went into class, but Evie walked past me without even a glance. It was so painful to have quarreled with her, especially as I felt ashamed of some of the things I had said. I felt that our friendship had been split at the roots and I wanted to mend it, but Evie didn't come near me. She spent every spare moment down at the stables. I knew she had no great interest in riding. It was Josh that drew her there.

I couldn't avoid seeing them together, as I had to go

to the stables every day to look after my own ponies and exercise them in the practice paddock. There was a light in Josh's brown eyes as the two of them talked, and the strain on Evie's face seemed to melt away under the sunshine of his smile. I guessed they were happy to dwell on the bond that Agnes had made between their families. Josh's inheritance of a single spark of her fiery compassion would inevitably bring him and Evie closer together. Yet I noticed that Evie was careful not to touch him, or flirt with him, or send off any of those little signals of possession that girls put out around attractive guys. She didn't behave in any way that suggested she was anything more than a friend to Josh. How could she, when she was still in love with Sebastian? But at least she wasn't alone.

I tried not to begrudge them their pleasure in each other's company, though I felt so miserable myself. And there was no one else I could turn to. Helen was more and more in a world of her own, obsessively writing long letters to her father or scribbling secrets in a notebook. The friends I'd had before Evie arrived at school had dropped away from me since I had taken up with "those two weirdos." And even worse, I still hadn't had a letter from Cal. I was sure now that I never would.

The days dragged past, and my free time hung heavily

on my hands. I tried to keep myself busy, of course. When lessons were over, I had my horses to look after, as well as my own corner of ground in the walled garden, which I tended out of a dull sense of duty. But everything that had once kept me busy at Wyldcliffe felt flat and empty without Helen and Evie.

In desperation, I started going to choir practice at lunchtime, as a way of killing time. At least music was a pure expression of the soul, and I hoped it might be uplifting. To my surprise Velvet was there too, mocking and mutinous in the back row, setting the other girls off into fits of giggles as she imitated Mr. Brooke's hesitant voice and awkward manner. I wished I could be a carefree, laughing schoolgirl like them, but I had another path to tread. And so I sang, and brooded and waited, and missed my friends. And every night, the drums sounded deep in my dreams, but I listened to them in vain; no clear sign or message came to me through that savage, pulsing music.

It was almost a relief when the following Saturday, Velvet created a diversion. She showed up at the stable yard to welcome a superb black gelding that her father had arranged to be sent over to the school for her. He was called Jupiter, and must have cost a fortune, with his aristocratic breeding and high-stepping legs. He skittered proudly on the cobbles as he was backed into his stall, and I sensed the envy from the other keen riders who were hanging around to have a look at the new arrival. Celeste and India, who fancied themselves elegant horsewomen, looked furious that Velvet had yet again stolen their thunder. But I thought the animal was far too showy for the kind of rough moorland rides we had around Wyldcliffe, and I told Velvet so.

"You're only jealous," she said carelessly. "He'll be fun, won't you, Jupiter darling? Dad has to have the best of everything, so he was hardly going to send me a fat old nag to ride. Anyway, you can try Jupiter out tomorrow. We'll take him and Starlight out for a proper gallop over the moors."

She seemed to expect me to drop any plans I had and immediately fit in with hers.

"Um . . . I'm sorry, I . . . um, haven't finished my biology assignment. . . ." I hadn't forgotten Miss Scratton's warning not to stray outside the grounds, and anyway, I wasn't really that keen to hang out with Velvet. For a moment she looked annoyed; then she shrugged.

"Whatever. I can find someone else." Velvet glanced over to one of the other girls standing about in the yard. It was Sophie, one of Celeste's set, a harmless but weak and anxious girl who was constantly bossed around by her so-called friend. "Hey, Sophie, isn't that your name? Would you like to come for a ride with me?"

"M-me?" stammered Sophie. "Do you really mean that? I'd love to."

"It's a deal then." Velvet smiled her most charming smile, and I could see that Sophie had just found someone new to hero-worship. My heart sank. I didn't think Velvet's influence would do Sophie any good at all.

Despite my troubles and worries about my friends, I had been constantly aware of Velvet's presence at Wyldcliffe since the beginning of term. It was like knowing that a wasp is hovering nearby, getting ready to sting. I could see that Rick Romaine's daughter was bored and restless at the school, and in the mood to look for trouble. Although Miss Scratton had promised a new era of modernization, she couldn't produce this single-handedly in a few days. Wyldcliffe had been run in a certain way for over a hundred years, and it wasn't going to change instantly. There were still the daily prayers, the old-fashioned uniform, the heavy academic workload as we prepared for exams, and the strict routine and antiquated deference to the mistresses. Not only that, the building itself was so gloomy and silent, with its heavy Gothic windows, its marble pillars and stairs, and endless passageways, that just being stuck in the school while the sun shone outside felt oppressive. There was still plenty for Velvet to kick against.

Another week began, and although I felt as though I was drifting in my own private quest, with no real purpose or certainty, Velvet seemed to be pursuing a clear plan of her own. She had gathered together a little group of admirers who started to call themselves the Wylde Babes. They turned up their collars and hitched up their skirts in imitation of Velvet, adopted a slouching, sulky posture during class time, and indulged in boisterous jokes during recreation periods. Velvet quickly had Camilla Willoughby-Stuart under her spell, and Julia Symons and Annabelle Torrington-Jones and a few others, and soon poor spineless Sophie was drawn into her crowd. Velvet gave the girls designer clothes and bags from the piles of expensive stuff she had brought with her and made out that they were all great friends, but there was a coldness under her manner to them. It was as if she was the leader and they were her servants, ready to do whatever she commanded. And Velvet seemed older than the rest of the girls in our year, with all her talk of wild parties in New York and Buenos Aires and Monte Carlo, her boasts of how screwed up she'd been when she'd checked into rehab, and how she hated her mother. I didn't know how much of what she said was true, and although I tried to be friendly and polite to her, I knew I didn't want to get sucked into her little crowd. However, my lack of interest seemed to make her even more determined to get me involved.

"Come with us, Sarah," she challenged me one evening when we were both in the dorm, changing into clean shirts before supper. "We're going to sneak out and go skinny-dipping in the pool after lights-out tonight. And we've got a bottle of vodka that I smuggled into school in my suitcase. It will be cool."

"It will be *freezing*," I replied. "And as for guzzling vodka, you can do what you like, but don't go making Camilla and Sophie and the rest of them drunk. You'll only get them into trouble."

"But I *want* us to get into trouble," she said. "That's the whole point."

"That's easy for you, Velvet. You want to get chucked out. But I don't think the other girls' parents will be very happy if they get expelled."

"Oh, don't be so *good*," she sneered. "I don't care about their parents. I don't care about anything except getting out of here."

"Well, you should. Wandering about after lights-out isn't a great idea."

Velvet narrowed her dark eyes and frowned. "So how come you were out of your bed the first night I arrived?"

I froze, but tried to look unconcerned. "What do you mean?"

"I woke up with a headache and couldn't get back to sleep. You weren't there, and you were away for ages. So what were you up to?" she asked. "You weren't going off to meet Evie's stable boy by any chance, were you? Trying to cut her out of the action?"

"Don't be ridiculous."

"Have you two quarreled about something? Sophie told me that you were inseparable last term, you and Evie and that other girl, what's her name, Helen Black?" Velvet stretched out lazily on her bed and added, "That's an interesting girl. She looks kind of crazy, but she's actually incredibly beautiful in that fragile, spaced-out kind of way. I wouldn't mind getting to know her better."

"Please don't," I said, oddly alarmed at the idea. "Stay out of Helen's way."

Velvet laughed mockingly. "Good dear Sarah, protecting her friends from naughty Velvet?" Then her expression changed, and her eyes glinted oddly. "That's what everyone tries to do. But it never works. They all get hurt in the end."

My heart began to race. I didn't understand why, but I

actually felt slightly afraid of her.

"What do you mean?"

She ignored me. "Look, are you coming down to the pool or not?"

"Sorry—not interested." I fumbled to fasten my blouse and hurried out of the room. But why was I so keen to get away from Velvet? She was just an overindulged show-off, a misfit. *I should be sorry for her,* I told myself, and tried to forget all about it.

I couldn't, though. The hungry expression in Velvet's eyes had reminded me of something I had seen before, but I didn't know what. I couldn't shake her out of my mind, so after supper—Evie ignored me and Helen wasn't there—I went to the small classroom near the math room where the new computers had been set up. A few other girls were using them already, either looking things up for class or playing games. I sat at one of the desks and tapped my password into the computer, hoping that no one else would notice as I typed Velvet's name into the search engine. A host of entries came up for her and for her father, Rick Romaine. I scanned them quickly.

Rick Romaine, controversial lead singer of heavy-metal band the Screaming Angels. Arrested several times for drug offenses. His 2002 concert was stopped by police after

a fan was crushed and killed. Accused by parental cam-
paigners of "corrupting youth" with his occult-influenced
act . . .

Velvet Morgan Moonlight Romaine, daughter of Rick and
Amber Romaine (who famously said that giving birth to
Velvet at sixteen was the biggest mistake of her life). Velvet
was voted one of the decade's teen style icons in Vogue,
released a number one record with her father, has modeled
in New York and Milan. . . .

This was mostly stuff I already knew, though I felt a
swift pang of pity for Velvet. Having your mother thinking that your birth was a mistake wasn't a great start in
life. Then another entry caught my attention. It was on a
blog called CelebSpy and it read:

Velvet Romaine has already been in trouble for drugs
and underage drinking in her short life, influenced by
her parents' wild lifestyle, and she checked into rehab at
age thirteen. But CelebSpy hears that darker rumors are
surrounding the teen. Her younger sister, Jasmine, was
killed in a car accident when Velvet's then boyfriend, singer
Jonny Darren, was at the wheel. No charges were brought,
but the word is that it was actually Velvet who was driving.

A short time later the pair broke up, and Darren committed suicide. She was sent to an exclusive Swiss boarding school to make a fresh start but had been there only a matter of months when a fire broke out that led to the dreadful scarring of one of her classmates. It was deemed to be an accident, but CelebSpy's informants are whispering that Velvet was involved in the fire—as a prank that went horribly wrong. In another incident, her mother's personal assistant was recently injured in a freak accident at Velvet's lavish sixteenth birthday party when a balcony over the dance floor collapsed. Coincidence? Is the shadow that hangs over bad boy Rick Romaine tainting his daughter's life? Is everyone who comes into contact with her fated to be hurt?

I was fascinated, then felt disgusted with myself for reading such trash. They were just digging for dirt, finding old stories and serving them up with a freaky new twist.

All the same, I resolved that I would do my best to keep Velvet away from Evie and Helen. Even though the three of us seemed to have fallen apart, I wouldn't let anybody hurt them. I would die for them first.

Fifteen

The next day Sophie, Annabelle, Camilla, and the rest of Velvet's little gang appeared at breakfast bleary-eyed, yawning conspiratorially, so it looked as though Velvet had carried out her midnight plans. Sophie looked worse than the others, and seemed secretly uncomfortable in their company. I guessed she was as timid of Velvet as she had been of Celeste's snobbish bullying. But at least she had survived this little escapade with nothing worse than a sick headache and a guilty conscience.

I wished so much that I could be with my own friends, but Evie wasn't at breakfast, and although I caught Helen's eye, she only nodded faintly and went back to reading a letter she had hidden on her lap. Another one from her father, I guessed. I noticed that from time to time she winced and rubbed her arm where the mark was hidden under her school shirt, as if it hurt. I glanced up to the high table to see if Miss Scratton had noticed too, but she was looking away, deep in discussion with Miss Dalrymple and Miss Clarke. The loss of our Guardian's advice added to my sense of isolation.

It was over two weeks since we had made our protective spell with Miss Scratton, and there had been no further sign of threat from Mrs. Hartle or the coven. *So it must have worked*, I told myself, and tried to feel positive. But my heart whispered another story, asking what was the point of being safe if I had lost my friends.

Perhaps it was because I was lonely that I started to brood so much about Maria. I had no one else to turn to, and the feeling that she was somehow watching over me in the background grew more intense. It was what I wanted to believe, of course, trying to convince myself that I wasn't entirely alone. But there was a real connection between us, I was sure. Had Maria been trying to answer my call through the Talisman the night after my quarrel with Evie? The strange flash of light and heat that had glowed from the necklace when I had called her name must have meant something. Why not try it again? I forced myself to resist that temptation, reminding myself that the Talisman wasn't mine. Soon Evie would realize that she couldn't simply let go of her heritage and would reclaim it from me, and I had to be able to return it to her with a clear conscience.

Maria still occupied my thoughts, though. I couldn't help wanting to know more about my great-grandmother as curiosity, loneliness, and desperation ate away at me. I wrote to my mother asking for any further details that she might have about Maria or her family. *Seek and ye shall find*, I thought to myself half-flippantly, as I posted the letter. I didn't really have any high hopes that my mother could tell me more than she already had, but it was worth a shot. As I waited for Mom's reply and followed the daily routine of study and prayer and the never-ending discipline of the hourly bells and the mistresses' scrutiny, I reminded myself that Maria had done all this too when she had been a pupil at the Abbey, surrounded by the same green-gray hills.

It occurred to me that there might be records of Maria right here in Wyldcliffe. There were plenty of dusty old photographs on display in the corridors and classrooms that gave glimpses of the school's history: photos of old lacrosse teams and school picnics and long-dead mistresses, and a picture of a German plane that had gone off course during the Second World War and crash-landed on the school playing field. And going further back in time, there was a faded sepia photograph in the entrance hall of the very first students to arrive at Wyldcliffe. It was dated 1893 and showed a dozen serious-faced girls, all dressed in long, heavy skirts, with thickly curling hair and black buttoned boots.

I tried to work out exactly when Maria would have been a student at the school. From what I already knew of our family history, it must have been just after the First World War, which Maria's generation had called the Great War. I didn't really know what I was trying to find out, but at least my amateur researches gave me fresh energy. On the next Sunday morning, after church, I went to the library and leafed through the collections of archive material. As Miss Scratton had said, Wyldcliffe was proud of its long history, and successive librarians had hoarded records of the school's triumphs and achievements. There were many bound volumes containing copies of old school magazines, full of sentimental poems and reports of examinations and the names of prizewinners. I scanned their yellowing pages, but I didn't find Maria's name anywhere. And then, one day, I spotted something in the volume labeled 1919.

At the bottom of a page full of Nature Notes and First Aid Tips, there was a small notice headed News. It listed a few small events that had no doubt seemed of great importance to the girls of nearly a hundred years ago: the birth of a litter of kittens in the stable yard; the acquisition of a new piano for the use of the senior students; a French verse competition. And then, underneath the rest, it said, *Miss Maria Melville returned to school last week after her sojourn in the infirmary. She had suffered a broken ankle when riding near Blackdown Ridge.*

I was so excited to see Maria's name in print. It made her more real, somehow. As I read the little notice again, something stirred in my memory. Blackdown Ridge was where the great stones stood on top of the moors, like gigantic fingers pointing up to the sky. Not only that—it was where Helen had been taken when she had tried to pass through the door of Agnes's study. Was there some link? I had been to the circle of standing stones only once before, and it was an eerie, haunting place, quite a long ride over the hills from the school and not the usual route for a ramble either on foot or horseback. Why had Maria gone there, I wondered, and how had she met with her accident?

A sudden, overwhelming desire to visit the place gripped me. I looked at my watch. There was still time to get there and back, and we were allowed to ride out on a Sunday, though I might need permission to go so far.

Something told me that Miss Scratton might refuse that permission, as she had advised us to stay on the school grounds. I was torn in two. I desperately wanted to go to the Ridge, and yet I also respected Miss Scratton's advice. Although she had warned us not to make any contact with her, I decided I would go and see her. If she gave me her permission to ride to the standing stones, I was sure nothing could go wrong. A pang shot through me as I remembered the journeys I had taken with Helen and Evie to Uppercliffe Farm, and to Sebastian's old home, Fairfax Hall, and I wished they could be with me now.

Quickly I made my way to the High Mistress's study and knocked on the door. There was no reply, but as I was turning away in disappointment, I saw the art mistress, Miss Hetherington, walking down the corridor. She stopped and smiled at me. "Are you looking for Miss Scratton? I'm afraid she's out this afternoon. She's taken half a dozen of the students from the top class to have tea at St. Martin's Academy, to make arrangements for the summer dance at the end of term. Are you looking forward to it? I think it's a splendid idea, don't you? But I'm surprised you aren't out riding on a day like this. It's such glorious weather—just perfect for the first of May!"

Miss Hetherington's natural-sounding enthusiasm

swept through the somber corridor like a fresh breeze. I had forgotten that it was the first day of May, the traditional beginning of warm weather and new life. I was so relieved that I could have laughed out loud. Everything sounded so normal. Miss Scratton had gone on a visit to the local boys' school. Students and staff were looking forward to a dance, and it was a lovely day for a ride. It felt as though everything that had happened last term really was fading away and the sun was shining on Wyldcliffe at last.

"Yes, I am—I mean it is," I babbled, then turned and rushed to the stables. Starlight snickered happily as I saddled him up and clattered down the drive. As I passed through the school gates I held my breath, but there was no catastrophe. Nothing would happen, I was convinced, nothing could touch me. The air was warm and sweet and the soft green moors were inviting. In my excitement I ignored any tug of caution and cantered away in the direction of the moors, and the stone circle on Blackdown Ridge.

It was farther than I had thought. I let Starlight walk the last mile as the land rose steeply and the view on either side of the Ridge opened up. The sky seemed endlessly high above the turf, and the valleys that dipped away on either side of me spread out to the horizon like billowing green waves. But the sight that lay ahead was the most impressive of all. Stark and black against the pale blue sky, a jagged ring of rough-hewn stones stood in a broken circle, like a vast primitive crown on the top of the moors.

As I rode up to them, it was already late in the afternoon. The warmth had gone out of the sun, and the megaliths cast long black shadows over the heather. I slithered down from Starlight's back and walked into the center of the circle. Men had dragged the stones here, huge blocks of granite and limestone, for some lost, hidden purpose. I felt my soul stir as I gazed at their stark beauty. There was a deep silence and stillness as I walked under their shadow, but I wasn't afraid.

Here, out on the hills, I felt free of all the worries that had haunted me since I had come back to school. This was my real Wyldcliffe, and my real world. I knelt down and pressed my hands into the black peaty soil and worshipped the wild land's Creator. Here I had nothing to fear. I was a child of the earth, and I belonged. Here I could do no wrong. Suddenly it didn't seem such a betrayal to borrow the Talisman's power. All I wanted to know was the truth about Maria. Surely it would do no harm?

I slipped my hand inside my shirt and drew out the Talisman. Now I would try its depths again, and call out to the Gypsy girl whose blood ran in my own.

Looking out to the north where the hills marched into the distance, I held up the silver necklace. It twisted in the breeze, and the fading light caught the edges of the crystal. Now it gleamed deep and intensely colored, as dark as the black earth, as dark as a Gypsy's eyes.

"Maria," I called. "You walked this land. You stood on this earth. You saw these stones. If you can hear me, or see me, send me a sign."

Nothing happened. The air grew dim, and cold, until I was shivering, but not with fear.

"I am your daughter's daughter's daughter," I cried. "Speak to me. Come to me."

The light changed. On the far side of the circle I saw a girl lying at the foot of the tallest stone. She had blood on her face and was wearing some kind of circlet on her head, like twisted leaves. Fierce-looking men were hovering around her, anxious and protective.

"Maria?" I whispered.

As if in reply, a terrible roar of anger ripped open the divide between the past and the present. I heard a storm of drumbeats, and then the sun wavered and went out, and the land was covered in shadow.

Sixteen

Maria Melville's Wyldcliffe Journal
April 10, 1919

As we stepped into the shadows of the caves, Zak stayed close to me. The men were grim and silent. They stooped and walked in single file down the narrow tunnel that led deeper underground. Every noise—the stealthy pad of feet, the scraping of boots against the rocks, a low gasp of breath—was magnified, echoing and rippling through the dark. I had never been underground before. I had imagined that the caves would be suffocating and enclosed. It was strange, though, because it didn't feel like that at all. I felt curiously at home in the deep weight of the earth. Some of the men had lit glowing torches that burned red and smoky, but I felt that I could almost see in the dark.

My feet didn't slip on the rough stone. I was safe and sure-footed, sensing when the passage would twist and turn, and I felt convinced that we would find Zak's father any moment, clutching a broken leg and glad to be rescued. And so to start with I wasn't afraid. Not then, not yet.

Soon the passage widened out into a flat area, like a rough-hewn room, before coming to an abrupt stop. There was nowhere to go except back along the passage we had already come down. One of the men, the leader who had spoken before, said in a hoarse voice, "Our Brother is not here. We must go farther to where the evil spirits dwell. Who can show us the way?"

There was some hurried, muffled speech in the crowd, then one voice called out, "The Conjurer must show us. Fairfax. He is a magician with power over the spirits. Let him show us."

"Fairfax! Fairfax!" The men murmured their approval.

I watched as Fairfax slowly pushed his way forward to the leader. He said, "I have some poor tricks, Josef, that's all, enough to earn a penny in the marketplace. If you wish, I will put them at your service for the sake of your Brother. But no one here must ever speak of this deed. Do you swear it?" His blue eyes glittered oddly in the torchlight, and his handsome face looked hard and threatening. For the first time, I thought that perhaps he might be capable of doing evil. "Do you swear?" he repeated.

Josef spoke first. "We swear." He drew a dagger from his belt and lightly scored the palm of his hand until he drew blood. Spitting on his hand, he then offered it to Fairfax. "We swear in blood."

Fairfax grasped Josef's hand firmly. "So be it."

Now I began to be afraid, not of the caves, but of this blue-eyed stranger and the powers he was going to call upon.

Fairfax strode up to the blank wall of rock that barred our way and laid his head against it, as though he was listening for something. Then he began to search the surface of the wall with his fingertips, feeling closely for any cracks or crannies. I remembered how he had broken the piece of mirror and miraculously made it whole again. He began to speak rapidly in a strange language that sounded like curses. He closed his eyes, and sweat stood out on his brow. He ground his teeth and cried out loud, "As I will it, so shall it be!" The next moment the cave wall fell, like a sheet of water. Everyone stumbled backward, amazed, coughing and gasping in the dust. A way through had opened up, a low tunnel streaked with red and silver *in the layers of stone. The taste of fear was in the air, whether of the new path that lay before us or of Fairfax's diabolical powers, I couldn't be sure.*

"We go onward," Josef growled. "Anyone who turns back now is an outcast."

One by one we passed under the shattered archway and entered the newly opened tunnel. I don't know how long we walked down it. Everything began to seem like a dream that I could not wake from, but at last the walls around us opened out and curved away. We had reached an underground cavern. By the light of the torches I saw that it was full of twisting pillars of crystal and rock, like columns in a temple. A few feet away a black lake spread out into the shadows. The company stopped and waited. My heart began to race. Something was going to happen.

There was a presence in the cavern, something that didn't belong in the world above. I had laughed at old Rebekah's tales of evil spirits, but now I wasn't so sure. Anything seemed possible in that deep place.

"We have come for our Brother. Release him." Josef's voice rang out in the cave and echoed many times. "Release him, release him, release him. . . ."

There was no answer. Then a rumbling, groaning sound began to fill the cavern. Grim shapes, like lumps of half-finished clay, began to move in the flickering torch-light. I did not know their name then, but I do now. It was the Kinsfolk, the creatures of the earth, and they had been woken from their long sleep. A sound of fierce drumming filled my mind like madness—

I can't! I can't describe what happened next! It comes back in my dreams, again and again, but I want to forget it. I wish I could tear it out of my memory like Fairfax tore me from the grasp of those monsters and got me out of there.

Afterward, as I lay bleeding on the Ridge under the shadow of the stones, I heard their screams and fevered drumming as they discovered that they had been cheated. And I know that the Kinsfolk will never rest until they find me again, or until some other unfortunate girl is forced to take my place as their dark and cursed queen.

Seventeen

The sounds of screams and drumbeats died away, and the figures of the girl and the men that I had seen faded into the air.

I was lying in the center of the stone circle, alone on the hilltop. The sun was beginning to set, and the twilight was heavy and blue. I stood up and pushed my hair out of my eyes and realized that I was cold, as though I had lain on the damp ground for hours. It was time to get back. But what had I seen? Had it really been Maria at the time of her accident on top of Blackdown Ridge?

A sudden noise startled me—Starlight stamping his hoof and neighing. I went over and caught hold of his bridle and murmured soothingly to him. The next moment I saw that I was no longer alone. Another rider was climbing up to the Ridge. I stood at the edge of the stone circle and watched him approach. The newcomer was a teenage boy who sat astride his heavy, powerful horse as though riding was as natural as walking. He wore rough jeans and an open shirt, and his untidy dark hair was ruffled by the evening breeze.

He was coming closer.

I dug my fingers into my pony's mane for warmth and steadiness and waited until the boy came to a halt only a few feet away. I looked up at the familiar face and tried to speak, but my mouth was dry and my courage failed me. He dismounted in one quick movement, then stopped and stared at me questioningly. For a moment we simply stood there, taking each other in. A lonely bird high above the Ridge called out a few achingly sweet notes.

"Sarah."

"Cal."

He stepped closer, but I moved back, confused. "Cal—what are you doing here—I thought you'd gone—I—I thought I'd never see you again—"

"Didn't you trust me?" he asked, frowning. "I told you I would come back."

"You said you were going to write to me." I didn't mean it to sound like an accusation, but I couldn't help it. I thought Cal would react with angry pride to the sting of my words, but he shrugged his broad shoulders and spoke quietly.

"I'm not much good at writing things down. Not much good with words at all. I did write, though. There was something I wanted to ask you."

"But I never got a letter."

"I know. I never sent it. I didn't want any of the teachers at your posh school getting hold of it and sneering over my ignorance." For a moment a sullen, defensive look flashed over his face.

"Cal, no one would—"

"Oh yes, they would. We belong in different worlds."

I felt sick with disappointment. Why had he come if he only wanted to quarrel? I couldn't help being who I was. I would have swapped all my family's money for Cal's freedom.

"Do we?" I said bitterly. "So why did you come back?"

Cal pulled something out of his pocket. He looked at it for a moment, then handed it to me. "To give you the letter myself," he said.

I took the crumpled paper and opened it. The writing had been crossed out as though he had tried many times to find the words for what he wanted to say. I held the letter with unsteady hands and tried to read as quickly as I could.

Sarah—

Something has happened to me. I never minded moving on before. I am used to being on the road. But now my mind is looking back, not forward. I keep thinking about you and the strange events out on the moors when I rode with Sebastian and the Brothers.

More than anything I keep thinking about you. What are you doing, Gypsy girl? Are you safe? Are you happy?

There is something else I want to ask you. I should have done it before my family left Wyldcliffe.

One day, I will ask you.

Cal

My heart was beating so fast that it hurt. "What— what did you want to ask me?"

Cal let go of his horse's reins and came closer. I felt my face burn as he looked at me as though I were the only person on the earth who mattered. "I wanted to ask—" Cal's voice was husky and tight. "I wanted to ask if you would mind me doing this."

He bent over me, and his lips brushed mine questioningly. Something seemed to explode in my head, as though my whole life had fallen into place and I knew the meaning of everything, I knew the person that I was really meant to be. I kissed him back, and we belonged, like two wild creatures finding shelter in each other.

"Oh, Sarah," he said at last. "You don't know how much I wanted this."

"But you never said anything—I didn't know—I thought I would never see you again. I thought I had to forget you."

"Helen said that maybe you and Josh—I know he cares for Evie, but I thought you still . . ."

"No! That was silliness, childish—it was over long ago, really." I looked into Cal's anxious face and murmured, "None of that was real. It was just a dream. But I've stopped dreaming now."

He smiled at me joyfully, his fierceness and pride softened by a glow of relief. We kissed again, and every kiss burned my soul clean. I was healed of all the muddled feelings that had plagued me, as Cal held me tight.

"I've dreamed of nothing but you. I couldn't forget you, Sarah. I kept telling myself that it was impossible, with you at school and me having to be with my family, but I couldn't forget. I know we're so different—I've no money—"

"That doesn't matter," I protested. "I don't have any money either. My parents are rich, not me. We're young. None of that is important. Only this is important." I sighed and leaned my head on his shoulder. "I want this to go on forever."

"It will, if you want it. I won't change," Cal whispered. "I'm so glad I found you."

"And I'm so glad you came back. Oh, thank God you did!" I burst into tears.

"Hey, don't cry," he said in concern. "You mustn't cry. I just want you to be happy."

To be happy. That was what Sebastian had said to Evie. *Be happy.* It was what we were all chasing. Helen was looking for a family, Evie looking for consolation in her grief, and I . . .

I realized that all my life I had wanted to belong somewhere that I would find for myself, away from my parents and the protective, slightly deadening blanket of their money and position. And out here on the eternal hills, surrounded by nothing but the earth and stones and the vast splendor of the sunset, far away from the school and its snobbery and its records of failure and success, here with Cal—strong and young and hard—I had found what I had been looking for. We were so different and yet we understood each other. "I'm crying b-because I'm so happy," I gulped. "Does that sound stupid?"

"Not stupid at all." He smudged my tears away, then drew me even closer to him, and it was so sweet and good that I wanted to stay out there all night under the bright stars and never go back to school.

"Let's stay here," I whispered. "This can be our place, where no one can find us."

"Don't tempt me." Cal reluctantly let me go. "We mustn't. We can't stay here any longer. It's time to go back; it's getting late and you'll be in trouble with the school."

"I don't care."

He laughed. "But I do. I'm not having them say you're going off the rails associating with riffraff like me. Besides, what about those women who were after you last term—the coven? And Helen's mother? Is she still dangerous? You shouldn't really be on your own."

"I'm not on my own," I replied seriously. "I'm with you."

Cal quickly became serious too. "And I'm with you now, Sarah, if you really want me. Whatever happens, we'll be together."

Together. I would never be alone again. Now I could face anything.

Eighteen

We rode back down to the valley side by side, our horses steadily pacing across the rough ground. I told Cal about everything that had happened—the sign on Helen's arm, and the strange message on the door of Agnes's study: *Listen to the drums.*

"And there was the sound of drums in my dreams," I said, "but I don't know what it means, or what they are trying to tell me. I don't even know who is doing the drumming. But then I had this feeling that it was important to find out more about my great-grandmother Maria—do you remember I showed you her picture? It said in the school records that she'd had some kind of accident up here on Blackdown Ridge, so I rode up here and I used the Talisman—"

"You've got the Talisman?" asked Cal in surprise. "But doesn't it belong to Evie?"

I sighed. "Yes, but she doesn't want to have anything to do with the Mystic Way anymore. I think it was partly my fault. I haven't helped her like I should have. I'm glad at least that Josh is looking out for her." I explained what Josh had discovered about his connection through Martha to Agnes's healing powers.

"If anyone can help Evie, it's Josh," Cal replied. "He walks a straight path, under the sun. It will be hard for him, though. Evie is still full of grief for Sebastian. But she won't forget her sisters."

"Do you really know that?" I asked hopefully.

"It's what I feel, in here," Cal said, touching his chest. "My mother has the Sight. That is a gift for women. I don't claim to know anything, but I can't believe that Evie will abandon the Talisman. She loves you and Helen— and Agnes. She won't throw that away."

"I hope you're right."

"But what about Maria? What happened to her up on the Ridge?"

"Some kind of accident, I guess." I shrugged. "I thought I saw her before you arrived. A young girl in the stone circle, with blood on her face. She was in pain and these men—oh, I've realized something! They were like the ghost men who rode with you and Sebastian—the Brothers! They were trying to protect her, and then I heard these awful sounds of screaming and shouting and drums beating—and then—" I glanced at him shyly. "Then you were there."

"Do you think what you saw was anything to do with the coven?"

"I don't know." I explained what Miss Scratton had done to help to protect us against the remnants of Mrs. Hartle's power.

"So you're safe," Cal said, looking relieved.

"It seems that way. But I am still worried about Helen—and that weird sign on her skin."

"The old folk would say it was a sign of the evil eye," Cal said abruptly. "Do you believe that?"

"The Book said something like that. But Evie said it could be psychosomatic, a manifestation of Helen's subconscious. I don't really know what Helen thinks. She's even more closed up and secretive than ever."

"Well, whatever it is, you won't need to ride out alone now."

"Why not?" My heart jumped painfully, daring to hope.

"Because I'm going to stay around Wyldcliffe for a bit. My uncle had to come back here to see about a piece of business, a horse he was buying. That gave me a good excuse to come with him and ride this way again. But I told my mother the truth. I said I needed to see you again, and if you wanted me to I would stay here in Wyldcliffe as long as I could."

"Oh, Cal—but doesn't she need you?"

"My uncles will take care of her and my sister. I said I would find some work and send them money if I could. My mother is fine about it. I told you, she sees most things. She knows how I feel about you." He laughed. "She said I've been like a sick cat the past few weeks and she was glad to see me go. So she gave me her blessing, and said a young man has to follow the wind, whatever direction it blows." He paused and looked thoughtful. "She gave me a message for you too."

"What was it? What did she say?"

"She said, 'A promise is forever, and is only broken with a curse.'"

I fell silent, wondering what she had meant. The words cast a shadow on my happiness.

"Don't look so sad. She sent you a gift too." We had reached the school gates, where we halted our horses and dismounted. Cal felt inside his shirt pocket and took out a little packet wrapped in torn paper. He handed it to me, and I opened it quickly. Inside was a piece of red silk ribbon, intricately embroidered with flowers and ears of corn.

"It's from her wedding outfit," Cal said in a low voice, tying it clumsily in my hair. Then he gazed at me in wonder. "How is it you don't know that you're beautiful?"

He drew me to him for one last kiss. I knew that I would be in terrible trouble for being out so late, way past supper time, but just then I didn't care. At last, though, I made myself say good-bye.

"I'd better not come into the school," Cal said. "The teachers won't like it."

"Miss Scratton wouldn't mind, I'm sure."

Cal looked at me sternly, clear-sighted again. "Miss Scratton won't be here for long. You can't rely on her. You have to look out for yourself. And for your friends. They are lost in mist. You have to be the one to see the way."

"I'll try."

"I'll meet you here tomorrow evening as soon as you can get away."

"But where will you stay tonight?" I asked.

"There's an old shepherd's hut up on the moor. I've got a blanket and some food. I can stay there and make a fire in the stove. The place is empty now that lambing is over, and at least it will be shelter. Then tomorrow I'll look for work, laboring, odd jobs, anything. Anything that will keep me here, next to you. Sarah, I—"

"Yes?"

He seemed to change his mind about what he was going to say, and just smiled. "I'll see you tomorrow." The next moment he rode away and melted into the hills. I scrambled onto Starlight's back and jogged down the drive, amazed by this unexpected gift of joy. But as I reached the deserted stable yard, I heard the muffled sounds of crying.

"Are you okay? Who's there?" I called.

A girl was sitting on an upturned bucket and sobbing. It was Sophie. She saw me and gasped, "Oh . . . thank God . . . it's you."

"What's the matter?"

"Oh, Sarah . . . it's . . . it's Helen."

"What are you talking about? What's happened to her?"

"She—she's had an accident," Sophie stammered. Then she covered her face and wailed hopelessly. "And I think she's going to die."

Nineteen

I truly thought I was going to die. The echoing cavern, with its twisted stalactites and eerie lake, would be the last place I would ever see. I thought it would be my tomb.

Miss Scarsdale says I must make myself remember. I must tell the truth, and then I shall be free. I trust her, so here is the end of my story, though I am trembling as I write. Oh, why can't I conquer this fear? I wanted to be like the Roma, strong and free, but why am I so weak?

Miss S. says I must not blame myself. "You have touched mysteries," she said, "and the fire of such secrets can scorch and wound. Healing will come, when you remember and face all that you have seen." And so I plod on with my task, wishing that I could see Zak, wishing that I could go home.

The cavern was not merely an empty cave. It was the beginning of an underground kingdom, where a crack lies between this world and other mysterious realms. This is the home of the Kinsfolk. They are earth creatures, who are bound to dwell in darkness until the end of time. All this Fairfax told me later. He is truly a great magician, yet he is somehow dreadful and frightening too, as though his heart has died.

But I knew nothing of this then. That night, deep in the hidden places of the earth, all I knew was what I saw and heard.

As Josef called out for Zak's father to be released, the Kinsfolk began to crawl into the light of the men's torches. Their shapes were grotesque, with heavy shoulders and deformed heads. They had iron collars round their necks and chains trailing from their wrists, and their bodies were squat and misshapen, like crudely carved figures.

"Never . . . ," they breathed, and although I wasn't sure how they spoke, I understood what they said. "Never. He has fallen from the sky world. We will take him. It is our blood right."

The Kinsfolk began to beat their drums. The sound

was terrifying, yet it made me want to move and run and dance. I seemed to be transported into a kind of trance. I saw the windswept moors spreading out under the sky, and sturdy ponies carrying short, strong men across the land. The men were naked apart from animal skins around their waists, and they called to one another with guttural cries as they thundered past. I saw mountains and high rocks, and a waterfall pouring over a gorge. I saw trees growing, unfurling fresh green leaves on their branches. It seemed that the whole world of earth and sky and water was pulsing with new life, and that the drums were beating in my heart, and that I was at the center of the wild world.

And then I was back in the cavern, and I realized that the creatures had left off their drumming and had surrounded me. Their stringy arms and gnarled hands reached out to touch me. I stumbled back away from them and fell down. The cap tumbled off my head, and my hair hung loose and my disguise was at an end.

"What's this?" snarled Josef. "A girl?"

"I'm sorry," I cried. "I wanted to help."

Then the creatures of the earth said, "Take the man. Give us the girl in his place."

Everyone stared at me. The earth men spoke in harsh

voices to one another and pressed around me, touching my clothes and hair and stamping excitedly on the ground. I understood what they were saying. "She has come at last! A queen for the Kinsfolk! She must stay in the earth instead of the man. Let him go!"

The silted mud by the side of the lake bubbled and stirred, and then a heavy shape was thrown to the surface. It was Zak's father, choking for breath like a gasping fish, white-faced under his layers of mud, but alive. His Brothers caught hold of him and embraced him, and he staggered to his feet.

"We will take the girl," the creatures hissed again.

"No!" shouted Zak, but Fairfax called for silence with a swift, sharp command.

"The girl shall stay, as your queen," he declared. "Take her."

I struggled in terror as the creatures took hold of me with their scaly hands. Their eyes never blinked or left my face, and before I knew what they were doing, they had torn my clothes so that they hung from me like leaves from a willow tree. One of them pushed a bronze circlet on my head. I wanted to scream but seemed to have no breath or will. I heard Zak shouting, "Maria, Maria, come back! Don't touch her!" The men muttered anxiously, but Fairfax watched in silence. Then one of the Kinsfolk stepped forward.

He was carrying a stone knife. He pressed it lightly against my cheek, and the blood began to flow. The drums started again, until the noise was a tormenting frenzy in my body and blood and soul.

"Down into Death!" the creatures screamed, and one of them got ready to plunge the stone knife into my heart. "No, no!" Zak shouted, but another voice rose above the confusion.

"AS I WILL IT!" Fairfax roared. The stone knife shattered into bits. The cavern began to shake and rumble. Heavy rocks began to fall from the roof. One fell on my leg, and I cried in pain. Fairfax snatched hold of me and Zak and pulled us to him, flinging his cloak over us. I heard him chanting strange, ugly prayers and curses and then—I don't know how—the whole cave seemed to fall around me and there was a wind like a hurricane and I thought the end had come.

It seemed only a moment later that we were flung out onto the hillside, under the standing stones. Fairfax, Zak, his father, and the Brothers were all there. I was bruised and bleeding, and everyone crowded around me in concern. The furious screams and howls and drums of the

Kinsfolk still seemed to echo around us, but above all that I heard someone call my name. At first I thought it was my mother. But it was a girl calling, "Maria—Maria—speak to me." I don't know who she was, but her voice haunts me now.

There. I have told my tale. As Josef said, we had walked through the darkest night and seen evil spirits. Fairfax told us briefly about the Kinsfolk, forgotten cave dwellers left over from a time when the world was younger. He said he had bound them in a sleep that would last many winters, and that they would not trouble me again. I didn't truly understand all that he said, I only felt glad that I was free and that Zak's father was safe. Zak hugged me for joy, and then we hardly knew whether to laugh or cry, but clung to each other. The men sang in praise of Fairfax. They called him "Brother" and carried him on their shoulders. I was grateful to Fairfax too, of course, so grateful, but he troubles me. He is not like other men. He is like a black flame in the night. How did he know about such things as the Kinsfolk? How did he get us out of there? What strange paths has he traveled?

I think I must have fainted out there on the moors after our escape, as I don't remember going back to school. When I woke up in the infirmary, the nurse scolded me for riding out alone. She said that I had been thrown from Cracker and that my ankle was broken, and thank heavens that young Gypsy fellow had found me out in the lane and brought me home, and maybe they weren't such bad people after all.

No one at school knows the truth, only Miss Scarsdale. I had to tell her, even if she thought I was delirious. She took my story seriously, though, and made me write it in this book. Now I can let go of it, she says, like a bad dream. One day, she says, someone will read this and be glad of it.

There. I have almost done. I am ready to let this go into the past. It is over. I do not have to be afraid anymore.

One thing remains. I have kept the bronze circlet. It is beautiful and not like anything I have ever seen before. How could such strange and frightening creatures have offered me something so lovely? There are things in these tangled events that I do not understand.

I arrived at Wyldcliffe as a girl, a child. I see now that I had been indulged and petted all my life and thought that I could pick and choose my pleasures as I fancied. I thought I could be friends with Zak and defy Miss Featherstone and pay no price for my rebellion. Now I see that life is not so simple. I am no longer a child. Whatever choices I make will bear consequences. I must learn to choose wisely.

My choice is this. As soon as I am well I will look for Zak. There is a bond between us that I cannot forget. If his family has already moved on, I will wait until they return to the valley next spring. I can put up with this school if it will bring us together again. And I will study and learn, and take something worthwhile from here into the great world. I do not need Daphne and Winifred's friendship or approval to do that. I will not let Wyldcliffe defeat me.

But this is not part of my tale. I have reached the end of my story. When I am well again I will hide this where it will not be found until the right time has come. There is a time for all things.

If one day you are reading this, whoever you are, I hope that you will have the courage to accept these mysteries. I hope that you will not have to enter the underground world. I hope that you believe me.

These things happened in the spring of 1919. My name is Maria Adamina Melville, and every word is true, I swear.

Twenty

I didn't want to believe Sophie. It couldn't be true. "What's happened?" I demanded. "Where's Helen?"

"They've taken her to the infirmary, but I saw her, I found her, it was so awful." Sophie began to cry again.

"Where did you find her? What do you mean?"

"She was lying on the front steps of the school, all twisted and—and—I think she'd fallen from one of the windows or something. Oh, Sarah, her face was so white and horrible!"

"I must go and see her. Where's Miss Scratton?"

"I don't know. I think she went over to St. Martin's, didn't she? Miss Hetherington is with Helen. She told me to look for you and tell you to go over to the infirmary."

I didn't bother to ask any more questions. Hurriedly

I put Starlight in his stall and made sure that he was all right, then raced into the school with Sophie trailing behind me. I flew up the marble stairs to the sickroom and burst in without knocking. Evie was perched on the edge of a chair next to Helen's bed, looking scared, and Miss Hetherington was talking to the nurse.

"Thank you so much, Sophie," Miss Hetherington said when she saw us. "You've been very helpful. You've had a shock, though, so go down to the common room with Nurse. She'll give you a hot drink and sit with you for a while. You'll soon feel better."

"But what about Helen?" Sophie asked fretfully. "Isn't she dreadfully ill?"

"She's had a nasty accident, but the doctor says that fortunately she hasn't broken anything. Don't worry, Sophie, she'll recover. It's not as bad as we first thought."

Sophie looked doubtful but allowed herself to be led away by the nurse. I went closer to Helen's bed. She was lying with her eyes closed and her fair hair smoothed neatly onto her pillow. Her arms lay thin and bare on top of the covers, like a child's. She had a bruise on her cheek and a bandage on one hand. The weird mark on her arm was clearly visible, an inky pattern against her white skin. Miss Hetherington sighed. "Silly child, getting a tattoo in the holidays. And now this."

She looked at us kindly but questioningly. "I wanted to talk to both of you. It appears that Helen accidentally fell from the landing window in the dormitory corridor down to the steps below and knocked herself out. She's incredibly lucky to be alive. Heaven only knows how she managed to do it, leaning out too far, I suppose." She paused. "Unless, of course, it wasn't an accident. I'm aware that you three were constantly in one another's company last term. Do you know of any reason why Helen might have done this on purpose? Was it some kind of cry for help?"

A memory of Helen deliberately stepping off the steep gables of the Abbey roof in the dead of night flashed back to me. She had been testing her powers of using the air to "dance on the wind," but another uneasy thought struck me. Helen had hinted before of wanting to end her life, when she had lived in the orphanage. Surely she hadn't been thinking anything like that again? Had she been so terrified by the mark on her arm that she was looking for a way of escape? Why hadn't I made her talk to me about it? So much for trying to look after my friends. With a sinking heart I felt that I had done nothing but let them both down since the term had begun.

"I found this in her pocket," added Miss Hetherington.

"I don't know whether it means anything to you." She handed us a bit of paper covered with Helen's intricate handwriting.

I hover in the star-filled sky, flying free,
Skybird, high above the earth.
You cut my wings, and I fall
Like swift black rain.
Skybird, skybird,
Full of secrets,
Full of sorrows.
I am falling so fast
Falling out of my body
Into the deep blue arc of night.
The stars are ready to welcome me.
Let me fall—let me be free—let me go—

"It's one of her poems," I said. "She writes stuff like this sometimes. But that doesn't mean—"

"I wondered—isn't this a plea for freedom?" The art mistress had a strange, guarded look on her face. "It made me think that maybe Helen had meant to hurt herself."

"I can't believe that," said Evie shakily. "She has her father now, she has us; it must have been an accident."

"I'm sure you're right," Miss Hetherington replied. "We can only be thankful that the result was not worse."

"Has—has she woken up at all?" I asked.

"She regained consciousness earlier, when the doctor was here."

"And did she say anything?"

"She talked a lot of nonsense, just rambling," Miss Hetherington said dismissively.

"But what about?" I persisted. If Miss Hetherington was connected with the coven, she wouldn't tell me, and if she was simply a teacher, as I hoped and believed, she wouldn't mind my questions. Either way, I had to ask. "What did Helen say?"

At that moment the nurse returned and came over to Helen's bed and she answered my question. "Oh, poor Helen," she said. "She talked about the wind . . . and dancing, and something about, I don't know, a priestess. It really didn't make any sense, did it, Miss Hetherington?"

"A priestess?" I repeated.

"Yes, that was it," the nurse replied. "But Helen's always been, well, rather oversensitive, hasn't she?"

"Anyway," the art mistress said briskly, "I'm glad we've had this chat. The doctor said it was all right for Helen to sleep now."

Miss Hetherington sent us away, saying that we could come back in the morning.

As soon as we were out in the corridor, Evie said in a stricken voice, "It wasn't an accident, was it? It was her, Mrs. Hartle! She's broken through our protective spell, hasn't she?"

I shook my head. "I don't know. Perhaps Helen falling really was just an accident—"

"Don't! That's the kind of stuff I wanted to believe, but it's no use, is it? The coven won't let us go as easily as that. You were right all along, Sarah. That mark on Helen's arm—I knew it was a sign of danger, I just didn't want to face it. And Helen's poem—she must be so unhappy. Oh God, I'm so sorry, I've been so selfish."

"I've been just as bad—I'm the one who's sorry."

"No, you were trying to make us face things and be prepared for what was out there, but I refused to listen. I should have—oh, I should have done it all differently." She bit her lip and muttered, "I wanted to be happy after everything had been so awful, and I thought I could just make myself happy by ignoring what was going on. But it doesn't work like that, does it?"

"I think perhaps happiness comes when you're not looking for it," I replied. "We can't force it." I had Cal to thank for teaching me that. "But I don't blame you, Evie. I think I understand."

"Do you really?" Evie looked up at me, hesitating. "Sarah—can you forgive me? Are we still sisters?"

"Now and always," I said, hugging her.

"For eternity." She laughed, then quickly grew serious. "What do we do now?"

"We need to find Miss Scratton—but let's talk to Sophie first. I got the feeling she wasn't telling Miss Hetherington everything."

We found Sophie, hunched miserably over a cup of hot chocolate in the corner of one of the new common rooms that Miss Scratton had organized. A few younger girls were sitting around a table on the other side of the room arguing over some kind of board game while pop music played on the radio. The common room had been provided with books and magazines, but it remained a gloomy place, with heavy red flock wallpaper and a black marble fireplace. Sophie looked grateful as we went to sit beside her.

"I hope you're feeling better, Sophie." I felt sorry for her. She was weak and self-pitying, but she didn't deserve to be so frightened and unhappy. "And thanks for raising the alarm about Helen."

"It was terrifying, seeing her there like that. She was staring up, so still and cold . . ." Tears trickled out of Sophie's baby blue eyes. "I've had such a dreadful weekend, what with last night as well."

"Why, what happened last night?"

"Oh, it all started as a stupid joke. It was Velvet's idea. I know she wants to get expelled, but I don't, my parents would go mad." Sophie lowered her voice. "I thought Velvet was nice at first, but she's not. I think she's a bit crazy. I don't want to have anything to do with her anymore, but now Celeste and India won't speak to me because I hung out with Velvet, and I'm so, so miserable . . . last night was so horrible." She began to cry again.

"So what went on last night that was so terrible?" I asked.

Sophie groaned and blew her nose. "It was so awful. Velvet was going on and on yesterday about some weird idea about greeting the May, you know, because it was going to be the first day of May today. She wanted us all to meet her in the ruins at midnight to have some kind of dumb ritual for Bel—Bel something."

"Beltane. It's an ancient celebration," said Evie.

"Yeah, that was it. But I was fed up with getting out of bed in the middle of the night—she's dragged us out three times now, and it just makes me so worried about being caught. So I told her that May Day is about getting up early and washing your face in the dew and skipping about with flowers in your hair, not creeping around in the middle of the night, but she didn't listen. She laughed at me for being scared, and the others laughed too, so I had to go along with it. But I wish I hadn't."

"So what actually happened?" I asked, beginning to feel impatient with Sophie's rambling story. It seemed to be nothing more than Velvet showing off and fooling about.

"Promise not to tell anyone else?" she asked.

"Okay, I promise," I said. "Just tell us."

Sophie shuddered. "We all crept down to the ruins just before midnight, like Velvet had told us—me and Annabelle and Julia and the others. Velvet had got all these candles and stuff that she had taken from the cupboard in the dining hall. We all had to hold a candle and act in her horrible ceremony. I was cold, and I just wanted to get it over with, but Velvet was really into it. She had got dressed up in these black clothes and weird makeup, and she made us parade around the altar chanting, 'We call the spirits of the dead, we call the spirits of the dead. . . .' Over and over again like that. Annabelle was giggling like anything, but it made me feel scared. I couldn't help thinking about Laura and how she'd been found dead in the lake, just a few yards from the ruins, and how the place had once been a church. It seemed wrong, you know, sacrilegious. But Velvet wouldn't stop. She kept going on, calling out for the spirits of the dead."

Sophie looked nervously across to the girls in the corner, leaned closer to us, and whispered, "Then it got worse. Velvet seemed to get serious, sort of desperate. She said we had to perform a 'Rite of Freedom,' to get her out of Wyldcliffe. She made a circle in the ground with a knife, slashing at the earth, and said we had to stand in the circle and make vows of freedom. I didn't want to, but she made us."

"Why didn't you just leave?" asked Evie.

"I don't know, I don't know. I was frightened to stay and frightened to go. And then Velvet brought out a bottle of wine she had stolen from the kitchens and we had to drink it in turns and say, 'This is the blood of my enemies—the blood of my mother. I renounce her. I am now the daughter of the night.' I know it was stupid, really, but you can't imagine how freaky Velvet looked, saying all that stuff. And then she poured some wine on the ground and said it was an offering to the spirits of the dead.

"Velvet started to dance and writhe about, pretending to be, I don't know, possessed or something, and she said, 'With this blade and this wine I release every prisoner, every trapped animal, and every fettered spirit. I claim freedom for myself and everything around me.' And the others were holding hands in a circle and chanting, 'Freedom, freedom,' and laughing like it was just a big joke.

"But after that—I don't know whether it was the wine we had drunk, but something happened." Sophie paused and seemed to sink into herself, remembering. "Velvet went all—all weird, but perhaps she was just playacting. I don't know, but anyway she terrified me. She stood as stiff as a scarecrow and said, 'We take our freedom. We are the spirits of the dead. We are the Priestess.'"

"We are the Priestess?" Evie and I looked at each other in alarm.

"Yes, and Annabelle said, 'That's very funny, Velvet, you can stop now.' But Velvet just stared at us with these huge demented eyes and said it again and again: 'We are the Priestess, we are the Priestess, prepare for the end. . . .' And it was so real, like she really believed it. The next moment there was this great crash, and I nearly screamed. A massive stone had fallen from the ruins onto the grass. If it had hit any of the girls, they would have been dead.

"I'd really had enough, and besides I was sure we would have woken the whole school by now. So I pulled away from the circle, and then Velvet snapped out of it and was herself again, just laughing and showing off and drinking more wine. I didn't want to stay a minute longer, though, so I ran back to the school and flew up the stairs to the dorm. Thank goodness I didn't see any of the mistresses, but I had this awful feeling I was being watched the whole way. I was sure I was going to be caught. I felt terrible when I woke up." She sniffed. "Then all this horrible business about Helen. And I thought the summer term was going to be so nice."

We sat in silence for a moment, then Sophie asked timidly, "Do you think we'll get into trouble about that chunk that broke off the ruins? Aren't they worth millions?"

"I don't see how anyone will trace the damage back to you, Sophie," I reassured her. "It was probably just ready to fall after all those years, nothing to do with Velvet."

"I don't know," said Sophie uneasily. "She says she can make things happen, and maybe it's true."

"What kind of things?"

"She told us this morning that she had made that stone fall on purpose. And—and that she could make me throw myself in the lake if she wanted me to."

"Of course she can't."

"But she was there when Helen fell! I didn't tell Miss Hetherington, because I was scared to say anything. But I swear Velvet was there, looking out of the window, when I found Helen. She stared down at me and put her finger on her lips as if she was warning me . . . oh God, I wish she would get expelled and go away!" Sophie sniffed again and wiped her eyes, then looked at her watch. "I'm so tired. I'm going to bed early. The nurse said I need to rest and was excused evening prayers. You promise not to tell anyone what I told you?"

"Of course," we both said, and watched her leave. My heart felt as cold as a stone. "The Priestess—that's what Helen talked about too," I whispered. "It must be Mrs. Hartle's spirit manifesting itself."

"So it was Velvet who broke our protective seal and awakened her!" Evie groaned. "And then Mrs. Hartle was free to attack Helen. How could Velvet have been so reckless and stupid?"

"I don't suppose Velvet really knew what she was doing. She probably thought it was a laugh, a silly game."

"Some game," said Evie grimly. "If Velvet wants to dabble in the unknown realms, she might cause all sorts of damage."

"But do you really think she has any actual power? Isn't it just talk to make herself important and scare people like Sophie?"

Evie threw herself back in her chair and closed her eyes for a moment, trying to think. Then she sat up. "I remember Helen saying something once, Sarah, right at the beginning of all this. Something about everyone having a voice inside them, telling them the story of their own power, and that you can reach that power if you bother to find out how. Why would we be the only ones to unlock that part of ourselves? Why shouldn't Velvet be alive to her own potential, even if she doesn't exactly know what she's doing?"

"And those stories of what happened at her last school . . . that girl being caught in the fire . . ."

"Should we go and talk to her?" Evie asked. "Confront her?"

I shook my head slowly. "No . . . no, I don't think so. If it was only a fluke, there's no point, and if she is onto something—if she is stirring something up, it might be best to keep out of her way. She's done enough already. Let's pray that it was just Sophie getting scared." But somehow, I didn't really believe that. I looked at Evie and saw my own fear reflected in her face. "Oh, Evie, how are we going to get through all this?"

She laid her hand on mine. "We'll get through, if you guide us. *S* for Sarah, remember? Tell me what to do."

I took a deep breath. "The first thing is to find Miss Scratton. We need our Guardian now. We can't wait any longer."

Leaving the crimson common room and its murmur of voices and music, we walked down the silent corridor as quickly as we could. Soon we reached the High Mistress's study. As I raised my hand to knock on the door, I heard the sound of furniture being dragged around. I glanced at Evie in alarm, then tapped loudly on the door. It was flung open by Miss Dalrymple. For once she wasn't smiling.

"What do you want?" she said abruptly. "It's late. You should be getting ready for prayers."

"Um . . ." I took a risk. "Miss Hetherington asked us to . . . to give the High Mistress a message."

"The High Mistress cannot be contacted with any messages tonight." A cold smile spread across Miss Dalrymple's flushed, plump face. "Or for many nights to come."

"Why not?" Evie demanded.

"A little accident has occurred on the way back from St. Martin's. But I wouldn't worry about it if I were you. You're in safe hands." Her blank, toadlike eyes held a threat as she stepped nearer to us. I could smell the sickly perfume she used and see the powder on her mottled cheeks. Over her shoulder I saw that she had been ransacking the study. Books and papers were strewn all over the floor. What had she been searching for? "And I hear that poor Helen has had a mishap too," Miss Dalrymple went on. "You must be so concerned for her. After all, you're so close, aren't you? Almost—" Her voice quivered. "Almost like sisters."

Without warning Miss Dalrymple gripped my arm so tightly that I gasped in pain. "We're watching you," she whispered. "You need to be very, very careful if you don't want to get into more trouble than you can handle."

"Don't touch her," said Evie, flaming up in anger. "We know who you are and your disgusting friends. We're not frightened of you or your precious Priestess or whatever she calls herself now."

Miss Dalrymple's face registered a flicker of surprise; then she pulled herself together. She let go of me and assumed her usual, sickly sweet expression. "I don't know what you are talking about."

"But what about Miss Scratton? What have you done to her?"

"What have I done? Sarah dear, I think you must be

feverish. You need to calm down. If you carry on with your wild accusations, you might end up in trouble. And if you must know," she added with a bright smile, "our dear High Mistress is in the hospital at Wyldford Cross. Such a dreadful accident. Such a shame."

She shut the door in our faces and left us standing there, completely stunned. A single night and a stupid prank had changed everything. First Helen, then Miss Scratton had been struck down. Which of us would Mrs. Hartle and her minions attack next?

Twenty-one

"So it looks as though the coven has worked out that Miss Scratton is not one of them," Evie said.

"And Mrs. Hartle must be behind all this, acting as the Priestess or whatever she wants to call herself now," I added.

We were sitting at the door of the shepherd's hut the next day, talking to Josh and Cal in the early morning sunshine. Evie and I had gone there before breakfast on our ponies, accompanied by Josh. We had told the boys everything that had happened.

"So you think this road accident was part of a plan?" asked Cal.

The news had been announced at evening prayers the night before. Apparently the minibus in which Miss

Scratton and the students had been traveling on the way back from St. Martin's Academy had skidded across the road when a deer had leaped out in front of the vehicle. The girls had been taken to the Wyldford Cross hospital with minor cuts and bruises, but Miss Scratton had been admitted with serious head injuries. It was sickening even to think about it.

"I'm sure it must have been set up deliberately," I said. "Helen and Miss Scratton both have 'accidents' the day after Velvet stumbles into working a spell to release the spirits of the dead? It has to be Mrs. Hartle attacking them."

Cal frowned and looked puzzled. "But I thought that Miss Scratton had some kind of power. How could she be ambushed by Mrs. Hartle?"

"Miss Scratton is a Guardian," I explained. "She has lived at different times in Wyldcliffe's history, using different names, playing different roles. She's been a teacher, a healer, and a sister in the old convent. That's all we know, and she wasn't supposed to tell us that much. But I don't think she can just step in and put everything right. We have to do it for ourselves. She can guide us, that's all."

"But wouldn't she be able to protect herself from attack by Mrs. Hartle?" added Josh.

"I don't know—not if she was taken by surprise, maybe. Anyway, she's not invincible, is she? Her spirit might be from the mystic realm, but she lives in the human world. Her bones can be broken in a car crash like anyone else's. It sounds as though she's really hurt. I just hope she'll be all right."

"Didn't she say something about not being allowed to stay in Wyldcliffe?" Evie asked. "Because she had told us her secret—do you think this is how she is being taken away from us?"

We had so many questions, and there was no one to answer them for us. My head was throbbing from anxiety and lack of sleep. I tried to grasp hold of something positive.

"Even if we assume that both Helen and Miss Scratton have been attacked by the Priestess," I said, "the fact is that she didn't actually kill them. So that must be good news for us. Either the Priestess wasn't strong enough, and they managed to resist her, or . . ."

"Or perhaps she doesn't want them dead yet," said Cal. I shuddered, and he put his arm around my shoulders with awkward pride, conscious of the others watching us together. Evie looked across at us and smiled encouragingly, but Josh suppressed a sigh. He was being so patient with Evie—just good friends—but I could sense how much he longed to have the right to embrace her.

He got to his feet and looked out over the valley. "So Mrs. Hartle is back and Miss Scratton is out of the way, Helen's had a mysterious accident and Velvet might be involved as some kind of rogue element. It's not looking good, is it? You and Sarah are vulnerable to attack, Evie. You need to work together to be safe. You need Helen back with you."

"I agree with Josh," Cal said. "We have to do something to help Helen, not just for her own sake but for all of you."

I remembered what Miss Scratton had said the previous term: *If you stay true to each other, you will be strong enough for anything.* . . . And her more recent words now seemed to hold another message: *Do not break the Circle.*

She was right. We were linked together, and we needed one another. If one of us was hurt, we were all hurt. Our sisterhood was our bond and our strength.

"I brought this," I said, taking the Book out of my bag. It looked faded and insignificant in the sunlight, but I felt a vibration in my fingertips when I touched it. "I've found something that might help Helen get better quickly." A thought struck me. "You don't mind, Evie? I mean, it's okay to show the Book to Josh and Cal?"

"Of course. They're part of this now." She glanced up at the boys. "If that's what you want. Are you sure?"

"Yes," said Cal. "I'm sure."

"I'd walk through fire for you, Evie, you know that," said Josh, with sudden intensity. "And what I told you about Martha and Agnes might help. I belong in Wyldcliffe. Whatever I can do, whatever is inside me—it's all for you."

Evie blushed and said faintly, "Thank you, Josh— thank you so much."

He stepped back and tried to shrug the moment off, forcing his emotions under control. "Hey, I'm just glad to be here, if it helps. And I'm glad Cal has come back too." Josh looked at me and smiled with understanding in his warm brown eyes. "So, Sarah, what do you want us to do?"

I had already found the page I wanted. "A Charme to Cure a Friend." It wasn't a complicated ritual or spell, just a recipe for a simple cordial of the kind Martha might have made, and her mother and grandmothers before her. In my bag were the necessary ingredients and equipment—a bowl, some sealed jars, and a tiny green glass phial—which I had taken earlier from Agnes's little treasure store. Her secret study was still open in the attic, and I had got up at dawn to raid it in preparation.

"Distille the essence of Lavender for Cleansing, and Hawthorne

blossom for the Heart, and add to a Mixture of Rosewater and Honey. All the time saying the Incantation of Friendship, and burning aromatic Woods. The Flame of Friendship must heat the Mixture, and all due Ceremonie must be kept. Add the Secret Spices and offer all with Prayers and Supplications. . . .'"

Cal quickly made us a small fire in a ring of stones in front of the hut, and Josh watched in fascination as Evie and I prepared everything. We asked the boys to keep a lookout for other riders from the school, or anyone else who might be out early—farmworkers or enthusiastic hill walkers. They took up their positions, and then Evie and I reached into ourselves for faith and hope. We chanted the incantations under our breath as softly as the wind sighing over the bright hills. "Let Helen be as free as the air," I begged. "Let her be liberated from sickness." Step by step we followed the instructions to make the healing potion, and a little while later the glass phial was full of pale liquid. We put out the fire and cleansed the area, so that no one would suspect what we had done there.

"Bless this healing remedy," I said, and gave the phial to Evie for her blessing. She took the little bottle in her hands and prayed fervently, "Let it make Helen well again." Then she glanced over at Cal, who was still scanning the land for any unwanted intruders. "Your blessing, please, Cal."

He looked slightly surprised, but took the medicine from her and examined it. "Let it do its work," Cal said simply, then passed it to Josh.

The green phial lay on Josh's open palm. His hands were broad and strong, but I had seen the delicate carving of a horse that he had made as a gift for Evie on Valentine's Day, and how sensitively he handled the living animals under his care. Now he touched the glass bottle lightly with the fingertips of his other hand and said, "Helen, come back to us." A flash of light flared out from the phial, and I saw the wonder in Evie's eyes and realized that she hadn't quite believed that Josh could be connected with Lady Agnes until that moment. "Let this bring healing," Josh added, handing the bottle back to Evie.

"Let it be so," she whispered, and I saw so clearly that we were all connected, in one endless circle of life and death and renewal, an endless circle of love.

My mind pulled back sharply to the present. "Thanks so much, everyone," I said in a businesslike voice. "Now we need to get in to see Helen and give her this. We'd better get back to school."

We rode back in pairs, Evie and Josh falling a little way behind.

Cal stayed close to me. "I hope this medicine helps

Helen, but everything still feels so fragile," he said. "You need something more to protect you, Sarah. If Mrs. Hartle is on the loose again, anything could happen. I can't bear to think that you might be the next one she attacks. Let me sneak into the school grounds tonight. I could sleep in the stables to be nearer to you."

"No, if you get caught they'd set the police on you! You mustn't risk it."

"They can't stop me being with you when you're in danger," he growled.

"If she's going to attack me next, it could happen anywhere," I answered. "You can't always be there, ready to defend me. Evie was right about one thing; we have to be able to live, not creep about in hiding. I've got to finish this, Cal. I've got to put a stop to it once and for all so that we can all live in peace."

"Why don't you come away with me and get out of all this?" he asked abruptly. "We could join my family on the road, and be free in the ancient ways, with nothing to keep us apart." My heart beat fast. I saw myself riding pillion on the back of Cal's horse, my arms wrapped round his waist, or driving together in a beat-up truck, making our way on the old trails across the countryside, laughing with his sister and uncles around a campfire, telling tales and singing songs, then lying together in a narrow bed and waking up together in the morning. . . .

"No, I can't, it's impossible."

"Why not, rich girl?" he teased. "The Romany life too hard for you? Parents wouldn't approve?"

"It's not that. I've made a promise. To be true to my sisters and to be faithful to the gifts of the Mystic Way, wherever they might lead me. I have to see this through. And your mother said a promise can't be broken—"

"Except with a curse. You're right." Cal sighed. "But I wish you weren't." He slowed his horse to a walk, and we twined our hands together and rode side by side, not speaking, listening to the beating of our hearts.

When we got back to school, we left the boys at the gates with the horses and hurried to the dining hall for breakfast. As soon as the meal was over, Evie and I flew straight to the infirmary. We were eager to see Helen and give her the healing cordial. But the nurse barred our way.

"Helen's not at all well, I'm afraid," she said disapprovingly, as though any sign of illness was a criticism of her professional care. "She's got a high temperature and needs to rest. I can't possibly let you see her."

"Has she seen the doctor?" I asked, sickeningly disappointed.

"The doctor came late last night and said it's probably just shock—a reaction to the fall. He's given Helen something to make her sleep. I'm sure she'll be better soon."

"Has she said anything, has she been talking? Did she ask to see us?" Evie asked.

"No, no, and no," the nurse answered. "Now stop pestering me. I've nursed enough Wyldcliffe girls to know what to do. The best thing you can do for your friend is stop worrying about her."

It was easy to say and impossible to do. For a wild moment I suspected that the nurse was a secret member of the coven and was deliberately obstructing us from seeing Helen so that she could do some harm to her. But I had no reason to believe that. I put my hand on the nurse's starched sleeve pleadingly. "Please, Sister McFarlane," I begged. "Let me just see her for two minutes. I know you're looking after her beautifully, but we've been so frightened, it was such an awful shock. If you let me see her just for a moment, we'll stop worrying and we won't bother you anymore."

The nurse pursed her lips, as if making up her mind; then she relented. "Well, if it means so much to you. It's nice that you care so much. Just one of you, mind, and not for long."

"You go, Sarah," said Evie quickly, slipping the phial into my hand. "I'll wait here."

I followed the nurse into the bright, sunny infirmary. Helen was lying on her back in the nearest bed with the covers pulled to one side. She looked hot, and although her eyes were closed she didn't seem properly asleep. She moved her head restlessly, and her breath was quick and shallow.

"I think the sun is in her eyes," I lied, and the nurse bustled over to the window to adjust the blinds. As quickly as a conjurer I touched Helen's lips with the glass phial, and a few drops of the liquid slipped into her mouth.

"Well, you've seen her now," said the nurse kindly, turning back from the window. "You can see she's in good hands. Come back later, and I'll tell you how she is."

I had no choice but to leave, but at least we had done what we could.

Evie and I went to get our books ready for class, though I didn't know how I could possibly concentrate on Latin verbs that morning. When we got to our classroom, Velvet was showing off to a crowd of girls in the few minutes of freedom before the mistress arrived. Sophie wasn't there, but the others were hanging on to her every word.

Velvet saw me and turned on her most charming smile.

"Hey, Sarah, look at this." She ignored Evie. They hadn't got on since their first meeting. "It's so funny!"

I wasn't in the mood to humor Velvet. All I wanted was to ask her what she had been doing near Helen when she'd had her accident, but there were too many people around. "What is it?" I replied curtly.

"We're just looking at these latest photos." Velvet held out a garishly colored magazine. It was crammed full of glossy photographs of vacant celebrities and wannabes. Velvet held up the center spread. The headline read *Rick Romaine's Rebel Daughter!* She thrust it under my nose, and I saw the first few lines of the article.

Velvet Romaine, daughter of rock star Rick and supermodel Amber Romaine, has become a pupil at the country's most exclusive and prestigious school. Wyldcliffe Abbey School for Young Ladies is notoriously strict. Will this prim and proper environment cure Velvet of the excesses that have landed her in trouble so often? Or will this "Wyld Child" prove to be too much of a handful for the school authorities?

There was a big photo of Velvet standing on the steps of the school the first day she arrived at Wyldcliffe. In the background a thin, upright figure was slightly out of focus; a woman turning her face from the camera. It was Miss Scratton.

I remembered something. I needed to get out of there.

"And the photographers are still hanging round the village trying to get more pictures of me," Velvet gloated. "I must think of something suitably outrageous to do for them."

"I think you've done enough damage already," I said coldly.

"Hey, what have I done now?"

"Ask Sophie," I said, then turned to Evie. "I . . . um . . . left my Latin dictionary in my dorm. Will you come and get it with me?" She looked surprised but followed me out of the room.

"Did you see that photo of Miss Scratton?"

"Yeah, of course," Evie replied. "But why is it important?"

"It reminded me of something. Come on, before Miss Clarke turns up and stops us."

I hastily led the way past the library and down the dark passageways to the red corridor. Its walls were covered in faded crimson damask, and had once led to a magnificent ballroom, which was now closed up. Most of the rooms in that part of the school hadn't been used for ages, not until Miss Scratton had three of them fitted up as common rooms for the lower, middle, and senior divisions of the school. At the end of the corridor there was the padlocked door of the old ballroom, then another gloomy passage that was occasionally used as a shortcut to the locker rooms at the back of the building. The passage was hung with obscure paintings of dreary landscapes, interspersed here and there with old photographs. I walked along quickly, scanning the walls.

"Here it is." I stopped in front of a faded sepia photo, labeled *Wyldcliffe School, Armistice Day 1918*.

About forty girls dressed in identical soft-collared tunics were lined up in rows, smiling for the camera. They were holding flags and a sign decorated with rosettes that said PEACE AND VICTORY. On the back row, half a dozen mistresses were looking out more gravely, their faces etched with the cost of war as well as the relief of its ending. "Look—there!" I pointed to the teacher on the end of the row. She had turned her head as if trying to prevent the camera capturing her image.

"It's Miss Scratton, I'm sure it is."

"It's a bit blurred," said Evie doubtfully.

"But it's just how she looked in that photo with Velvet, can't you see?"

"I suppose so . . . it could be her, I guess."

"It is her, I'm sure of it. And that means she might have known my great-grandmother Maria. She was here just after the war ended."

"But how does that help us?" Evie asked.

"I've been thinking about Maria a lot lately, and I have this feeling that she is connected to all this. I think—I think I saw her up on the Ridge yesterday, near the standing stones. Don't you think that's strange, on the day that both Helen and Miss Scratton are injured?"

"Couldn't that just be coincidence?"

"I've told you, I don't believe in coincidence. And it wasn't just a daydream or anything like that. I—well, I hope you don't mind, Evie, but I used the Talisman, and then I saw Maria, or a girl at least, and heard this drumming noise. And Helen heard drums when she had her vision of her mother. And that message on Agnes's door: 'Listen to the drums.' I've been beating myself up for not working it out yet, but I just haven't been able to see where it was leading. But Maria keeps coming back to me, and perhaps she's the sign we need."

Evie looked slightly doubtful.

"I know it's not much," I admitted, "but it's all we've got. Perhaps there's a connection between the message on the door and the drums in Helen's dream and in my vision of Maria. Perhaps they are Gypsy drums? If we tried to contact Maria again—if you used the Talisman—perhaps we could find out if she is really behind the message and what it means."

"So you heard drums when you saw Maria?"

"Yes. And I'm convinced that Maria knew something that would help us. Please, Evie, let's just try to contact her. We've got nothing to lose, and it might lead to something."

"Of course. We'll do it tonight." Evie's face was set and hard, like a young soldier's. "I'll try anything and do anything for you and Helen. I won't let you down again, I promise."

Twenty-two

The day dragged past. All I could think about was using the Talisman. But we had to wait until night-fall, when we could get away from the other students and the prying eyes of the mistresses. The only relief to the usual routine was that it happened to be the day that the local village kids were coming to use the school's facilities. Some were going to play tennis, others would have music lessons, and some would be allowed to use the rather chilly outdoor pool. Evie had volunteered to help with the swimming, and I had agreed to go along with her. I had wondered whether the other teachers would use Miss Scratton's absence as an excuse to cancel her plans to open Wyldcliffe's doors to the local people, but apparently the event was going to take place as scheduled. And so after lunch, instead of going to the science lab for our normal afternoon classes, Evie and I went down to the pool. We found the sports mistress, Miss Schofield, looking even more bad-tempered than usual, glaring at an eager but slightly apprehensive group of about a dozen ten-year-olds.

"Well, I suppose you'd better get changed. And no messing about! You've got two minutes exactly."

The kids crowded into the old-fashioned wooden huts that had been built as locker rooms by the side of the pool. I rather reluctantly found myself an empty cubicle and went inside to strip off my uniform and get into my bathing suit. It was a soft, warm day, but the water in the deep marble pool still looked pretty cold. Evie was happy, though, temporarily distracted from our troubles by the lure of the water. She would have swum in any weather, but the pool was only filled in these warmer summer months. Eventually we were all ready. Most of the children were giggling and shy, but some of the bigger boys were trying to show off, pushing and butting into one another and threatening to jump in.

"Stop that!" Miss Schofield barked as she lined them up. "You will get in slowly and sensibly, and follow my instructions exactly. . . ." She obviously wasn't in favor of the new Wyldcliffe-for-all scheme, which boosted my flagging enthusiasm. I had never liked this bullying teacher, so anything she wasn't happy with seemed good to me.

"Ooh, it's cold," said a thin little girl with untidy hair, as she put her toe into the water.

"You won't feel it once you're in," I said encouragingly.

"It's gorgeous, honestly." Evie smiled. "And it's lovely to have you here. We're going to have great fun."

Miss Schofield glowered as one by one we helped the children to get in the water. There was lots of shrieking and splashing, but soon they began to enjoy themselves. Miss Schofield, although she was a snob and a bully, was an expert coach, and she took the stronger swimmers to the deep end and helped them with their technique. Evie and I stayed in the shallow end with the more timid children, playing games and trying to build up their confidence. The time raced by, and soon it was time for them to get out. "But we haven't done any diving," said a stocky little lad. "I can dive already."

"Show me," said Evie. He fearlessly threw himself headfirst into the pool and came up laughing and spluttering in a ring of bubbles. "Well done," Evie said, laughing. "Now watch me."

She did the most beautiful dive into the deep end

and glided along the bottom of the pool with her long red hair floating behind her like dark silk. As I watched her admiringly, the light around me seemed to fade. She wasn't coming up—she'd been down there too long—her slim body seemed suspended in the greenish water, like a frozen statue. Everything around me was dim and silent, except for the sound of my own heart beating. I watched, immobilized with fear, as Evie's body seemed to roll over lifelessly in the water. She floated toward the surface with her arms hanging awkwardly by her sides and her eyes gazing upward, seeing nothing, like Ophelia drifting to her doom. I felt the water choking my own mouth and breath, drowning my senses, and I gave a great gasp and cried out, *Evie!* The next moment the sun was shining again and the vision was over. The children were clapping as Evie surfaced gracefully at the far end of the pool, her diving display over.

"That was great fun, wasn't it?" she enthused as we got dry. "The kids are so sweet." Then she sighed. "If only everything could be, you know, normal like this."

"Yeah," I muttered. "If only." I couldn't tell her what I had seen. I couldn't tell my best friend that I had seen a vision of her death.

* * *

220

The children were given a tea of buttered toast and homemade cakes in the dining hall, and then they were ready to go home. We helped them find their cardigans and jackets and sports bags; then the whole party trooped down the corridor to the black-and-white-tiled entrance hall. "Ooh, look, it's so big! Do you sleep here? Can we come again?" Their innocence touched me. It was good to hear laughing, unself-conscious voices in that place, although when we passed Celeste in the corridor, she shrank back theatrically as though the children would infect her. "Miss Scratton, our High Mistress, says she wants you to come often," I said, trying to compensate for Celeste's rudeness. But the kids hadn't noticed, and they jostled happily out of the hallway and onto the drive, where their teacher was waiting to collect them. Evie and I walked with her, then waved good-bye to the children halfway down the lane, just beyond the school gates.

"Bye!"

"See you again!"

"Thank you!"

Their voices filled the air as they walked away toward the village. The spring sunshine had cooled, and the color had faded from the day. "Better get back inside," I said.

"Let's just watch them a minute longer," said Evie. Her

face was glowing, and she looked more beautiful than I had ever seen her. "I'd like to have ten children, wouldn't you?"

"Well, not all at once," I joked feebly, feeling more and more anxious. "I really think we should go. We can't risk anything happening before we try to contact Maria tonight."

"I suppose so." She turned away from where the crowd of children had now disappeared, and we walked back up the lane to the school gates. The western sky was filled with harsh light. I didn't know why I felt so nervous, but I pulled at Evie's arm and urged her to go more quickly. We reached the gates, where the old sign of the school's name still spelled out its eerie message among the missing letters: BE COOL OR YOU DIE.

I heard the sound of hooves, as urgent as my heartbeat. A black horse was galloping toward us out of the light. Its rider was a tall young man wearing a heavy cloak and hood. He had long black hair and eyes the color of a summer sky and a smile full of sorrow. Evie gave a little moan as though she had been hurt, then she stumbled forward.

"Sebastian! Sebastian—oh it is, it is you!"

He bent down from his horse and gathered Evie in his arms, and for a moment they clung together. Then

Sebastian pulled her onto the horse's back. It reared up and shrieked, and Sebastian's hood fell from his face. He no longer looked like a beautiful boy. This was not Sebastian Fairfax, neither in life nor in death. A ghastly, skeletal figure held Evie cruelly as she writhed in its grasp, trying to escape, but it was too late. The horse plunged and whinnied and galloped away over the slope that led to the moors.

"Evie, Evie!" I shouted as I ran after them, but they had already vanished.

One by one, they had been taken: Helen, Miss Scratton, and now, dearest of all to me, Evie. What were they going to do to her? Where was she being taken? The image of Evie floating in the water came back and overwhelmed me with horror. I was alone. We had been divided and crushed by the Priestess and her plots, and there was nothing I could do. I sank to the ground and cried like a lost child.

Then a voice in my head spoke. *A promise cannot be broken except with a curse.* I had made a promise to cherish and care for my sisters, through good and bad, hope and despair, whatever happened. I was the only one left. *S* for Sarah. This was my time. I had to use it.

Twenty-three

For once, I decided that I would try to trust the school authorities. Perhaps just this one time, if I told someone that I had seen Evie being abducted, the teachers in charge of our lives would behave as they were supposed to and call the police. I wasn't quite sure what the police could do, but it had to be worth trying.

I went straight to the High Mistress's study and knocked loudly, hoping that someone I could even half believe in, like Miss Hetherington or Miss Clarke, would be there. But there was no answer. I tried the handle, and the door was locked. Undeterred, I strode away and headed up the marble stairs to the mistresses' common room on the second floor. Classes had finished for the day and girls were pouring down the staircase, going to music and art clubs or on their way to the library to do prep. It was as though they all lived on the other side of a glass wall to me. My Wyldcliffe wasn't the same as theirs. Only Velvet and Sophie and Laura had unwittingly brushed against my world, and as I threaded through the chattering students, I wondered how long it would be before all the Wyldcliffe girls came under the shadow of the Priestess. Why would she stop at hurting the three of us? Why not destroy all that was young and good and hopeful?

I reached the door of the staff common room and was just about to knock when it opened. To my relief it was Miss Hetherington.

"Oh, please, Miss Hetherington, I wanted to see you about Evie."

"So you've heard already, have you?"

"Heard?"

"I'm afraid Evie's father has been taken ill whilst he was on leave in London. She's had to catch a train to go and see him straightaway. It's a long journey, but she'll get there later tonight, and I'm sure it will be a comfort to them both to be together."

"She's gone to London?" Miss Hetherington looked so sincere, but was she bluffing? "Are you sure?"

"Of course. Miss Dalrymple took the call from London

and arranged everything for Evie."

I bet she did, I thought grimly. So that was the way the coven was playing this. Miss Dalrymple and the rest of them must be obeying the Priestess's orders. They had obviously planted this story about Evie having to dash to London to cover up her absence.

"Are you all right, Sarah? You look rather pale."

"No, I'm fine," I answered. Miss Hetherington might simply be an innocent messenger, but she might equally be one of them. There was only one teacher in this place that I could really trust, and that was Miss Scratton. She was the person I needed right now. Trying to make a connection with Maria, as Evie and I had planned, would have to wait. But our High Mistress was still in the hospital at Wyldford Cross. I backed away from the door of the staff room, trying to look unconcerned.

"Oh well, I guess Evie will be back soon enough," I said. "Thank you. I'd better go and do my prep."

I headed down the marble staircase and walked to the library, but I didn't go in. I carried on walking until I reached the windowless red corridor. Its crimson walls looked almost black in the lamplight. I opened the door of our common room. Thankfully no one was there, so I went straight over to the corner where a new telephone had been installed. You were supposed to write your name in a book with the date and length of your call, but I didn't bother. I flipped through the telephone directory until I found the number of the hospital.

"Hello? Hello? Can I please speak to Miss Scratton?" I asked the receptionist, speaking as quietly as I could.

"Miss who?" said the woman at the other end.

"Scratton," I repeated. "She was admitted on Sunday afternoon. She's one of the teachers at Wyldcliffe Abbey."

"Do you know which ward she is in, dear?"

"No, I'm sorry—but she had head injuries. She'd been in a road accident. Is she okay? Is it possible to speak to her?"

"What did you say her first name was?"

"I didn't—I don't know—"

"Well, I can't seem to find her on the patient list."

"But you must!" I begged. "It's really urgent."

"Just wait a moment, I'll go and inquire. I'm putting you on hold."

Her voice snapped off, and some irritating music played in my ear. I waited nervously, expecting Miss Dalrymple to come in and snatch the phone from me at any moment, and I cursed Wyldcliffe's long-held rule forbidding cell phones.

"Come on, come on," I groaned under my breath; then the music stopped and the woman spoke again.

"Are you still there, dear? I've just spoken to the manager, and he's confirmed that we don't have a patient called Miss Scratton."

"You mean she's been discharged?" I said hopefully.

"No, dear. She couldn't have been discharged, as she was never here."

"Never there?"

"That's what I said. Sorry to disappoint you. Good night."

The phone went dead.

For a moment I stood there, blinking stupidly at the phone. Then I slammed it down and ran out, my mind buzzing with questions. Where was Miss Scratton? What did it mean, she had never been in the hospital? She must have been there after the road accident. But if she wasn't in the hospital, why hadn't she come back to Wyldcliffe to help us? I had to find some answers somewhere.

I raced down the corridor, opening classroom doors, looking for someone, anyone, but the school seemed deserted. One of the doors I opened was to a small music room. Mr. Brooke was giving a piano lesson to a golden-haired eleven-year-old with an earnest expression and heavy glasses. "Oh, I'm sorry," I mumbled. I turned and fled until I reached the library, then tried to smooth my uniform and pull myself together before going in. A group of eighteen-year-olds was sitting at a table, deep in study.

"Excuse me. I'm sorry to bother you," I said, "but can I just ask you something?"

One of the girls looked up, mildly surprised. It was one of Wyldcliffe's traditions that you didn't speak to older girls unless spoken to, but I knew Catherine Hedley slightly from home, as we had both ridden in the same summer polo matches. "Catherine, you went to over St. Martin's with Miss Scratton, didn't you?"

"Yes, I did, worse luck." She waved her wrist at me. It was bandaged heavily. "I can't ride for at least two weeks after the crash. But I'm lucky it was nothing more serious, I suppose. Why do you want to know?"

"Um . . . it's just that Miss Scratton was our form teacher, and some of us were wondering about . . . um . . . clubbing together to get her some flowers. Do you know what ward she was in? Did you see her being taken to the hospital? How was she? Was she very badly hurt?"

"I don't really know," said Catherine. "I can't remember much about what happened. We'd had a great time at St. Martin's, and when we were driving back everything seemed fine. Then I remember seeing a huge deer leap out in front of the minibus. The next thing I knew I was waking up with a pain in my wrist and the minibus wrapped round a tree."

"So where was Miss Scratton?"

"Miss Dalrymple said she'd already been taken to the hospital. Miss Scratton had been sitting at the front and was hurt worse than the rest of us. It's a nice idea to send flowers. I'm sure she'll be better soon, though."

"Miss Dalrymple was there?" I asked.

"Yes, she organized getting us all back to school."

"Oh, yeah—of course. Well, thanks."

I turned away and left them to their books. It seemed that Miss Dalrymple had a finger in every pie.

There were two possibilities. Either Miss Scratton, like Evie, had been spirited away by the Priestess and her followers against her will, or she was in league with Celia Hartle and had abandoned us just when we needed help.

The second suggestion was impossible. I believed in Miss Scratton. I always would. Besides, Miss Scratton had known something like this would happen to her and had tried to warn us about it. "I will not be allowed to stay long," she had said. And so she had tried to protect us with the spell we had made in the ruins, not foreseeing that Velvet's blundering would undo it. Miss Scratton had done everything she could, but now she was gone. There was no wise guardian to help me. But I wasn't the only one left. How could I have forgotten that I had one remaining sister who might be able to tell me what to do? I had Agnes, and I still had the Talisman. Somehow, I had to use it to reach her.

That night I crept out of the school one more time, tracing Evie's footsteps down the secret steps to the old servants' quarters and out to the stables. I was shivering under my jacket, and I told myself it was simply because I was cold. I was doing this for Evie, and for Helen, and I couldn't be afraid. When I had gone back to the infirmary before the lights-out bell, the nurse had told me that Helen had improved slightly and had just fallen asleep. "I'm not going to let you disturb her now," she had said with a smile. "She'll be right as rain in the morning."

I clung to that hope, and a hundred others. That Agnes would respond to my call. That I would find Evie. That no harm would come to me alone at night, with the Priestess roaming the land. Besides, I had the Talisman with me. I told myself again and again that it would protect me from the Priestess, but as I crept down the tree-lined drive to the school gates, I couldn't help feeling naked under the stars, as though Mrs. Hartle's spirit was watching my movements like a spider waiting for its prey.

When I reached the locked gates, two figures were waiting for me in the shadows of the lane.

"Cal?"

He threw a rope over the wall. I scrambled up and dropped down lightly to the other side, where he and Josh were waiting for me. Cal hugged me briefly and Josh nodded, grim-faced, his golden smile wiped away by the terrible loss of Evie.

"We'll find her, Josh, I promise," I said, moved by his pain. I had been worrying about Evie as my friend, my sister, my responsibility; for an instant I saw through his eyes, and felt his anguish. He had loved Evie all this time, and yet they hadn't even kissed; he had her friendship and gratitude, but nothing more. And now he might never see her again.

"We've got to find her," he replied, in a strained, broken voice. "We've just got to."

The three of us set off in the direction of the village. There was a thin frost underfoot; one of those sudden returns to winter that often happened in Wyldcliffe's northern valley.

The church tower looked pale and ghostly against the

sky. Ancient black yew trees stood at the entrance to the graveyard like sentinels. Cal took my hand. "The spirits of the dead lie here," he murmured. "Tread carefully."

"We aren't doing anything wrong," I replied. "We seek Agnes in the light where she lives in peace, not in the shadows."

He didn't reply but held my hand more tightly.

I led the way to the old-fashioned stone tomb, surmounted by the angel statue. We gathered around it in silence. The statue looked down on us with worn stone eyes.

When I had tried to call on Agnes once before, after my quarrel with Evie, nothing had happened. Agnes hadn't responded to me. But here at her tomb, this place of power and protection, some special gift might be granted by my sister of fire. I set a circle of white candles around her grave, their little flames flickering bravely in the night air. Then I sprinkled herbs and flower petals and anointed the place with water sweetened with subtle oils. The boys shifted behind me uneasily, looking around for any sign of danger.

"Great Creator," I said. "I stand here, innocent of any crime. I pray for my sisters Helen and Evie and our Guardian, Miss Scratton. They have fallen victim to our enemies. Let me speak with our sister Agnes for guidance."

I took the Talisman from my pocket and hooked it over the outstretched hand of the stone angel. "Agnes, receive your own. Speak to me."

Nothing happened. My stomach began to tighten. Would she answer? The wind was getting stronger, sobbing through the branches of the trees. The hills around us seemed cold and menacing, and I thought how frail my faith was in the face of such a bleak, hostile world. But it was a thread of gold, made not just for this moment, but for eternity. Although I was afraid, I somehow knew that we were all being cared for by a higher power, and that the whole of Creation was fundamentally good, not twisted and crazed like the Priestess and her Unconquered lords had made it for themselves. "I believe in you, Agnes," I whispered. "I believe in your message of love." I heard my heart pounding, and I seemed to hear Cal's heart pulsing in time with my own, a steady beat of youth and strength that would never give up. "Please, Agnes, please help me now."

The statue of the angel began to shine with a faint light. We saw it shimmer and change until Agnes was standing in its place. Josh gasped and knelt on the ground, shielding his eyes as the light grew stronger.

Agnes did not speak, but gestured with her right hand. The light spilled from her hand in white flames, and in the center of the flames we could see vivid images. The first was of Evie, just as I had seen her before, still and silent under the water, her hair floating around her face and her eyes glazed in death. I cried out and the image changed. Now I saw Helen in bed in the infirmary. She was dreadfully ill and thin and struggling for every breath.

"They told me she was better—but she's dying!" I gasped. "And Evie is—oh, Evie—"

Agnes laid her finger on her lips for silence and then gestured again. The flames glowed once more, and this time I saw a young girl with dark, curly hair. It was Maria, I was sure of it. She was lying with her eyes closed at the foot of the tallest standing stone, wearing a circlet of leaves like a crown. Then Agnes looked right into my eyes and pointed at me. A single word formed on her lips: "Seek." Her voice echoed through the graveyard. "Seek . . . seek . . . seek . . ." The next moment I was staring at the stone face of the angel, blank and meaningless.

I turned to Cal in a panic. "What shall I do? Evie— where is she? What's happened to her? And Helen looks so ill!"

"Was that other girl Maria?" asked Cal.

"Yes, I'm sure it was her. That's exactly how I saw her up by the standing stones. But what did Agnes mean? Seek—which one of my friends must I seek first?"

I felt pulled in every direction. Josh spoke unsteadily. "I'd tear Wyldcliffe to pieces to find Evie, but we still have no idea where to start. And Maria—wasn't that just an image of the past? At least we know where Helen is. Perhaps you should start by helping her."

His words made sense, though I was now gripped with a dread that Helen might already have been smuggled out of the school by Miss Dalrymple and the coven. I began to run.

"Wait!" Cal said, running after me. "We'll come with you."

"No!" I stopped for a moment. "If you want to help, go and—" I could hardly bear to say it. "Go and search the river for Evie. If she really is—if her body is there . . ."

"She's not dead, Sarah, I promise," Josh said, and for a brief moment a faint smile softened his expression.

"How can you be so sure?"

"I feel her, in here," he said, and he lightly touched his forehead. "And I see her, like a bright flame in the dark." I hoped with all my being that he was right and that his hidden link with Agnes would guide him now. "But we'll search for her, all the same," he added. "We'll go to the river."

"Thank you, thank you so much," I gabbled. "I'll see you back at school. I've got to get back to Helen now. I can't lose any more time."

For a moment Cal and I stood face-to-face. "I hate you going alone," he said, frowning. "It's not safe."

"I'm not alone," I answered. "I've got you." I reached up and kissed him, then broke away. "You'll try to find Evie with Josh? You promise?"

"I promise." He kissed me again. "And I never break my promises." Then he and Josh turned away in the direction of the moors, and I set off back to the Abbey, running as fast as if the Priestess and her hellhounds were already tracking me down.

The door of the infirmary creaked as it opened. I slipped into the white, clinical room, feeling numb. Nothing seemed quite real anymore. Racing back from the village, sneaking back into the sleeping school, wondering whether I would be caught on the stairs: none of that was real. Only Agnes's message was real. I had to seek out my sisters and save them.

A clock was ticking in the corner of the room. There were four white beds, and another door that led to the place where the nurse slept. Helen's bed was the only one occupied.

"Oh God, thank you . . . thank you. . . ." I was so grateful to find Helen still there that the shock of her appearance didn't immediately sink in. But she was just as I had seen her in Agnes's picture. Helen was lying rigidly on her back with her eyes open, seeing nothing. Her breath was coming in low, ugly rasps with long pauses in between each painful gasp. I felt her forehead and wrist. She was cold and clammy and her pulse was barely registering. A little voice in my head that seemed to come from another world told me I should call out for the nurse and telephone for an ambulance. But the adult world had let us down. Mrs. Hartle and the other corrupt teachers at this fine school had used Helen and Laura and the rest of us for their own ends. The doctors would be helpless against the force that held Helen in its relentless grip. It had nothing to do with conventional medicine; this was the Priestess's poison at work in her veins. Sophie had been right after all. Despite—or even because of—the attentions of the staff, Helen was near to death.

As I hovered over Helen's white face, strangely beautiful even in this extremity, Miss Hetherington's words came back to me. Did Helen actually want to leave this world? Would I be wrong to call her back, even if I could?

Disconnected images spun through my mind: Helen crying over her mother's submission to the Unconquered lords, Helen standing on the roof of the school and stepping into the void, Helen carrying us with her through air and space like a shooting star. Helen—loveless, tragic, misunderstood. She had never really been happy. Perhaps it would be easier than I had thought to let her go, and let her be in peace. Was that what she wanted? I hesitated, desperate to do the right thing.

My fingers closed around the glass phial that was still in my pocket. I had to try. I couldn't give up, and neither could Helen. She hadn't had her chance at life yet, and everyone deserved that.

I unsealed the little bottle and dropped some of the remaining liquid onto her lips, then dabbed her forehead with the rest. Helen stirred and moaned. Her arm shifted position on the white cover, and I saw the livid scar on her skin and noticed that her hand was tightly clenched. Taking her icy hand in mine, I kissed it, and her muscles seemed to relax and her hand opened up. She had been clutching a small round object. I had never seen it before, but I knew at once what it must be. It was the brooch that Mrs. Hartle had left with Helen as a baby, and it was the exact size and shape of the tattoolike marking on Helen's skin.

I remembered the words of the Book: "From where do such signs come? Many Scholars declare they are a Sign of great Destiny, with Death in their wake. . . ."

A sign of great destiny. This seemingly insignificant bit of jewelry, or whatever it was, had started all this trouble for Helen, I thought. I picked it out of Helen's open palm and examined it. Was the pattern in the center of the circle supposed to be crossed swords or a pair of stylized wings? Was it a sign of danger? And how—and why—had it transferred a perfect image of itself onto Helen's skin?

For a second I seemed to see the flames dancing on Agnes's hand when she had shown us the vision of Helen. An odd phrase came to me: *Fight fire with fire*. Without stopping to analyze it, I took the brooch and placed it exactly over the mark on Helen's arm, then pushed it into her flesh like a seal. At once, Helen sat up, her eyes wide-open in pain.

"Aaah . . . that hurt . . . ah!" She clutched her arm. The mark stood out red and angry. But the next moment she threw her arms around my neck and sobbed, "Thank you . . . oh, Sarah, thank you so much. I wanted so much to come back after I fell, but I couldn't. She was holding me—"

"Who was it?" I asked. "Your mother? Or was it Velvet?"

Helen stared at me with haunted eyes. "No, it wasn't. It wasn't like that."

"So what happened? Who was it?"

"I was in a deep, secret place," Helen said faintly. "And someone was keeping me prisoner." She hid her face in her hands and whispered, "It was Miss Scratton."

"Miss Scratton?"

"Yes. She was holding me back. She's working against us."

Twenty-four

Nothing made sense anymore.

The rest of the night passed like a slow-motion dream. First we had to face the nurse, who must have been woken up by the sound of us talking. She came into the sickroom to find me sitting on Helen's bed, and she furiously brushed away my explanations about being worried for Helen. "I've never heard of anything so selfish, bursting in here in the middle of the night like this! And Helen needing to rest so badly, you could have given her a real setback." Yet she was clearly surprised and pleased with Helen's pulse and breathing, and calmed down a little when Helen pleaded with her not to be angry.

"You don't know how Sarah has helped me," she begged. "Seeing her has made me feel so much better.

Please don't tell anyone. Don't get her into trouble."

Eventually the nurse stopped scolding and let me go to my dorm, but I couldn't sleep. Nothing made sense. Helen had been cured by a sign of evil, and Miss Scratton was the one who had trapped her spirit and body and dragged her to the brink of existence. So our supposed Guardian had fled and become our enemy. Now everything had another interpretation. Miss Scratton must have set up that road accident herself somehow, and then escaped to join the Dark Sisters. That's why she was never in the hospital. It was all a fake, and everything Miss Scratton had told us was a lie. *But she helped us*, I told myself. *I believed in her....*

I didn't know what to believe. I couldn't take it in. I kept saying the same words over and over again. "But the mark is evil, and Miss Scratton is on our side," until I got all mixed up. "The mark is on our side ... Miss Scratton is evil ... the mark is Miss Scratton...." I must have fallen asleep, because I plunged into a vivid dream.

I was with Cal. We were in the woods, and the earth was alive with light and warmth. The trees were newly crowned with fresh green leaves, and a swath of bluebells shone purple against the tree trunks. Between the trees a smooth lawn of grass was sprinkled with white flowers. Cal bent to pick some of them and twined their fragile stalks in my hair. Then we stood face-to-face, as though waiting to dance or speak, but we were silent, too full of strange new feelings to talk. He looked at me questioningly and then ran his fingers through my hair and down my neck. Our mouths searched for each other, and we trembled as we kissed, as though we couldn't believe that this happiness was really for us. I seemed to hear the trees breathing, and sense the grass growing, and the sweet, heady scent of the bluebells was as potent as wine.

The next moment everything shifted, and the grass became a boggy field of mud. From behind the slender trees an army of grotesque clay-colored creatures emerged. Their misshapen bodies and swollen heads filled me with disgust as they began to paw at me, pulling me away from Cal. I was slipping out of his grasp, leaving him behind. "No!" Cal shouted. "Come back!" Then his face changed, and he was reaching out to me and shouting, "Maria, Maria, come back! Don't touch her! No!"

I echoed his cries and called wildly, "No, no, no . . ." I woke up sweating, not realizing that I had shouted out loud.

"Sarah, what's wrong?" Ruby was sitting up in bed and staring at me in concern, blinking shortsightedly. "Are you okay?"

"Oh . . . yeah . . . sorry. Nightmare." I fell back on my pillows and wiped my face. I could still see those pawing, bony hands. I could still see the distress in Cal's eyes as I was dragged away from him. I could still hear the frantic voice calling Maria's name.

"What the hell was all that about?" Velvet asked, glaring at me from her rumpled bed.

"Nothing—a bad dream. Sorry."

"Sounded like you were having total hysterics. Mind you, I don't blame you." Velvet yawned and looked at her watch. "Oh crap, the bell will go in a minute. Might as well get up and face another perfect day in the madhouse." She got out of bed and started pulling clothes out of her drawers and throwing them down in a heap. "This place is enough to drive anyone crazy. I can't stand the thought of wearing this disgusting uniform for one more minute. If my parents don't get me out of here soon, I'll burn the place down. I'm not joking."

"I thought you were enjoying being the 'Wyld Child,'" I said, trying to cover up the confusion I still felt about my nightmare.

"Oh please, don't insult me," Velvet drawled. "Freaking out a few dimwits like Sophie and ragging ancient teachers isn't exactly hard."

"Velvet, don't go looking for trouble," I said, sitting up and pleading with her. "You don't know what you might stir up."

"Like what? Getting a detention? Getting the school picnic canceled or whatever it was that Miss Scratton promised all the good little girls for a treat?"

"No, it's just—Wyldcliffe is kind of different. Things go on that shouldn't."

"How interesting," she replied coldly. "Do tell me more." She stared at me with her deep, sultry eyes, and I wondered again just how much she really knew.

"What did you say to Helen before she fell through that window?" I asked.

"Me? I didn't say anything to her. I wasn't near the place. Why should I have been?"

Because Sophie isn't a liar. Because you were there when your sister died, and when that fire started at your last school, and when your mom's assistant got injured. Because I don't trust you.

It was hopeless. I couldn't say any of those things. "I just don't think you should do stuff that affects other people like Sophie," I said lamely. "She'll end up getting hurt. She was really upset after your little scene at the ruins the other night."

"Yes, she was," added Ruby. "It's not fair. You're rich

and famous, Velvet, so it doesn't really matter what you do, or what happens to you, but some of us want to do well at school and get into college and stuff like that. We need to get good reports."

"So it doesn't really matter what happens to me?" Velvet's expression hardened. "Is that what you all think? That I haven't any feelings, just because my picture gets into the papers?"

"Ruby didn't mean that—," I began.

"Forget it. You're right, Ruby. I shouldn't ask anyone to be involved with me. I shouldn't try to have any friends or any fun." Velvet's voice became harsh, and she began to tear her nightclothes off and fling her uniform on anyhow. "I'm a bad influence," she said savagely. "I should be the one who gets hurt. Everyone hates me, even my mom." She pushed her feet into her shoes, then stood up and leaned over my bed. Her face was so close to mine that I could see the soft texture of her creamy skin and smell the trace of the heavy, expensive perfume she always used. "I liked you to start with, Sarah. I would have been a better friend to you than that snotty redheaded Evie Johnson and crazy Helen Black. But it's too late now. So if we're not going to be friends, we'll have to be enemies."

"Don't be so—"

"Enemies," she snarled, and swept out.

I started to get dressed, churning up with every emotion. Deep down I was sorry for Velvet, but she scared me too. I didn't know what to think of her. Was she a melodramatic poseur or something more dangerous? But as I walked down the marble staircase I told myself there was only one person I needed to think about, and that was Evie. Helen had come back from the threshold of death, but Evie was still lost, and every hour, every minute was precious in the race to find her.

When I went into breakfast, I was surprised to see that Helen was there too, looking extremely pale and tired.

"Why aren't you resting?" I asked.

"I've persuaded the nurse that I am well enough to come back to school," she replied. "My fever has gone, and she couldn't find anything wrong, so she had to let me."

I was so glad to have her back, but she still seemed slightly feverish to me. There was a hectic look in her eyes, and she wasn't touching the food in front of her.

"Can I see it?" she asked in a low voice.

"What?"

"The brand—the thing you touched me with to release me last night."

I reached in my pocket for the little brooch. For some reason I felt reluctant to give it to her.

"Where did you get it from, Helen?"

A shadow seemed to fall over her face. "Miss Scratton gave it me, before she set off for St. Martin's. She said she had found it in her study and that it must have been left there by my mother, and that she thought I should have it."

"But why would your mother still have it? Didn't you see someone take it from you when you were a baby in the children's home?"

"That was only a kind of dream. Maybe what I saw wasn't true. Or maybe the home had just put it away safely and they gave it back to my mother when she came to collect me all those years later. Anyway, it doesn't matter. I've got it back now."

She took it from me and quickly pinned it to the slip under her school blouse.

"I don't think you should do that, Helen," I whispered. "It's a sign of evil, isn't it? If we can't trust Miss Scratton, we should be very careful of anything she gave you. And it came from your mother in the first place. That's all the more reason to fear it."

"But I was only a baby! Don't you think my mother

could have given me just one good thing?" Helen's voice shook. "It released me from Miss Scratton's hold, didn't it?"

"So why would Miss Scratton give it to you, if you could use it against her?"

"I don't know! Maybe she thought it was a worthless trinket. I don't know and I don't really care. It's a gift to me, from my mother, before she became what she is now. You can't stop me having it, Sarah. I won't let you!"

I had never seen her like this before, white and trembling and furious. I hated it when people like Celeste sneered at Helen and called her crazy, but the uncomfortable thought came to me that perhaps she really was on the edge of a nervous breakdown. But then again, anyone would seem crazy if they had gone through the stuff she'd had to deal with.

"It's okay, Helen," I said, aware that a few other students had turned to look at her. "It's okay."

I sat in silence, letting the moment pass. Then I busied myself with eating my breakfast, though I wasn't hungry.

"I can't stop you keeping the brooch," I said quietly. "But please be careful, Helen. We don't know what other powers it might have. I just want you to be safe."

"I am safe," Helen muttered. "But what about Evie?

Where can they have taken her? And Agnes just said that you had to seek? Nothing else?"

"No, just that." I sighed. "Seek and ye shall find. I hope that's true."

I didn't tell Helen that already, before breakfast, I had walked down to the pool, dreading and yet half expecting to see Evie's body floating in it. But there had been no one there except the gardener, cutting the lawns and whistling softly to himself. And Josh had said that she wasn't dead, despite the image of the drowned girl that Agnes had shown us. After going to the pool I had gone to the stables to see Josh, who was there already, working early. He told me that they had found no trace of Evie down by the river and that he was still convinced she was alive. He was planning to search over the moors again as soon as he had tended to the horses in the stables and could get away. That much at least I could tell Helen.

"Let's check out all the places on the school grounds that we know the coven has used before," I said to Helen, pushing my plate away. "There's the crypt under the ruins where we had our first battle with them. I'm going to cut classes and have a look down there for a start."

"I'll come with you," she replied quickly.

"No, it would attract too much attention if we are

both missing from class. You cover for me, say I'm doing errands for one of the mistresses or something."

The bell rang for the end of the meal. We stood for prayers and then fell into line as everyone filed out to get ready for the day's work.

"I'm just going to check the mail," Helen said, "to see if Tony—Dad—has written again."

We walked down the corridor to the black-and-white entrance hall. Here, on a polished table, the students' mail was set out each morning after breakfast. Helen found her letter. She opened it, and I could see the first few lines. *Dear Helen, Miss Hetherington called me to say you'd had an accident. I do hope you are feeling better. I've been worried. . . .*

Helen stuffed it into her pocket, looking pleased. "I'll write back to him later. Look, isn't that something for you?"

A small parcel stood at the back of the table, labeled *To Miss Sarah Venetia Rosamund Fitzalan, Wyldcliffe Abbey School for Young Ladies.* I recognized my mother's flamboyant handwriting and remembered with surprise that I had written to her at the beginning of term asking about Maria. It already seemed such a long time ago. I picked up the parcel eagerly, though something warned me not to open it in front of any other students. The bell was already ringing for the first period of the day, and girls and mistresses were crossing the hall on their way to various classrooms. I caught sight of Agnes's portrait hanging on the wall. She seemed to be watching me, encouraging me. She had shown me the image of Maria, and I was more certain than ever that there was some connection between Maria and everything else that had happened. Then I remembered that it was Miss Scratton who had moved the painting into the entrance hall so that it could be seen and admired—Miss Scratton who had gone back on everything she had promised us. My sense of certainty tumbled again, and I felt a swift pulse of panic run through me. How could I possibly find Maria? And how much more desperately did I want to find Evie? "Seek," Agnes had said, but it was like searching for a leaf in a great forest.

"Helen, when you get to class make some excuse about me. I'll see you later." I ran up the white marble stairs with the parcel under my arm. As I reached the dormitory floor, I bumped into Velvet. She was wearing riding kit.

"Careful!" she snapped.

"Oh—sorry—"

"Just get out of my way!" She ran past me down the stairs, with a dangerous look in her eyes. An image came into my mind of black smoke licked by dull flames, and the sound of girls screaming and sobbing filled my ears. I felt sick, and seemed to gag on the bitter smell of charred wood and metal. The next moment the sights and sounds had gone and I was alone.

I wanted to run after Velvet and have things out with her, but I couldn't let her distract me from what was really important. I turned my back on her and walked down the deserted dormitory corridor. Everyone had gone to class, so there was no one to see me pass through the door in the curtained alcove. I began to climb the hidden stairs to the attic, switching on the flashlight that we kept on the first step. No one would find me here, or see the contents of my parcel. I would look at it quickly, then start my search of the places where the coven might have taken Evie.

Shutting the door of Agnes's study behind me, I looked on the shelves where she had stored the ingredients for her healing spells. I found a box of colored candles, and chose four tall white ones and set them on her desk. Four lights for four sisters, four elements, four corners of the Circle. As an afterthought, I put a bloodred candle in the center and lit that for Maria, then turned off the flashlight. Then I sat down and unwrapped my mother's parcel, pulling away several layers of card and tissue paper until I found a dress made of soft scarlet material, embroidered all over with fruits and flowers.

"Oh, it's lovely." I sighed, gently stroking the fabric. Then I realized I had seen something similar before: the red silk ribbon that Cal's mother had sent me. This was the same kind of needlework. The dress was Romany craft, I was sure of that. Forgetting everything else for a moment, I turned impatiently to my mother's letter.

Darling Sarah, I do hope the term has started well for you. How is dear old Wyldcliffe looking in the spring sunshine? It was lovely to get your letter. I know you have always been fascinated by Maria and our Gypsy connections! You always used to ask me for stories about her when you were a child.

I am sending you this dress and I know I can trust you to look after it properly. It must be a hundred years old and belonged to Maria's mother (your great-great grandmother—just think of that!). I think it might have been a wedding dress, though I'm not sure. And I think the leaves are a kind of headdress to go with it. Anyway, I was going to keep the dress as a surprise for your eighteenth birthday, my darling, but as you are going to have a school dance (goodness—we never had such a thing in my day!), I thought you might like to wear it then. I think it would look rather gorgeous on you, much better than a boring old prom dress. It has been passed down as a memento of a different life, and now it is yours.

I don't know much more about Maria than I have already told you. Sadly, I never knew her as she died when I was only two or three. My own mother was always rather guarded about Maria, as though she didn't quite like talking about her. But you know how straitlaced poor Granny was, like all the Talbot-Travers side of the family. All starchy and stiff and old-school manners. I wanted very much to be close to her, but it just wasn't her style. At least I've been a different kind of mother to you, my sweet.

When Granny was so ill last year, her mind wandered a little and she sometimes talked about her own childhood, in a terribly rambling kind of way, but I did pick up a few things. Apparently Maria was very imaginative and got into trouble at Wyldcliffe for frightening the other girls with ghost stories about goblins that lived up in the caves on the hills. And I know that even though Maria married well (in terms of money and land and all the rest), she still kept in touch with the Gypsy people and did a lot for them. Apparently there was one particular friend she had called Zak. When I was little, I used to think that perhaps Maria and Zak had been secretly in love and I made up quite a romance about them, which made Granny dreadfully cross, as she thought this insulted her own father's memory. But from what I remember I am sure your great-grandfather was very dull and stuffy compared to Maria's Gypsy friend! Oh, and another thing, when Granny was reliving her memories in those last few days before she passed away, she went on about Maria and drums. It was quite odd. She kept saying something about "My mother told me to stay away from the drums." Granny was quite insistent and said it several times. "Stay away from the drums in the deep places of the earth." Of course, she was very muddled and ill by then, poor love. Oh, it's all rather sad, looking back on family history, isn't it? When all the people who have been before us have to go down into the valley of death and leave this world behind—

But I'm getting too gloomy! I meant this to be a cheerful letter to go with your pretty dress. I do hope you get the chance to wear it. If it doesn't fit, ask the school housekeeper to alter it for you. I'm sure she will help if you ask nicely.

Well, that's nearly all for now, my darling. I hope you are enjoying plenty of rides on Starlight—and Daddy is dropping hints that if you get a good report he

might keep one of the young hunters he is training up
and give it to you next season. . . .

The rest of the letter was just gossip and affection and bits of news from home. I read the parts about Maria again.

Stay away from the drums.

It was all making a pattern, but not one that made any sense. Then my eye was caught by a sentence in the letter. *I think the leaves are a kind of headdress . . .* I hadn't seen any leaves. I felt inside the layers of wrapping again, and my hand touched something cold and hard under the tissue paper.

It was the most beautiful thing I had ever seen, a delicate crown made of polished bronze leaves intertwined in an eternal circle. The dress was lovely, but this circlet was extraordinary; a miracle of craftsmanship that glowed a deep burnished color in the candlelight. It was hard to believe that it had started life in the earth, as a lump of lifeless metal ore.

My heart began to pound. I had already seen this bright circle crowning Maria's dark head in my vision by the standing stones. Yet it was old, older than the dress that had belonged to Maria's mother—hundreds, maybe even thousands of years old. Where had Maria found it?

What did it mean? And why had it come to me?

There was a glass-fronted cabinet on one of the walls, containing bottles of ointments and essences. I stood in front of it, just able to see a dim reflection of my face in the glass door. I watched myself, fascinated, as I raised the circlet in my hands and placed it on my head like a crown.

Everything changed. I saw with different eyes. I was no longer in the attic, but in a meadow filled with flowers. I wore a crown of ripe corn and scarlet poppies, and I was holding the hand of a young child, who looked up at me with trusting eyes. It was sunrise, and the whole day stretched out ahead of me in a long, golden vista. There was a clear pool at my feet, and I looked down and saw my reflection. I was beautiful—I was transformed. I lived now and in eternity; I was far beyond anything I had ever known, and the drums were beginning, driving into my heart and mind and taking me deeper into the magic. I was special, anointed, marked out for a great destiny—

"No, come back! Sarah, Sarah!" Someone was shaking me. "Sarah, wake up!"

It was Cal. He tore the circlet from my head, and I fell to the ground. Every trace of the glory had vanished. I was just Sarah again. The moment of vision was over. I burst into tears and sobbed in the dust. Cal knelt beside me, full of concern, but I was too angry to care. "Why did you do that?" I snatched the crown back. "It's mine, give it to me!"

He looked surprised, but then drew away from me and stood up. "Here, take it," he said abruptly. "But what the hell was it doing to you?"

I got up and forced myself to stop crying, and checked the circlet anxiously to make sure it wasn't damaged. "It wasn't doing anything, it was just—you don't understand."

"Then explain. Tell me what's going on. What was happening here, Sarah?" Cal asked. His face in the shadows looked lean and tired. "You were in some kind of weird trance."

"I was trying to find out about Maria—"

"I thought finding Evie was your priority," he interrupted.

I flushed and snapped, "I know, but I can't do everything at once. I just feel it's important. Anyway, how on earth did you get in here? The staff will go mad if they see you."

"No, they won't—I'm officially Josh's new assistant. He told the school he's busy studying for college and can't come every day, so I will be doing some of his work in the stables instead. It gives me the perfect excuse to be here."

"And keep an eye on me?"

"I'm not spying on you, if that's what you mean." His voice was proud and hard. "Helen came to the stables just now to see Josh. She said she thought you'd be in Agnes's room and told me how to find it using the secret staircase. I wanted to help you, but I won't bother if you don't need me." We stood glaring at each other. I didn't understand why I was so angry with him. All I knew was that I hadn't wanted to return from where I had been and he had forced me to.

"I'm not used to needing anyone," I replied, every bit as proud and haughty as Cal.

"Fine. Do this your own way. But I'll tell you one thing—Josh isn't going to just hang around while you wait to get your 'feelings.' We searched the river right up to the waterfall, and across the marsh-bog last night looking for Evie, but there was no sign of her. He's going out on the moors again this morning to look for her, and if that doesn't work, he's ready to go to the police and tell them everything."

"What can the police do?" I muttered sullenly. "They won't be able to find Evie, or track down Miss Scratton either."

"I can't say I'm particularly fond of the police myself," Cal said with a hint of his old grin. "But they'll start some kind of investigation," he went on. "Josh is getting desperate, and he thinks anything that might bring Evie closer is better than nothing. But the authorities could close this place down if there's any more scandal," Cal added. "If they send you all home, how will you have any chance of finding Evie again or dealing with this evil spirit—the Priestess? You have to work fast. Maria is only a ghost—a memory, that's all. Evie is real. If she's alive, she needs you desperately. You've got to find her first."

I knew he was right, but knowing that annoyed me even more.

"I will find Evie, and without your help," I shouted. "Maria will help me. I know she will. The spirits of the dead can see us still—that's Romany wisdom, isn't it?"

"Fine," he shouted back, his pride flaming into anger. "If you're such an expert, you sort everything out with your dead great-grandmother. I'll go back to where I belong."

"Go then—I don't care! I know what I'm doing."

"I hope you do, Sarah," Cal said. "I really hope you do." Then he turned and left. I heard his footsteps on the narrow stairs. As the sound quickly receded into the distance, I wished I could take every word back, but it was too late.

I wanted to cry, but what was the good? I hardened myself against the terrible sense of loss that I felt. If Cal walked out of Wyldcliffe and went back to his family, I would never have the chance to explain or make things up with him. *Well, let him go*, I told myself, trying to rekindle my anger. Feeling anger was better than feeling despair. Our quarrel had been his fault too, I told myself. He had been ridiculously touchy and impatient. I glanced down at the thin circlet that I was still clutching in my hands, and at the soft folds of the dress that lay on Agnes's desk. I would never wear that dress for Cal now, but I still had the circlet. That would lead me to Maria, I was sure, and somehow, I was convinced, Maria would lead me to Evie. I would show Cal that I had been right, I would show everyone. . . .

I gathered up my treasures and held them against my heart, but they couldn't fill the emptiness that was in me now that Cal was gone.

Twenty-five

I found nothing that day. The crypt under the ruins was damp and empty, as though no one had been down there for months, and the secret grotto—the fancifully decorated cavern in the school grounds that led to the crypt—was deserted too. By the middle of the afternoon I was tired, and not just with sneaking about and trying to avoid being seen while the rest of the school went about its business. For the first time I started to wonder whether I really would find Evie. Josh's plans to go and report everything to the police began to seem inevitable. There would be publicity, a missing person's inquiry, and Evie's father would be dragged into all this, out of his mind with worry. And I would never see her again.

No. That couldn't be how it ended. I wouldn't let that

happen. I was strong, I told myself. I was Sarah. Even without Cal I could do this. I would see it through. My mind wearily checked over every possible place in the school where I should still search for Evie, or where I might find some clue, and then it struck me that I had been so stupid. Of course, I still had the Book. It might contain a spell that would teach me all I needed to know. *To Finde that which is Loste*—it had to have the answer in its illuminated pages.

I had returned the Book to its hiding place in Starlight's stable after we had used it to make the healing potion for Helen. I hoped that I wouldn't bump into Cal again. I just wasn't ready to face him, but I was lucky, and when I reached the cobbled yard no one else seemed to be around. Quickly I let myself into Starlight's stall. My faithful pony whinnied with delight, anticipating a gallop, but I gently quieted him, then pushed the straw to one side and lifted the loose brick where the Book of the Mystic Way was hidden. I took it out and sat cross-legged with my back to the wall and rested the leather-bound tome on my knee.

When I tried to open it, though, I couldn't, however hard I tugged at the cover. Feeling a surge of panic, I laid my hand on the green leather and willed, "Open. Open to me," as I had when I'd unlocked the door of Agnes's study. Then the Book sprang apart, its pages flapping as though in an invisible wind. The intricate writing and drawings and symbols became a confused jumble as the pages flipped over rapidly, before coming to a sudden stop. Now the Book lay open on my knee, but the writing on the page didn't look like a set of instructions for a charm or a spell. Instead I could just about decipher the cramped letters to read the following message.

"Beware! Oh ye who seeke the Truth and Lighte, ye must know this: There are those who brush against the Mysticke Way, as a lost sheep may brush against an Oak Tree in its wanderings. These Women are neither true Sisters of the Sacred Elements, nor Servants of the Shadows, and yet if they stray too far, they may take all to Ruine with them. Let it be knowne that these Women are called Touchstones. With them it is as though the Lightning strikes them, yet they feel it not, and see not whither it leads, nor whence it came. An Elemental Power such as Fire may touch this Woman to reveal itself, and yet she will know not by what she has been touched.

Some Touchstones may live in simple innocence, never questioning why Marvels occur near them: why, by example, a well may gush over with wholesome Waters when they chance to pass, or why good harvests come to their village, or why the Fire in their hearths burns up brighter and longer than any of their Neighbors'. But there are others whose Heartes are not so pure, and through them, great troubles may come. With them, the Fire burns the harvest, the Waters of the stream dry up, and the Wind blows in such wild measures as to blow down their Neighbors' houses. Such a one may come to know themselves to be a Touchstone. Then they seek not the Wisdom or Discipline of the Mysticke Way, only its glory. Indeed they may choose to use the power that they unwittingly attract for Destruction and Evil, and in doing so may be sucked into the Shadows, where they can do great Harme.

All Life flows in magnetick energy (which doth unite the Elements), from Birth to Death, from the Earth to the Heavens, from one Heart to Another, like a great and sacred Dance. A Black Touchstone usurps the right path of the Dance and destroys its flow and no good can come of this, like wickedly damming a River to create a terrible Floode that washes all living creatures away with its mighty Force.

I had to read it more than once to understand what it was saying, and even then I couldn't quite accept what

I knew in my heart to be its message—that Velvet was a Touchstone. The fire at her last school, the tragic accident with her sister, her boyfriend's suicide, even her part in Helen's fall from the window—they all made a kind of sense now. Velvet in some way attracted untamed energy, a kind of overspill from the elements, and the darkness in her own heart turned this to a negative, destructive force. *They all get hurt*, she had said, and now I knew why. I leaned against the rough wall of the stable. It was all too much. I couldn't deal with everything by myself. And now I had quarreled with Cal—over what? A dream?

The time for dreams was over.

I went to look for Helen and found her sitting alone in the common room, curled up in an armchair. She had a book of poetry in her hand but was staring into space, her mouth moving slightly as though chanting to herself. She gave a start when she saw me.

"You didn't find Evie, did you?"

I shook my head and sank into a chair next to her.

"Helen, what really happened when you fell from the window? Did Miss Scratton make that happen too? Or was it your mother?"

Helen's face clouded. "I don't know. I'm not sure."

"Was—was Velvet there before it happened? Did you see her?"

"Yes, she was. I remember seeing her. Why?"

"Sophie said that she saw her looking down from the window after you had fallen." I rapidly told Helen what I had just read in the Book and what my suspicions were about Velvet. "She seems to have some way of making bad things happen. And if she gets drawn into the path of the coven or your mother it could be even worse."

Helen held her head in her hands and gently rocked backward and forward, trying to remember.

"It was Sunday afternoon," she began. "I'd been lying on my bed in the dorm but I felt restless, so I went out into the corridor and walked up and down, just pacing aimlessly. No one was around. It felt so hot and stuffy, so I opened the window—the arched one opposite the staircase that looks over the front drive. I wanted to get some fresh air.

"I remember looking out at the moors in the distance, and I wished I was up on their heights, letting the wind push me wherever it liked. I wondered where my mother's spirit was roaming, and if I dared try to dance on the wind again. I hadn't been able to do it when we were trying to get into Agnes's room, but I got this idea that if I could send myself through the air to wherever my mother was and surrender to her, she might be satisfied. If she destroyed me or took me into her power, or whatever it is that she wants, I thought perhaps she would leave you and Evie alone at last. At that moment it seemed that it didn't really matter what happened to me, as long as you two were safe."

"Oh, Helen, you mustn't ever think that—"

"I couldn't see how else you were ever going to get free of her. Anyway, as I was standing there trying to decide what to do, I heard someone coming down the corridor. It was Velvet. She had a riding whip in her hand. She stopped and looked at me oddly, like she guessed my thoughts. And then—it's hard to describe. A wind blew up, like a freak storm. The window kind of fell out of the wall, and I fell too. I didn't have time to think, but I knew I would be smashed to pieces on the steps below. Then the next second—well, I was floating. Floating peacefully. I wasn't in my body anymore. I was in a great white space, and I was dancing, like in a dream. But I wasn't alone. There was someone I was dancing with . . ." Her voice trailed away.

"What happened then?"

"There were people and voices. They were fighting over me. I wanted to be free—and they wouldn't let me alone—I don't remember exactly. Then Miss Scratton was there, saying, 'No, not yet, it's not your time. You have to wait for the Priestess. You must become the Priestess.'

"After that the white space vanished. Everything went dark. I wanted to come back, but Miss Scratton wouldn't let me. She was holding me, and it hurt. It hurt me in my mind." Helen looked at me unhappily. "I don't know if I can ever dance on the wind again."

"Have you tried since then?"

She sighed. "Yes, this morning when you were searching for Evie. I wanted to get to the place that Evie is being held, to find her, even if it meant being in danger. But it was like last time, I couldn't do it. Something is watching me and holding me back. I'm really sorry."

"Do you think it's Miss Scratton again?"

"I don't know. It was like—I can't explain—like someone was sitting on my wings, if that makes any sense."

It made sense, but we still weren't any closer to knowing what to do, or exactly how Velvet fitted into everything. I jumped up and began to walk up and down impatiently. "But even if Miss Scratton is preventing you from doing that, surely we have other powers?" I said. "What could we do to attack the Priestess and her coven—or disarm Velvet—before they hurt Evie?"

"We can't use our powers for attack, only defense. Only for the common good."

"But I made the earth shake, down in the crypt in our first battle with the coven, and I destroyed a wall, and tore up rocks on the hilltop—"

"Those battles were forced upon us, Sarah. We can't be the ones to start the conflict."

"But we have to do something! The Priestess has already attacked us. She has taken Evie. We have to fight back."

"What are you going to do? Cause an earthquake at Wyldcliffe? Lock Miss Dalrymple in a mound of earth until she tells you where Evie is?" It sounded absurd like that, but it wasn't a million miles from what I had been thinking. "Anyway," Helen went on, "what does Cal think we should do? He sees straight. You can trust him."

I sat down again, feeling raw and stupid. "I don't know. You'll have to ask him," I said.

"Have you quarreled? Oh, Sarah, don't, please don't!"

I was surprised by her distress and tried to shrug the whole thing off. "People do quarrel sometimes," I said. "It's not the end of the world."

"It could be the end of our world! Everyone who has come into contact with the Mystic Way has some part to play. It's all for a purpose. We all fit together like the pieces of a jigsaw. Everything is connected. Lose one part of it and we could all be lost." She tried to calm down and control herself. "We need Cal. You need Cal."

Need. That word again.

"I can look after myself. I don't need a guy to lean on. I don't need Cal."

"Haven't you ever seen a rose growing on the side of a house? Accepting support isn't a sign of weakness. It makes you stronger." Helen sighed deeply. "If I had some-one—anyone—I wouldn't waste a second of it in anger."

I didn't know what to say, but I knew she was right.

"Sarah, I've lived my life in a kind of dream," Helen continued. "Even here and now, talking to you isn't as real as things that I see in my mind." She rubbed her head as if in pain. "Sometimes I really do think I am going mad and that I can't carry on. I don't know if I can get to the end of all this. I just have to believe that I will, and that I'll find what I am searching for. Evie and Sebastian—they were doomed from the start. But I know that Cal is real. What he feels for you is real. And if I had that, I'd hold on to it like—like a stone. A stone in my pocket that would always remind me of what is real and true and eternal."

"Oh, Helen, I feel so—"

I never got to finish what I was going to say. A crowd of giggling girls burst into the room.

"My God, did you see her? She was in such a state!"

"She doesn't look so hot now, does she? I reckon that photo will be in all the papers tomorrow."

"And after all that showing off about being such a brilliant rider!"

I went over to them. "What's happened? What's the big joke?"

"Oh hi, Sarah," said Marion Chase, who'd always been friendly with Celeste. "It's Velvet Romaine. She's landed herself in big trouble *and* made a complete fool of herself *and* got her picture taken by one of those photographers still hanging around in the village."

"What did she do?" asked Helen.

"Only gone and stolen Miss Scratton's horse and taken it out on the moors," Marion sniggered. "But she managed to get herself lost up by the peat bogs and has come back to school half-dead and covered in mud and the horse is practically lamed."

"And Velvet thought she was going to look so cool!" Marion's friends laughed. "She really will be expelled now. She never properly fitted in here, did she?" Their spiteful faces sickened me. They had been so keen to suck up to Velvet when she had first arrived, and now they were crowing over her downfall. And they were supposed to be ladies. What had happened to the ideals of selflessness and honor and loyalty?

"She's a Wyldcliffe girl," I said coldly, "so we should be sticking up for her, not laughing at her because she made a mistake. Come on, Helen."

We left them staring at us openmouthed. I knew they would turn their venom on me as soon as we were out of sight, but I didn't care.

"I need to get hold of Velvet," I said, as we marched down the corridor. Although I had said that about sticking together, I was actually furious with her. I knew from my father's work that even a slight injury to a horse's leg could lead to it being crippled. And in that case it would be shot rather than left to live a life of pain. "She'll be okay, but if she's hurt that horse . . ." I found myself blinking back tears, remembering how Miss Scratton had summoned the beautiful white mare to carry the body of Mrs. Hartle from the hilltop battle. How at that moment we had turned to Miss Scratton as our friend and our rock. How all that had been a lie. Somehow, in my jumble of emotions, Seraph stood for everything that had been free and good and innocent, before the world grew so dark.

We crossed the entrance hall. Girls were hanging about there, waiting for the bell, and I caught snatches of their conversation. ". . . so selfish, that poor horse . . . stupid, really . . . I hope they do chuck her out. . . ." It seemed as though the whole school was talking about Velvet. We raced up the stairs to the dorms.

"Please do not run on the stairs!" Miss Clarke, the Latin mistress, reproved me as I reached the second floor. "Ah, it's you, Sarah. As you were not in class this afternoon, I want you to come and see me after supper to collect the work we did."

"Yes—of course—sorry."

I forced myself to walk sedately the rest of the way. When we reached the dorm, Velvet was lying huddled on her bed. Her clothes were filthy, and she had a long scratch down one cheek. Ruby was hovering next to her.

"We want to talk to Velvet," I said. "Can you leave us for a bit, Ruby?"

Ruby must have seen how angry I was, as she scuttled out of the room without another word.

"You can break your neck for all I care," I said. "But don't go hurting innocent animals. You had no right at all to take that horse out. It was totally selfish and irresponsible."

Velvet pretended to yawn in mock boredom. "Oh, enough with the lecture already, Sarah. Don't be such a pain. I swear Seraph is okay. It's just some cuts and bruises. Josh checked her over and said it wasn't as bad as it looked. Of course, according to Celeste's dumb friends, I practically killed the stupid animal on purpose."

I was relieved by the news of Seraph, but I hadn't finished with Velvet. "And what were you doing next to Helen when she had her accident?" I went on. "Did you push her—or make her fall?"

"I've no idea what you're talking about," Velvet replied, sitting up and starting to brush the mud from her riding trousers. "I told you before, you and I have nothing to say to each other."

"Oh, I think we do," I said. "We know about the fire at your last school. We know more than you think."

"So you know that I wanted Gina to end up scarred for life? That I wanted my boyfriend dead, and my little sister smashed up in that car? I suppose you read in some scumbag newspaper that I was jealous of Jasmine and wanted her out of the way and neatly arranged it all? It's not actually that easy to stage a car crash, if you hadn't noticed. God, it makes me sick that people believe that crap. You know nothing about me—nothing!"

"I know that it makes me sick when people lie to me, and hurt my friends," I replied. "How did Helen fall? Tell me!"

"How would I know? Ask her." Velvet threw a glance at Helen, who was standing to one side. "Face it, Sarah, it was nothing to do with me. Helen tried to chuck herself out of the window, didn't she? Everyone says she's nuts. You can't blame me for that." She burst into a noisy storm of tears. "They try to blame me for everything. But I can't help it . . . I can't control it . . ." Then she shook herself angrily. "Why are you asking me all this stuff anyway?" she demanded. "What do you really know?"

I hesitated. Part of me wanted to tell Velvet everything, to warn her that she was a Touchstone. I wanted to help her if we could, but I didn't think she would listen. She was too angry and bitter for that. It wasn't help that she wanted; it was to lash out at the world that had hurt her, and to hurt it back in return. She was watching me intently, like a cat. "Does it happen to you too?" she whispered. "Do you have any . . . powers?"

"We're all powerful, aren't we?" I replied evasively. "Just being young is powerful."

"No, I mean special stuff. Not like my dad's stage shows, all that voodoo and hocus-pocus black magic. Dad loves it, but I know it's only an act, even though he claims to be descended from a witch who was hanged God knows how long ago. That's just all show business. But I do think there is some kind of force out there, controlling things, making things happen. Weird things. Wouldn't you like to know more about that?" The expression in her eyes was wolfishly hungry, and I knew then where I'd seen that expression before—in Harriet's tormented eyes when she had been possessed by Celia Hartle's dark spirit. Velvet radiated the same despair and greed, but even then I wanted to believe that it wasn't too late for her. If there was any way we could help Velvet, and stop her blundering further onto a path of darkness, it would be worth the risk.

"We do know some things," I said, lowering my voice. "Helen was the first to get in touch with her powers."

"Tell me!" Velvet grabbed my arm. "What can you do?"

I looked at Helen for guidance. She looked calmly at Velvet and said, "We are only servants. The powers are only to be used for the common good."

"That doesn't sound like much fun."

"It's not about fun," I said to Velvet.

"What do you do? Where do you meet? Is that why you sneak out at night? I've been watching you, and reading up about stuff. You need four corners in a Circle, don't you? So it was you and Evie and Helen—who was the fourth? Is it one of the teachers?"

I felt uneasy. Velvet's guesses were too close for comfort. How long had she been spying on us to find all this out?

"Our secret sister is Lady Agnes," Helen said.

"The dead girl in the old painting? No kidding? You're not winding me up?"

Helen shrugged. "I never lie. The truth is more powerful than any lie."

But I wasn't sure that Helen had been right to tell Velvet about Agnes. It seemed to me that Velvet was interested in power and excitement and mastery over the people around her, not healing or wisdom. I couldn't trust her—not yet. "Look, Velvet, forget we said anything. Just try to stay out of trouble, and we'll take care of the rest. Then maybe we can talk later." I tried to walk away, but she hung on to my arm.

"You can't leave it like that! You have to tell me! I want to be part of it. I want to have powers and control things, make stuff happen." Her expression darkened. "I want to get revenge. You can help me to do it."

"Let go—"

"But you need me now! I know you're up to something, and I want to be in on it. Life sucks, but at least this is interesting. Let me in, Sarah. Evie's gone and she's not coming back. I could take her place."

I stared at Velvet, shocked. "What do you know about Evie? What do you mean, she's not coming back?"

"I know enough not to believe that story about her rushing off to see her dad. Don't you want to know where I got to on my ride? I think you'll want to hear what really happened."

"Okay, tell us. But hurry up!"

Velvet let go of my arm and stretched out on her bed, taking her time, completely at ease now. "I skipped class this morning and went straight down to the stables. Josh was working there, so I sneaked into that kitchen garden near the yard and waited until he had gone off for five minutes. There was no one else around, so it was easy to saddle Seraph and lead her through the practice paddock and down to the school gates. I thought stealing the High Mistress's horse might be bad enough to get me expelled, and at least I would have some fun doing it.

"The only person I saw was the gardener. 'Where you off to, miss?' he asked. I said I'd got permission to exercise Miss Scratton's mare for her, and he believed me. It was gorgeous weather, and I was looking forward to a real gallop over the moors—you were right about one thing, Sarah, Jupiter hates the rough ground and is no fun to ride round here. I could tell that Seraph was a marvelous horse, and even though she was a bit big for me, I knew I could handle her."

"So where did you go?" I asked.

"I didn't really have any plan, so I just thought I would stick to the main track that led away from the school. It was signposted Beacon Hill—do you know it?"

"That's the old hilltop fort," Helen said. "There's nothing left of the fort now. The hill was a kind of temple in ancient times."

"Well, I think I must have reached it, because I'd climbed higher and higher until there were the most amazing views. Really you could see for miles, and I started to think that Wyldcliffe wouldn't be such a bad place if you could just ride and think and be free like that. There was something kind of peaceful up there . . . anyway, I was enjoying myself. I laughed to think of the rest of you stuck in class back at school, and I was wondering what you'd say when you found out what I had done. Then I thought I should get something to prove it to everyone. I began to wonder if I could ride over to the boys' school, St. Martin's or whatever it's called, and sneak in and talk to some of the students, get one of their phone numbers or something as a kind of trophy. I'd even managed to telephone one of the paparazzi guys before I'd set off and told him to get over to the village later if he wanted a photo of me cutting school. I know it's tacky, but everyone does it—how do you think the paparazzi know where to hang out to get the pictures for the magazines?"

"I don't know and I don't really care," I said. "What happened then? How did you get Seraph into such a mess?"

"I'm trying to tell you. I didn't do it on purpose. Anyway, I set off again in the direction that I thought would take me to St. Martin's, but that's when everything changed. Something weird happened." She hesitated. "I swear this is true, even though it sounds mad. The light kind of changed. Shimmered. I don't know how to describe it. As though all the color was being sucked out of everything. I heard a woman's voice singing from far away. It made me want to run straight to whoever was calling out like that. Seraph began to sidestep and toss her head up and down; then she reared up and shot off as though she was a racehorse in the direction of the voice.

"All I could think about was clinging on and not

falling off. I didn't know where we were heading or how to stop Seraph. She seemed to have supernatural strength, and my arms were aching with trying to hold her back. I was worried that we might be near the bogs on the far side of the moors, because I'd heard stories of people getting lost there and never coming back. We must have been near them already, because the ground started to get soft and marshy and Seraph kept plunging into pools and splashing mud everywhere. I just closed my eyes and hung on. Eventually we started climbing up again and the air seemed fresher. There was a big slope ahead of us, covered in trees and shrubs, and an old house behind the trees. We skirted around the house and its park, and then Seraph went galloping madly up the slope, crashing through rough gorse bushes and cutting her legs badly."

My heart seemed to have slowed right down as Velvet was telling her story. I seemed to be watching her and Helen and myself from a distance. I looked out of the window, where the day still shone bright and calm. Soon it all would become clear. Soon I would be out on those hills myself, seeking my destiny. *Seek and ye shall find.* I just needed one more piece of the jigsaw.

"What happened then?" asked Helen.

"Seraph clattered to a halt and threw me off. I was on the hillside just above the house, and I had crashed into some kind of monument."

I knew what she was going to say next. I knew what she was about to see.

"It was an old stone tablet covered in moss, but I could see that there were letters carved in it—a name—"

"Sebastian Fairfax," I said.

"How do you know?" she asked, startled.

"I know," I said. "Go on."

"The writing said something about 'To the memory of Sebastian Fairfax, a beloved son,' and as I was looking at it, I realized someone was standing behind me. I thought I was going to scream, but I couldn't, and I had to turn around even though I didn't want to. And then I saw him."

"Who was it?" I asked, although I already knew.

"He was beautiful," Velvet said simply. "I've never seen anyone like him. He was wearing kind of theatrical clothes, riding kit and a long black cloak. And he had these amazing eyes, blue like . . . I can't describe them. He was perfect."

"Did he speak to you?" asked Helen.

"Yes," she said. "That's the whole point. He said, 'Tell your friends that Evelyn Johnson is trapped in the deep places of the earth, and neither fire nor water will save her. Tell them that she needs her sisters.' And then—then— his face changed, as though he was crumbling away to dust. And the next minute he just vanished." She looked at us with a kind of triumph. "So you see, Evie won't be coming back. You'll need me now. You have to let me in."

"Do you think we'd give up on Evie so easily?" I replied furiously. "What kind of friends do you think we are?"

"Oh, I don't know much about being friends," Velvet replied. "I've got such a natural talent for making enemies. So what's it to be, Sarah? Am I in? Will you let me into your little secrets or not? Friends, or enemies?"

I couldn't trust myself to speak.

"No one will ever take Evie's place, Velvet," Helen said in a quiet voice. "And it is you who must choose whether you are for us or against us. We can't make that decision for you. Come on, Sarah, let's go."

She led me out of there, and we left Velvet staring at us with resentment burning in her eyes. I was shaking, and Helen took my hands in hers. "Sarah, you can't care for everyone, or save the whole world. Velvet will find her own path. Your task is to find Evie. What are you going to do?" Her pale face was full of sorrow, like a saint in an old painting. Who did Helen pity most at that moment—Velvet or Evie? Or was her pity really for me?

The deep places of the earth. Sebastian, or his shadow, or a memory of his love, had tried to tell us where Evie was hidden. She was trapped in the earth—but where?

Earth for Sarah.

S for Sarah.

I remembered the words in my mother's letter and the warning they contained. *Stay away from the drums. Stay away from the drums in the deep places of the earth.*

Listen to the drums. I was beginning to understand. The drums connected everything, the drums that I'd heard when I had seen Maria. I knew I had been right when I had told Cal that Maria held the key to the mystery. She must have known those deep, fearful places herself, where Evie was now lost. *Stay away,* Maria had once said, but I had no choice. It was my task to seek them out. I had to find Maria, and when I did, I knew that she would lead me straight to Evie and into the heart of the danger.

Twenty-six

I got ready as though we were going on a picnic, filling an old backpack with warm sweaters, a map, my flashlight, and a piece of rope I found in the stables. Anything that might be useful. Hidden at the bottom of everything was the bronze crown. It was too precious to leave behind. Underneath my riding clothes I was wearing the Talisman. It was all totally surreal.

It was also ironic that Miss Scratton's relaxation of the rules meant that our year was now allowed out for a short walk or ride after supper, as long as we signed out in the book in the entrance hall. So we were allowed to leave the school and face her and her Priestess as the day began to fade. Helen and I jogged on Bonny and Starlight down to the school gates. Two Wyldcliffe students going for a ride on a lovely spring evening, that was all.

Helen had fallen in with my plans without any argument or discussion. Although she didn't usually like riding, she was a natural horsewoman, far better than Evie would ever be—but I couldn't think about Evie. It hurt too much. This was our last chance to find her, and I couldn't get it wrong. Instead I rode next to Helen and tried to distract myself by admiring her straight posture and delicate profile. She looked as though she didn't quite belong in this world, like a medieval knight riding into battle, doomed and proud and sad.

We rode through the village, and I remembered how we had first met Cal there. I remembered how he had been wary at first, and how my feeble attempts to use some Romany words had softened him. Then he had smiled and called me "Gypsy girl," and I had felt that I belonged. I ached to see him again, with his rough brown hair blown by the wind and his watchful eyes older than his years. I longed for his rare smile that was just for me. I knew now that I had wanted him from that very first moment. Well, I had messed that up. If only—but it was best not to think about what might have been. I wouldn't get another chance.

We paused for a while by the scrubby patch of land

where the Gypsy camp had been. This was the moment to turn back and return to school in time for evening prayers. But instead, we went on, following the long winding path that led to the moors. The path took us steadily higher. It began to feel cold. Here on the high ground the spring came late, but it was still so beautiful. I hadn't realized before just how much this place was part of me—the wide sweep of moorland, the jagged outcrops of rocks, the swoop and cry of the birds. It was my own land, it was in my heart. Eventually the black stones on the top of the Ridge came into sight. We reached them and dismounted.

"Ready?" Helen asked.

I nodded. "I'm ready."

We stood in the center of the ring of stones and faced the late sun. Pink and gold clouds swelled over the far horizon. The birds fell silent. We could hear nothing but the breath and sigh of the wind. I held the Talisman up to the sun, and it burned with reflected light.

"Maria," I said. "You showed yourself to me in this sacred Circle. Tell me now where to find the deep places of the earth. Tell me how to find our sister Evie. Holy powers, show us the truth."

The sun was blotted out. It was night, deep midnight, and the stars trembled above us. At the far side of the

Circle, next to the tallest standing stone, we saw a young girl and a woman dressed in black. Their faces were veiled, but they were beckoning us toward them. The girl pointed to the ground; then they vanished and so did the stars. The radiant glow of the bright evening flicked back on again like an electric light.

"There's something over there that they want us to see," I said eagerly. "Come on!" We ran to search the ground, but there was nothing unusual. I dropped to my knees and pressed my hands against the turf, letting the earth below speak to me. I closed my eyes, concentrating intently and asking for guidance. I heard a girl laughing. I saw her riding a plump hill pony. *"Come on, Cracker! You can't catch me, Zak!"* I saw her slumped against the stone, the circlet on her head, the blood on her cheek. Maria was calling to me.

"Dig!" I panted. "We have to dig." I tore at the earth with my bare hands, then pressed my fingers into the wet soil. "Mother Earth, show us your secrets," I begged. "Reveal your treasures." The earth crumbled loosely under my hands until I could move it aside as easily as sand. Soon I had carved out a shallow hole at the foot of the stone. I reached in and found a handful of tarnished coins. Next to them was a small stained bundle, wrapped in waxed cloth. My hands shook as I opened it. The bundle contained a few torn pages, covered with clear, round handwriting. "It's from her! It's from Maria!"

I smoothed the crumpled papers on my knee. *Maria Melville's Wyldcliffe Journal*, it said at the top. I began to read, with Helen looking over my shoulder, as the day began to slip away into oblivion.

> *If one day you are reading this, whoever you are, I hope that you will have the courage to accept these mysteries. I hope that you will not have to enter the underground world. I hope that you believe me.*
>
> *These things happened in the spring of 1919. My name is Maria Adamina Melville, and every word is true, I swear.*

We had reached the end of Maria's journal. I smoothed the papers and folded them up again. Now I knew where to go and what to do. Maria's story had given me the final piece of the puzzle; the location of that underground world where Evie was a prisoner. The caves at the White Tor—that was where we would find the threshold between this world and the dark places of the earth. I loved and pitied Maria for her story, but most of all I was grateful.

"But what about these creatures—the Kinsfolk—are

they still living in the caves?" asked Helen. "Or is it just her now—my mother?"

"I don't know." I was reluctant to tell Helen that I had already caught glimpses of Maria's tormentors in my dreams. Maria had said that Sebastian had bound them again in sleep, but hadn't Velvet's reckless game released all bindings? Whatever had once slumbered in the dust of the earth might be awake, and the thought made me feel faint. I didn't doubt Helen's courage, but maybe I doubted my own. The Priestess I already knew, and I thought I could face her again, but idea of those shrunken, wizened bodies filled me with disgust. I felt their hands reaching for me, as they had grasped Maria. I saw their hideous faces and felt their icy breath of death. I sensed them waiting to claim me.

I had been so desperate to discover the secrets that would lead me to Evie, so intent on saving her, and now that I seemed to have what I needed, I wasn't sure that I could do this. I looked across the valley to the opposite ridge where the White Tor rose against the sky. I knew, in my deepest self, that if I went on this journey to the underground kingdom I would return changed. Or perhaps I would not return at all. I went over to where Starlight was waiting patiently and leaned my head against him and prayed for strength to do this thing.

I was not like Evie. I didn't belong in some great romance. I was just Sarah, the best friend in the background, nothing special. Good old Sarah, always there to help everyone else. That's what best friends were for. I had promised that I would do anything for my sisters—the words had been easy to say, but how hard it was to actually do it. Because I knew that in order to save Evie, some sacrifice would be asked of me.

Now I had to make the hardest decision of my life. To go on, or to go back.

"Sarah?" Helen called softly. "Are we going? What are we waiting for?"

The sun was setting over the wild, wide land that I loved so much. I loved the wind on my face, and the high call of the birds, and the deep life and history of the ancient hills. The rocks that lay like bones underneath the heather and gorse spoke to me of power and strength and eternity. Was I really strong enough to give up all of this and never see it again?

And Cal—if I didn't return from the caves, he would never know how I felt. Never know that I was weak enough to be stupidly angry and then regret it. Weak enough to need him. Weak enough to fall in love.

But I had made a promise, and that promise couldn't be broken.

The sun had almost gone. Night began to spread over the moors. Out there, in the land that I loved, Evie was lost. That was the only thing that mattered.

I had made my choice. I would leave everything that was dear to me and enter the underground world, for her sake. I would not turn back. I would walk into the valley that was called Death.

"I'm ready," I said to Helen. "Let's go to the White Tor."

"But you're not going alone," said a gruff voice. It was Cal, standing in the center of the circle, his hands clenched by his sides. Josh was next to him, holding the halters of their horses.

"Cal," I said, amazed. "I thought you were leaving."

"I changed my mind."

"But how did you find me? How did you know I would be here?"

Helen walked over to me, her eyes shining. "I did it," she said. "I told Josh that we needed them both."

"You shouldn't have said anything." I felt embarrassed and confused. "I can manage on my own."

"It's not weakness to need someone, or to love them. Josh loves Evie. You love Cal," said Helen simply. "Love makes you stronger. What was the real secret of Agnes's great power? Her love for Sebastian, that was all. And we will need all our powers on this night. This is the beginning of our battles, not the end."

I was scarlet in the face and I could hardly look at Cal. "I'm so—so sorry about that stupid quarrel," I stammered.

"It's hard for me to say I'm sorry," he replied, looking down and scuffing the ground with his foot. "But I am. You don't know how sorry. I thought I had lost you, and it was killing me."

"I hated quarreling too."

Cal stepped closer to me and said in a low voice, "Sarah, I have to tell you something. The real reason I came back to Wyldcliffe."

"Why? Cal—what's wrong?"

He looked straight at me. "I'm in love with you," he said. "I'm in love with Sarah Venetia Rosamund Fitzalan. So you're stuck with me now, if you'll have me."

I didn't say anything. I had no words for that moment. We kissed, and with that kiss we sealed something between us forever, that no quarrels or misunderstandings would ever undo. It was hard and real and eternal, like a stone in my pocket.

"Let's go, Sarah," said Helen. "It's time."

Then we mounted our horses and rode like four avenging angels across the darkening valley. We rode as close to the edges of the peat bogs as we dared before veering away and up again to the higher ground that led to the Tor and the caves. As soon as we came under the shadow of the great crops of limestone, we slipped off our horses and tethered them to a straggling thorn tree.

"Don't worry," whispered Cal, seeing me glance at them anxiously. "I'll come back for them later, whatever happens. I promise."

I smiled fleetingly at him, touched by his concern, then looked around to examine the place we had arrived at. It was the first time I had been to White Tor, but I recognized the biggest cave mouth from pictures I had seen of it. It was just as Maria had described in her journal. I silently sent her a message of thanks.

Josh led us into the cave, eager to get closer to Evie at last. He had explored some of the cave systems in Wyldcliffe before and knew some of their physical dangers—airless tunnels and deadly crevices as well as the constant threat of rockfalls or underground flooding. But there was nothing Josh could do to guard us against the evil spirits that inhabited those hidden places. We simply had to trust one another and walk blindly into the dark.

Josh went ahead, and we followed him down the first tunnel. Soon we reached the place that Maria had mentioned—a wide flat area like a small chamber of rock. This had been blocked off on her journey and Sebastian had used his powers to open the way to the underground kingdom on the other side. But we had no need to do the same. A doorway had already been opened in the rock wall, a perfect arch with smooth, polished edges. Runes and spells were carved around it, grotesque signs with unknown meanings. I didn't like this open, welcoming door. It was too much like walking into a trap.

We crossed its threshold all the same—we had no choice. Cal squeezed my hand briefly as we went in single file into a new tunnel that was much narrower and lower than the first. Our flashlights created huge unexpected shadows on the walls as we moved forward.

Ahead of me I could see that Josh was stooping down, and behind him Helen was also walking along with bowed head and stiff arms. I guessed that she, who belonged to the air and the light, was suffering most in this narrow space. At least I was with Cal. Even here I felt warmed by his love. He had come back to find me, to swallow his pride and start again, and he was taking this journey for the sake of me and my friends. Wherever he was, I was at home. How could Helen keep enduring her loneliness? I wondered. But when she did find love, I knew it would be deeper than most people could only dream about. *A love beyond the confines of the world*, hadn't Miss Scratton promised? I wondered what she had meant and when this would happen for Helen; then I remembered that Miss Scratton had told so many lies and that maybe this had been just one more.

"Wait!" Josh whispered. "We've reached the end of the tunnel—be careful."

We emerged one by one into the cavern where Maria had been nearly a hundred years before. The beam of my flashlight wasn't powerful enough to reveal the whole of the vast cave, but I caught glimpses of high rock formations and clusters of crystal and shining yellow stalactites. The air was very cold and the underground lake gleamed black, as slick as oil. I couldn't make out the far shore, which was lost in shadow. Water dripped unseen, like a dull heartbeat. Now all my terrors came back to me, and I dreaded to feel the clutching hands of the Kinsfolk dragging me away at any second.

Torches sprang into life as though lit by an unseen hand. They were stuck into niches in the rocky walls and spread their light over the sides of the cave. But the lake—there was something evil by the lake. A low stone trough full of water stood at its edge. It was a crudely carved coffin.

"No—no—no!" Helen moaned. Then I saw it too.

Evie was lying in the stone coffin, under the surface of the water. Her lips were slightly parted and her eyes were closed. Her skin was white as swansdown and there was no life in her at all. So it was true. My vision had been right. Evie was dead and our quest was useless. The whole world seemed to shudder to a halt, and I sensed my grief like a rock in the distance ready to crush me, but for the moment I was numb, holding off the pain.

Josh stumbled forward with a desperate cry. He plunged his arms into the stone trough and lifted Evie's body from the water. His face was frozen in agony as he sank to the ground, cradling her in his arms.

"Evie—come back, come back," Josh murmured, stroking her wet hair. "My darling, my love—" He seemed to be willing her back to life, but she hung limply in his embrace. Then he raised his eyes and looked around wildly as though searching for someone. "Agnes," he called. "If you can hear, help me now! Your spark of healing power—it lives in me—help me!"

Help me . . . help me . . . help me . . . The words echoed around the cavern. Josh touched Evie's face, as if in blessing; then he kissed her wet mouth.

"Look!" I gasped. Evie's eyes fluttered, and the breath shuddered through her body. She sat up and threw her arms around Josh's neck and the next moment we were all crowding round to embrace her, crazy with joy, laughing and crying and forgetting to be careful or afraid.

"And so you have come. Welcome." A thin, dry voice cut through our celebrations. I saw that in the middle of the lake there was a small island. A cloaked figure was standing there. I steeled myself for seeing the hateful thing that had once been Helen's mother, the deadly Priestess.

"Welcome," she repeated as she slowly turned to face us, letting her hood fall from her face. "I am the Priestess. You are the Priestess. We are the Priestess." But it wasn't Celia Hartle's spirit that was confronting us.

It was Laura.

Twenty-seven

Laura? But it can't be—"

I remembered Laura van Pallandt as pretty and spoiled and not very clever, always hanging about with her cousin Celeste and following her lead. She'd had thick, honey-colored hair and a wide-eyed, slightly startled expression, as though life was constantly taking her by surprise. *But she's dead*, I kept saying to myself. *Laura's dead, this can't be true. . . .* I forced myself to look at the apparition's gray face. Her eyes were bloodshot and her hair was the color of withered leaves, but it was the girl I had known, I was sure. "Laura!" I cried again.

She turned her blank red eyes to me. "Laura . . . Laura . . . ," she repeated monotonously. "Yes, that was my name. But that life has gone; I am no longer like you.

I serve the king of the Unconquered lords and his Priestess. I am the Priestess," she chanted. "We all belong to the Priestess. You belong to the Priestess."

"I don't," said Helen defiantly. "I don't belong to anyone." I had heard her say that once before in sadness, but now she sounded proud.

"You will all belong to me."

A new voice rang out. Laura sank down, fear and pain flashing over her face. Some force was pushing me to my knees, making me bow down to all that remained on earth of Celia Hartle, once the High Mistress of Wyldcliffe, leader of the coven of Dark Sisters and now the most faithful servant of the Unconquered lords. As she stepped out of the shadows, Cal fell next to me with a groan. Helen struggled; then her body bent and she too did unwilling homage to her mother. Evie collapsed to the ground, where Josh tried to shelter her in his arms.

Mrs. Hartle's face was shrunken like a skeleton, and she was shrouded in swirling mist. Dust and ash seemed to fall from her as she moved toward us, gliding over the water without sinking into its black depths. She flicked her wrist and a whip of dark fire lashed out. Cal and Josh were blown off their feet, and the next second they were chained to pillars of stone.

"So," she sneered, "you have brought your boyfriends? Helen, you surprise me, I didn't think you'd ever attract anyone. Especially someone so very charming." She stroked Josh's cheek with her bony hands, and he flinched at her touch. The next moment she had gagged both of the boys with another flick of her wrist. Cal and Josh writhed and struggled to get free, but they were helpless. I wanted to run to Cal, but I couldn't move from where the Priestess held us on our knees. I groped in my mind for an earth spell to shake the ground beneath our feet and break the stone they were chained to, but my thoughts were sucked away by Mrs. Hartle's poisonous presence.

"Leave them!" said Helen. "They are our friends. That's something you wouldn't understand."

"Let me tell you what I do understand," Mrs. Hartle said in a dangerously soft voice. "You have all rushed here to save your beloved *friend*, as I knew you would, but you have achieved nothing. You have done exactly as I planned, exactly as I wanted you to do. I've had you watched. I have been calling for you, Helen, looking for you in your dreams. I summoned you to Blackdown Ridge, the night you came back to the school. I wanted to give you a chance to give up your tiresome meddling in the mysteries, and join my great cause. But of course, you had to resist. You fled, and set yourselves up against me, all of you, even that simpering fool Agnes, the traitor, who cannot rest in her cursed grave."

"What is it you want?" I asked desperately. "Why did you take Evie? Why is Laura here?"

"So many questions!" she replied, amused. "The first one—so very interesting. The heart of all philosophy! What do I want? The great question of life. And yet why should I tell you?" Another dart of fire flashed from her, and I felt as though I had been struck on the face. "But then again—why not? It will be amusing to see you grovel before the heights of my ambition.

"I wanted to become immortal as Sebastian had promised," she began slowly as though remembering something from a long time ago. "You and your friend Evelyn Johnson prevented that from happening. Yes, you were clever. Clever or lucky—I wonder which?"

"We stopped you because we had right on our side," I said. "Evil never wins, not in the end."

"No one ever wins in the end, not in this world, because death takes everything away, even from the victors. When Sebastian failed me, I had to seek another way of evading death's grip, and I found it. My master is the greatest of the Unconquered lords, he is their Eternal King, and I am his Priestess. By serving him I will live forever in the shadows."

"Who wants to live in the shadows when they have known the light?" Helen said defiantly. "And even the Unconquered lords will not last forever. Time itself will be destroyed at the end of all things when a reckoning will be made. Then you'll have to pay for what you've done. The Great Creator sees everything."

The smoke and mist around Mrs. Hartle's figure seemed to shudder for an instant as she wavered in doubt. Then she laughed. "I hope you'll be there to see that moment with me—if it should ever happen, which I doubt. Your gods are silent and spent. Only power is real."

"Power is real," Laura echoed in the background. "The Priestess will triumph."

"How does Laura come into this?" Helen asked, keeping her eyes fixed on her mother's face. "What have you done to her?"

"Why do you ask, my daughter? You were there the night that the coven sucked Laura's soul, harvesting her strength and energy to feed Sebastian and keep our hopes alive."

"Only because you made me!" Helen cried. The guilt and anguish that she felt was plain to see, and I realized what a burden Laura's death had been for Helen to carry.

"You could have refused to be at our ceremony," said Mrs. Hartle. "Yes, Helen, you are just as responsible for Laura's death as the rest of my Dark Sisters, simply by your presence. You saw me drink too deep of her youth, and she died. But her soul could not pass. It had been forced from her body by our mysteries and was under my command, so when her body died she remained trapped between this world and the next. And when the girl Velvet made her mockery of a spell on the ancient altar, she released not only the bonds you had tried to lay on me, but Laura's spirit. In her last living moments I owned Laura's soul, and so she now exists under my command."

"Didn't choose . . . had to . . . join the Priestess . . . ," Laura intoned.

"Let her go!" I shouted. "Stop tormenting her—and Helen too. Let them both go."

She laughed at me. "Let them go? You will all join me, willingly or not. Those who resist will be overcome and yoked to me as Bondsouls. Laura is my first Bondsoul, and there will be many, many more. Through them my power will swell, like a spider spawning her brood, and my master will be pleased. We will have an army of them, and Wyldcliffe will be destroyed." Mrs. Hartle looked coaxingly at Helen. "But if you come to me willingly, Helen, like my Sisters in the coven, yours will be a different destiny. You could be the chief of my handmaidens and share my glory."

"Nothing on earth would make me join you," Helen said.

"Except the one thing you really desire," Mrs. Hartle replied, her voice soft and low. "A mother's love. Come to me and I promise I will love you through all eternity." Her face changed, and she grew young and beautiful. She held her arms open tenderly. I looked at Helen in alarm. Would she be able to resist this offer of the only thing she had always wanted?

Helen gasped. "Cruel! You're so cruel! Don't pretend you can love me. No one can. No one!"

"I have always loved you, my child, though destiny drove us apart," Mrs. Hartle whispered, and for a moment I believed her. But as Mrs. Hartle reached out for Helen I saw the wild glint in her eye that betrayed her grasping desire for Helen's powers. "We can start again, daughter," she murmured. "Come to me."

Helen stumbled to her feet and walked toward her mother as though hypnotized.

"No, Helen, it's all lies, don't listen to her," cried Evie, but Helen ignored her.

"I do love you!" she sobbed, as she stood face-to-face with Mrs. Hartle. "I've loved you all my life! I'd do anything for you."

I felt crushed. We would all be lost if Helen turned her back on us and joined her mother, and Helen would only be hurt, again and again and again. We couldn't let it happen. Cal and Josh writhed to get free of their bonds, and Evie looked on in fear as Helen wept. I tried to connect with the Talisman that still hung around my neck, hidden under my clothes. *Let Helen see the truth, Agnes*, I begged silently. *Let her know that we love her for herself, not her powers. Don't let her be deceived. . . .*

"At last, my child," Mrs. Hartle said. "At last you have learned wisdom."

"I—have learned—that I can't be like you," Helen replied with a great effort. "I've loved you and hated you, and now I have learned to live without your love. Here— you gave me this, but it has only brought me trouble. Take it back and forget that you ever had a daughter." She unfastened the wing-shaped brooch from where it was pinned to her shirt and offered it to Mrs. Hartle. "Let this be the end between us."

Mrs. Hartle stared in surprise at the gleaming token

in Helen's hand, and a strange expression passed over her face. A struggle seemed to be going on inside her, as if she had one last chance to choose good instead of evil, truth instead of lies.

"So you have found the Seal," she said in a whisper. "The one good thing I ever gave you. Hide it, before—" Then she broke off, and her expression changed. "I have no time for this. Will you join me or not? This is the last time I will ask you to join me of your own free will."

"I have already made my choice," Helen said at last, as though every word caused her pain. She looked at us, then back at her mother. "I choose to be loyal to my friends. I choose my freedom—to say no to you." My heart was breaking for her. She looked so fragile and defenseless, yet she was being so brave.

"You have chosen defeat! You have chosen despair!" Mrs. Hartle's anger blew away the illusion of her appearance, and she was once again a haggard wraith. "So be it. From this moment you are nothing to me."

"And you are nothing to me," said Helen, her face set like a stone. "We will never serve you, and you will never be free of your own wretched choice! We have nothing more to say to each other. Now stand aside and let us go!"

"Do you think you can dismiss me and come and go as

you please?" Mrs. Hartle shrieked. "How dare you!" She flung her daughter away from her, and Helen fell back to the ground next to me. Then the Priestess laughed, mad and terrible and frightening. "I won't allow any of you to escape, not even through death's gateway. You will stay here, in the hidden places of the earth, and all your powers will serve me!"

She seemed to pace up and down between us, weighing up our strengths and weaknesses, seeing into every secret of our hearts. "Welcome, sister," Mrs. Hartle said to Evie. "You bring me gifts of fire and water. It will be sweet to have your powers and those of your precious Agnes as my own, a fine revenge on you for allowing Sebastian to evade me. But you won't be so lucky, I promise. There is no one left to rescue you.

"Helen, you bring me new pure secrets of the air, first and greatest of all the elements, the breath of life, the essence of creation. And even you, little earth woman," she added, sneering at me. "Even you bring your muddy strength to my altar. When I return with my Sisters, we will drain your souls and your powers. You will be like Laura, bound forever to your mistress. Until then, I have other servants to guard you. They awoke with Laura, and I have gathered them to me in the shadows, as all things shall come to me in the end."

The lights dimmed. She glided back over the water to the island in the middle of the lake, and her darkness seemed to engulf poor wretched Laura, who vanished from our sight.

"Awake, creatures of the endless night!" Mrs. Hartle called. "Stand over my prey."

Crawling from the farthest shadows, a horde of misshapen creatures emerged. Their heads lolled over their squat bodies, and they wore iron chains at their necks and wrists. They had leathery skin like mummified corpses. Evie hid her face from them as they surrounded us, but I knew what we faced and I made myself look at this new enemy.

The Kinsfolk. The ancient, crawling creatures that had attacked Maria.

They came closer, smelling of death. Some carried spears tipped with bronze, others had crude clubs and drums and leather pouches slung over their shoulders. I felt sick as they came near and the leader pointed his spear toward Evie.

"The girl is ours," he seemed to say. His twisted mouth barely moved, but I could understand his thoughts. "She was lying in the stone bed, asleep in the water. You promised her to us as a new queen for the Kinsfolk."

"Fool! I am your queen now," said Mrs. Hartle. "I stirred your wills and minds with the promise of the girl, but your task is to keep her prisoner until I am ready to deal with her, not enjoy her yourselves. Guard the others too."

"Promise-breaker!" he grunted. The rest of the Kinsfolk took up his words and beat their spears on the ground. "Promise-breaker! We curse you, Spirit Woman! Curse you! Curse you forever!"

"Silence! The girl is mine!" Mrs. Hartle raised her hand and cracked a whip of fire at one of the Kinsfolk. He began to burn like a dry torch, screaming in agony and flinging himself into the lake to put out the flames. There was silence. Perhaps it was only then that I truly believed that Mrs. Hartle was capable of killing us all.

"The girl is mine," she repeated coldly. "They are all mine, as you are. Guard them until I return, or your service to me will be more painful than you can imagine. The males you can kill. Be satisfied with that."

There was another murmur of discontent, but the leader bowed stiffly to Mrs. Hartle. "The Spirit Woman has spoken," he said. "The Kinsfolk hear your words."

"Then do your work well!" She shrouded herself in

mist and faded from sight, and the cloud of her presence was lifted. The chains that held Josh and Cal dissolved into smoke, and we were released from our humiliating kneeling position. We all clung to one another as Mrs. Hartle's grotesque servants moved in closer, like merciless hunters.

There was no way out past their savage weapons. There was no way out at all.

Twenty-eight

The Kinsfolk swarmed forward with inhuman speed and strength, and the next moment they had overpowered Josh and Cal, holding them down with sharp flint knives pressed against their throats. Then the leader raised his arm to hurl his spear into Cal's heart, as his people chanted, "Death! Death! Death!"

"No!" I screamed, and threw myself blindly at the leader's feet. "Stop! You mustn't do this, please, I beg you."

The creature paused and turned the black slits of his eyes on me. "It is a blood payment for the Kinsfolk warriors. It is our right. The Spirit Woman gave these men to us."

"I'll give you something better if you spare their lives," I said wildly.

"What?" he demanded. "What will you give?"

"I—I'll be your queen," I stammered. Images flashed into my mind, of Maria sobbing, and long hands grasping for me in a glare of red smoke. I heard the drums, I felt the stab of the knife, and I thought I was going to be sick. Terror pulsed through my whole body, but I couldn't turn back now. I had led my friends into this, and I had to help them. Fumbling in my bag, I dug out the bronze circlet. "Here, this is yours. Take it and take me. But you must release my friends."

The creatures gibbered with excitement at the sight of the coronet, but Cal groaned, "Sarah, you can't. I won't let you!"

"They'll kill you if I don't! What choice do we have?"

"We are all free to make our choices," said Helen, as though seeing a vision. "Sarah has chosen a hard path. But we can't stop her. None of us can. It is her time. It was written—S for Sarah."

Evie looked white and unhappy, but she whispered, "I believe in you, Sarah. I trust you to make the right choice."

"Accept my offering," I implored the leader, handing him the circlet. "And let my friends go free before the Priestess returns."

"You will do this for the Kinsfolk?" he asked. "To save your own people?"

"Yes," I replied. "I promise. And I never break my promises."

"You bring the lost crown back to the Kinsfolk," the creature said with a low bow. "We will defy the Spirit Woman and release the others. But you must stay in the earth kingdom with the Kinsfolk, and wear their crown. This is your promise? Agreed?"

"Agreed," I said. "But you must let my friends go quickly so they will be safe."

"The Kinsfolk will show them the secret path. It leads from the earth kingdom to the stone circle in the sky world."

"I can't leave you here, Sarah," Cal said in anguish.

"You have to! The whole point is for you to get out. When Mrs. Hartle comes back, she'll kill you and Josh and make Evie and Helen her slaves—and me. I have to do this. At least it gives the rest of you a chance. Go! Just go!"

"Sarah's right," said Josh reluctantly. "She's our only hope now. We have to do as she says."

I hugged them one by one, and finally Cal.

"You've given me so much," I whispered. "Enough for all eternity." His eyes met mine, and I understood everything. Cal was the one who knew me, right the way

317

through. The one I had no secrets from. The one who loved me. Not for being good or strong, but just for being me, all of me, good and bad. And now I had to keep my promise. I had to let him go.

"I love you," I whispered. "This isn't the end for us."

"It can't be," Cal said. "I won't let it be the end. I'll wait for you at the standing stones—I'll be there for you—when you get through this—" His voice broke and he couldn't speak.

"I'll get through it," I said. "Wait for me." I smiled, then turned from him to hide my tears. Josh gently pulled Cal away, and there was nothing more to say.

It was time.

I was ready.

"You must take the secret path," said the wizened leader to Josh. "My folk will guide you." Two other tough-skinned creatures, bent and wiry, led the way with torches in their hands. They pulled on one of the stalactites, and with a great rumbling an entrance opened up in the cave wall. This was the way back to the light, but only for Josh, Helen, Evie, and Cal—they were all leaving me behind.

I didn't watch them go. I closed my eyes until the sound of their footsteps had been swallowed up. And then I was alone in the deep places of the earth, and I had to fulfill my vow.

The rest of the creatures dragged me to the far side of the cavern. A huge pillar of rock spread out in fantastic shapes like a tree of stone. Simple red lamps hung from its branches. The leader lit the lamps with a torch and they began to smoke. A heavy, drowsy smell filled the air. And then it began. The drums. The chanting. The long cold hands reaching for me, tearing at my clothes and tugging at my hair. Maria had known this and been terrified. Sebastian had rescued her, but I had to bear it. Then the leader's fingers brushed against the Talisman, which was still hanging around my neck, and he sprang back. "Aaeee! The girl wears a stone of power! She has great magic!"

Their drumming and singing became even wilder until the music echoed through the cave. One of the Kinsfolk took a long, coarse piece of cloth from his bag and tied it around my shoulders like a robe. Then they bound me to the tree of stone and began to whet their knives and sharpen their spears. Every instinct made me want to scream, but the heavy smoke crept into my mind, whispering of ancient stories and deadening my terror.

Listen to the drums.

Until now, I had listened to those drums with my head,

not with my heart. I had heard only what I thought I would hear—fear and savagery and the dreadful unknown. But now, at last, in that deep place under the sacred earth, I listened with my secret soul. I listened, and on the other side of my fear, I finally understood. The drums were a call to life, and a lament for the Kinsfolk's long servitude, not a war cry. They were beating in rhythm with my own heart, and I understood that another fate was unfolding in this secret cavern, not simply my own.

"Who are you?" I asked. "Where have you come from?"

"I am Kundar," the leader said. He touched his scarred chest. "I am the head man. We are earth people. Slaves. The new queen will set us free." He reached into his pouch. It was full of red powder like ground clay. He spat on his fingers and made a stiff paste with it, then drew a shape like an eye on my forehead. "See with Kundar's eyes. See like the Kinsfolk."

The smoke and torches and the cavern vanished and I was standing on Blackdown Ridge. The farms and homes of Wyldcliffe were no longer there. The towers and gables of the Abbey didn't exist. The only landmark that was familiar was the ring of standing stones. Down in the valley below, I saw some wooden huts thatched with straw. Riding across the land was a group of men; short and stocky but strong and free, galloping on their shaggy hill ponies and shaking their bronze spears in the sunlight. Their hair was dark, tinged with red. As they came closer I could see that some of them were wearing intricate neck-laces and armbands, and their clothes were made of skins and woolen cloth. Women and children rode clinging behind them and young men ran barefoot alongside the riders, almost as swiftly as the horses.

When they reached the stones, the riders dismounted and the whole tribe stood in a circle. They carried green branches, which they waved in the air as they sang and chanted. Then a young girl, of maybe fourteen years old, was picked out from the crowd. A cry of excitement went up. The people threw the branches to the ground. The girl stepped forward, looking pale and frightened, but proud. A fine metal circlet was placed on her head. "Down into death!" they cried. "The new queen goes down into death! She brings back life for all!"

Then the picture changed with a swirl of color. Now I saw the people sitting together, sharing a meal around a fire outside their huts. A woman was milking a goat. Chil-dren played and tumbled in the grass. The next moment the place was filled with screams as yellow-haired men on horseback galloped through the village, scattering the food and slaughtering the men, who had been caught unawares. They snatched the women and children, hauling them away and throwing them over the backs of their horses. Sounds of lamentation filled the air.

The last picture showed a band of the men who had been defeated by the invading tribe. They were roped together and wore chains around their wrists and necks. Dead bodies were heaped up at the edge of the peat bog on the moors. The victorious tribesmen threw the corpses into the black mud, where they sank slowly into the marsh. Then the living prisoners were also thrown into the bog, weighed down by their chains, sinking, slowly suffocating, swallowed up by the earth.

"No . . . ," I protested, coming back from the vision. "It's too cruel, I don't want to see any more. . . ."

"It is a true sight. These things happened. We were cursed by the men who killed us and took our women. We could not die and pass to the land of fathers. So we slept in the earth and changed to bog men, caught between this world and the next. Every hundred winters we wake for a little time, and dwell in the caves of the earth kingdom. We feel pain and shame. We look for the new queen, but we do not find her. But now the Spirit Woman has bound us with fire and magic. She makes us slaves."

"She wants to make all of us her slaves," I said.

"She is an evil spirit. Not like our queen. Only the queen brings life to the Kinsfolk."

"How?" I asked, my heart racing. "What do you want me to do?"

"The queen goes down into Death. She finds the living Tree that never dies. She comes back with a gift from the Tree. It is a sign that the Kinsfolk are safe, for many winters. Then the queen is safe too."

"And what if she doesn't—doesn't find the Tree?"

"Then she is not the real queen," Kundar replied simply. "She stays in the earth with Death."

Now I knew the truth about the Kinsfolk, and this truth would either lead me to triumph, or to destruction.

Kundar raised his hands high over my head, holding the bronze circlet. I looked up at it, and it seemed to me that even in that lightless cave the sun shone through the leaves. *Mother Earth, help me*, I begged silently. *Great Creator, protect me.*

I looked at Kundar's strange, deformed face, which somehow still had an air of tired dignity. His eyes were black and brilliant in the torchlight. The drums began. His face changed to a grinning mask. But his eyes were full of love. They were the eyes of an untamed boy with a proud, deep heart, someone who knew me, good and bad. . . .

"I'm ready," I whispered. "I'm ready."

Kundar placed the circlet on my head, and the creatures of the Kinsfolk rushed forward to strike with their polished stone blades. Pain stabbed though me, such pain—

I fell.

I was falling, falling like a leaf in the wind.

I was in a deep trench that had been dug in the ground, lying on my back. I opened my eyes. Far away, stars glittered overhead. I saw Cal in the stars, then my mother's face, then the shape of a white swan. Pain was pinning me down. I was bleeding. My life was pouring away into the wet earth. Someone came to stand at the edge of my grave. It was Kundar. He threw a handful of dust onto me and said sorrowfully, "Down into Death."

Then I saw Evie, looking down at me sadly. "For your long voyage," she said, as she threw a handful of earth into the tomb. The stars turned again. Helen took Evie's place. "For the way ahead," she said, and she threw in a faded garland of flowers. Then the earth began to crumble from the sides of the grave, filling up the space as rapidly as water floods a stricken boat. I was drowning in the earth,

I couldn't breathe, there was dust in my mouth and death in my lungs. *The Tree*, I thought faintly. *I never found the Tree*. Then panic engulfed my mind as the black earth smothered me, and every light and sense and sound was extinguished forever.

Twenty-nine

Into the earth you went, my sister,
Into the earth you sank.
The stones were calling you,
The hills held your heart.
Into the earth you went.

Fear crushed you, stole your breath.
Earth held you like a lover.
Who will see with your eyes now?
Who will comfort those you left?
Into the earth you went.

The grass grows, the river swells,
But the birds are silent.

White swan, leaving us.
You have gone, my sister.
Into the earth you went.

Into the grave you went,
Down into death's arms.
When will I see you again?
A white swan flies across the moon,
And is silent.

It was Helen's voice, waking me from a long sleep. I opened my eyes. I was in a forest, surrounded by tall, slim trees. Bluebells shimmered like a violet mist in the distance. White flowers dotted the rich grass. I was wearing a long green gown, embroidered all over with flowers and fruits and intertwining leaves. The bronze circlet was on my head, and there were roses in my hair. A silver charm hung from my neck. I had seen it before; twisted silver strands clasping a bright crystal. Of course, I remembered. It was the Talisman. I remembered everything.

"Use it well," Evie said. "It is your time."

I spun around to find her, but she wasn't there. I was alone in that hushed, secret place. All the colors seemed more brilliant than I had ever known, as though blue and yellow and green had only just been thought of at that moment. The air was so pure that it made my head sing. Here everything could grow, and be renewed, and find peace.

A white peacock stepped slowly across the grass. I followed it and we soon left the forest behind. The land rolled away into a lush valley, with ripe corn growing in fields as golden as the sun. Scarlet poppies brushed against my ankles as I walked through the fields to a wide, glittering lake.

In the middle of the lake, on a grassy mound, a huge tree was growing. It was like the tree of stone that I had seen, but this was alive. It was the living Tree. Its bark was golden and its leaves were every color from pale green to deepest red. As I stood and gazed at it, I heard the rustle of new leaves unfurling, and felt the swell of its fruit growing. This was the root of all trees on earth.

The peacock wandered idly by the banks of the lake, pecking in the grass for seeds. I didn't know how I could cross the water to reach the Tree. It was deep and clear, too far for me to swim. If only Evie were here, I thought, then I remembered her words. *Use it well.* I unfastened the Talisman and trailed it across the water. "Please let me pass," I said. "I am a child of the earth. I mean no harm."

A spray of ivy at the water's edge began to stretch and grow, curling itself around like twisted wire, spreading out across the water to make a swaying green bridge. I ran across it to where the Tree was growing and breathing and living.

"Welcome, little sister," said a voice, though I couldn't see who had spoken. "You have great courage. This is your reward."

A single leaf twirled down from one of the upper branches, hovering on the air, until it rested on the palm of my hand. "Go," said the voice, "and be a queen."

The next second I was slammed back into the darkness. A mildewed grave cloth covered my face and there was a weight on my eyes. For a moment I panicked. Had the Kinsfolk tricked me? Was there no way back? Making a great effort, I moved the hand that still clutched the precious leaf, then I heard voices.

"She moves . . . she wakes. . . ." I felt hands pulling me upward and tugging the cloth from my face, and then I was back in the cavern. The ropes that had bound me were lying in shreds on the ground, and I was standing in a circle of the Kinsfolk. I was still dressed in green, and in my hand was a delicate leaf, fashioned out of bronze. It was the gift from the everlasting Tree. I had done what I had promised.

"Here is your sign," I said shakily. "Another piece for your crown."

"She brings a gift! She is the true queen!" Kundar took the bronze leaf and twisted it into the circlet on my head. Then the Kinsfolk swarmed around me, touching my robe and crown and feet and hands. And as they touched me they stood up straight and broad, their chains and collars falling from them. They were no longer hunched and wizened but were the men I had seen through Kundar's eyes, Wyldcliffe's original inhabitants hundreds or thousands of years ago, before they were murdered and cursed. They had dark eyes and red hair, and were crowned with garlands of oak leaves and ears of corn. "You bring life. You free the Kinsfolk. The queen has come!"

Kundar looked at me with eager, glinting eyes. "Now we will sleep well. Now, when the earth ends, when time is finished, and all come back from Death, our womenfolk will know us. Speak your wish. The Kinsfolk serve you."

There was only one thing that I wished for. "I want to see my friends. I must go to them."

Kundar bowed. "You are the earth queen, but you live in the sky world too. We will take you to them, then sleep again until you call."

"If you ever need me, I will come back," I said.

"That is your promise?"

"Yes. I promise."

He made a funny clicking sound as though he were laughing. "Come," he said. "Now we will go to the stone circle." As Kundar turned to lead the way, I could only hope that I would find my friends there, waiting for me.

I pushed past a tangle of brambles and ferns and stepped out of a hidden cave mouth into the night air. We had reached the end of the secret underground tunnel that led from the cavern to the foot of Blackdown Ridge. The wind was fresh and the sky was black, dusted with stars. Was it really the same night that we had entered the caverns under the White Tor? It seemed that I had lived a whole life since then. Kundar came and stood next to me, while the rest of the Kinsfolk folk hung back in the shadows.

"We are in the sky world now." He looked up at the stars. "The stars have changed. All things change."

"I shan't change," I said. "Stay here please, Kundar. I'm going to walk up to the Ridge. I might need you."

I made my way up the rough slope as quickly as I could in my long gown. The sound of low voices carried on the night air, and soon I saw Cal and Josh, Helen and Evie sitting on the ground. They were overshadowed by the megaliths and talking softly. I suddenly felt shy and not sure what to say, and pulled the circlet from my head. But Helen saw me and jumped up. "I knew you'd come back." She smiled and kissed me. "I knew you'd make it."

"Thank God!" Evie rushed to hug me. "Oh, Sarah, I'm so sorry for everything. If I hadn't been stupid enough to be fooled by Mrs. Hartle's lies and deceptions, I would never have caused you all this trouble. I should have known that it couldn't be Sebastian waiting for me by the gates. I just wanted to believe that miracles might happen."

"Miracles do happen," I replied. "Just not how we expect them to. It was Sebastian—or a vision of him—who told us where to find you. But it was Josh who called you back to life."

"I know." Evie glanced at Josh with wonder in her eyes, before turning back to me. "When I was asleep in that stone coffin, it was as though I was drowning in dreams. I seemed to see Sebastian again, as clearly as when he had been alive. But he was different, so gentle. He told me that he had been permitted to reach out to help me just once because I was in mortal danger, and that now my sisters were searching for me, and someone else too, who—well, someone who loved me as I deserved to be loved. He smiled at me and his whole face was full of light—just light and beauty—and then he was gone. And I knew that I wasn't ready to follow him yet, not even into all that beauty. I wanted to come back to the world. Then I heard Josh calling me. Oh, Sarah," she whispered. "I know now that Sebastian has left this world forever. I mean really know in my heart, not just my head. He won't come back again. There's a time for everything, isn't there? A time to grieve, and a time to heal. And I've been given a second chance, and I'm so grateful for everything. . . ." I hugged her tightly. We had all learned so much about ourselves and one another in these past weeks and days. "Thank you so much," Evie said as she let me go. "Thank you for what you did for all of us."

"And thank you for this." I gave the Talisman back to her, then I hugged Josh too. "I couldn't have saved Evie without you," I said. "Helen was right. We're all in this together now."

Finally I stood before Cal.

"Sarah—oh, Sarah," he said hoarsely, staring at my strange robes. "What have they done to you?"

"It's fine, I'm okay—"

"I thought I was going to go mad, sitting here waiting for you. I wanted to go back down to the caves, but the others stopped me. I couldn't bear you to face that alone."

"I wasn't alone," I said. "I was with the Kinsfolk. They are my people now."

Cal took the bronze circlet from my hand and placed it gently on my tangled curls. "And you're my queen," he said, kissing my forehead and drawing me to him. "Now and always."

"For all eternity," I whispered, and Cal sighed with relief.

"Come on," he said. "Let's get back to the school and away from here."

But at that moment there was a deafening rumble of thunder. A shape of thick mist formed in the air, and Mrs. Hartle appeared out of the gloom, wrapped in a fume of fog and bitter ash. The Priestess had returned.

"How very touching," she sneered. "How this love of yours makes you all so weak and sentimental. Fortunately, I am not troubled by your infirmity. So you escaped the caves and came to the stone circle. Very well, it makes no difference to me where I take your souls. Here is as good as anywhere else."

I couldn't understand how she had found us, but she seemed to read my thoughts.

"Laura stood guard unseen in the cavern and heard

your secrets," she went on. "She reported to me and told me of your plans to spoil my own. Oh, it was wrong, Sarah, very wrong to tempt my loyal servants away from me, little earth woman. What will I do with you as a punishment, I wonder?" Her voice drawled as she spoke, but I sensed the rage behind her words. Yet her anger gave me strength, as though it had lit a fire in me.

"You may be a priestess, but I am a queen now," I declared proudly. "I have been down into Death and returned with a gift from the living Tree. My people are waiting in the caves below. I don't take orders from you anymore."

"A queen! A queen!" she mocked, glaring at my crown and robe. "For a rabble of savages and a garland of tin?" She drew herself up to her full height. "This time I am not alone. This time my Sisters are with me. And this time there will be no escape."

Ranks of cloaked and hooded women were walking silently up the Ridge. They reached the sacred stones and stood in a menacing circle, blocking our way and waiting for instructions from their mistress. Mrs. Hartle raised her hand, and I knew what was coming—the flash of cold fire like a whip that would chain us again as prisoners.

"You first, child of mud!" she cried, and aimed her first

blow at me. But Evie threw herself in the way and held up the Talisman. It caught and broke the force of Mrs. Hartle's spell into a thousand droplets of light and blasted it back into her face. She screamed with shock and fury. "Take them! Take them and bind them."

The Dark Sisters drew long white knives from under their cloaks and came rushing toward us. But creeping behind them were the shapes of men, moving as stealthily as cats.

"Kundar!" I called. "Defend us now!"

The Kinsfolk took the coven by surprise, knocking their weapons from their hands and throwing them to the ground. Some of the women fought back, and there was a clash of metal and wood and the terrible screams of battle. The women tried to grab hold of us, as the Kinsfolk formed a protective circle, jabbing at them with their long spears. Then the Dark Sisters drove in heedlessly, throwing themselves wildly onto the spears in their frantic attacks. There was a confused mass of people fighting. I saw Helen knocked to the ground and Cal wielding a battle-ax that belonged to one of the Kinsfolk. Evie and I struggled to reach Helen, desperately plunging through the press of bodies toward her. Then the three of us clasped hands, murmuring protective incantations as we crouched together in the onslaught. But the fury of the coven was no match for the skill and cunning of Kundar's men, and the Dark Sisters began to lose heart as they were repelled again and again, wounded by the deadly spears.

Soon many of the women had turned and fled, despite Mrs. Hartle's frantic commands. Only about half a dozen of them remained, ready to fight to the death for their mistress. I thought I glimpsed Miss Dalrymple's face among them. Kundar and his men got ready to charge.

"Wait!" I called, scrambling to my feet. "Wait, Kundar! We don't want any more bloodshed." I turned to Mrs. Hartle. "We will never give in, but we don't want to fight, or hurt your followers. Stop this battle now—go back to your shadows and leave us in peace."

An uneasy silence fell. The Dark Sisters looked at their Priestess for guidance.

"Earth woman!" she spat. "Thing of mud and rocks and dust! You will not tell me what to do! I could crush you in one hand!" she screamed crazily. Then she flung her arms into the air and ground her teeth and muttered, "My master . . . great lord . . . send me your lightless power . . . send me your bitter ashes from beyond the grave. . . ."

The sky, which had begun to grow lighter, changed. The stars were blotted out. Thick, choking blackness filled the air, and I could hardly breathe. The Kinsfolk groaned and writhed on the ground, and all around me I heard the sounds of my friends gasping for air. Mrs. Hartle cried out in a terrible voice, "AS I WILL IT!" She pointed at us, and fiery sparks shot from her fingers. They turned into monstrous serpents that coiled themselves around us. Cal tried to reach for me, but my arms were pinned to my sides. I couldn't move. The breath was being squeezed from my lungs. I was going down into death once more. She would win, the Priestess would win and the light would be diminished. That couldn't happen, I wouldn't let it. . . .

Do not be afraid. For some reason I remembered Miss Scratton's words. *Do not be afraid of what you see. They are simply dreams and visions. Remember that, do not be afraid.*

And despite everything that had happened, I believed her. I still believed in Miss Scratton.

"They're not real!" I shouted. "They're just our fears! Don't be afraid, and she can't hurt us." Already I felt the serpents' coils slipping from me, and the darkness lifted. The next moment my eyes were dazzled by a light coming from the eastern side of the stone circle, and I thought confusedly that the morning had come and it was the sun. But a voice spoke to me out of the light. "Well remembered."

It was a voice I knew. I blinked and saw a woman in a gray robe sitting on a white horse. The light was coming from her.

"Miss—Miss Scratton?"

She laughed. "That is not my real name, Sarah. I hope to tell you what it is one day. But first there is work to be done."

Then the light dimmed, and Miss Scratton appeared as she always had looked, although there were shadows under her eyes. She rode forward into the circle of jagged stones, and the others saw her too. Mrs. Hartle let out a long hiss at the sight of her, and the snakes crumbled into smoke.

"You tried to hold me back from my task, Celia," Miss Scratton said pleasantly, as though greeting a colleague in the staff room, "though you could not keep me away for long. It was ingenious of you and your loyal followers, I admit, faking that car crash and capturing me, making it look as though I had deserted your daughter and her friends. But a faithful messenger was sent to them, one who knew what it was to love even beyond death, and so they found Evie. You must have thought that Evie would be the bait to lure Sarah and Helen into your trap, but together they were more powerful than you can ever be.

And as soon as even one of these girls called on me in her heart, I was able to return. I am their Guardian, and I will not let you harm their young hopes."

Mrs. Hartle didn't reply but blasted a spray of black fire at Miss Scratton, who repelled it with a word of Power. The remaining Dark Sisters yelled and launched a fresh attack on the Kinsfolk. Cal and Josh snatched up fallen clubs and knives from the ground and pressed forward into the battle, trying to keep the women away from us. For a moment I stood paralyzed, watching in horror. Mrs. Hartle and Miss Scratton were fighting in a fury of light and sparks and smoke. I wanted to help, but didn't know how; then I saw that Miss Scratton was edging her enemy all the time a little nearer to the tallest of the standing stones, the great pillar that pointed up to the heavens like a black finger. An idea flashed into my mind. I dodged one of the women who was lunging toward me and shouted, "Evie! Helen! The Circle! Make a Circle!"

Evie was still holding the Talisman. She thrust it toward me. "Here, take one side of the chain! Helen, you hold another." I saw what she was trying to do. We all laced our fingers into the chain so that it was held in a taut silver circle with the Talisman dangling from it.

"Mysteries of Earth and Air and Water, come to us now," I called. "Agnes, our sister, help us. Let no harm cross our Circle!"

"Let no harm fall!" the others echoed. "Help us now!"

The Talisman glinted in the faint starlight. Our Circle was complete. There were four of us. Four girls, all so different, but united in love and strength. Agnes smiled radiantly and said, "Do not be afraid!" We held fast to the Circle, and everything began to spin. Wind and rain and lightning crashed around us. I knew what I wanted to do. I reached inside for everything that gave me strength. My friends. The land. The deep earth. My crown of leaves. My Gypsy boy. I directed all that strength toward the great black megalith where Miss Scratton and Mrs. Hartle were still locked in a bitter conflict.

Listen to me, I urged silently, *stone and earth, bone and rock, open to my will. Let it be so. Let it be as I see it in my mind. Let the rock open.*

There was a thunderous noise as the earth tore apart, and the huge stone split in two. Mrs. Hartle screamed, staggering backward into the cleft in the rock. Her face was blotted out by the shadow of the two halves of the primeval stone, and although she struggled, she could not move away from that spot.

"Earth take her!" I cried. "Bind her now!"

My sisters took up the cry. "Bind her!" Then we chanted together: "Bind the wolf, bind the shadow, bind the lost spirit. . . ."

"Helen!" Mrs. Hartle shouted in desperation as she felt her victory slipping away and defeat edging closer. "Don't do this to me! Let me go!"

But Helen carried on chanting, although her eyes were filled with pain. "Bind the dark spirit, bind the murderer, bind the evil tongue. . . ."

"Traitor!" Mrs. Hartle snarled, and flung a last bolt of poisonous fire at her daughter. Helen deftly caught the smoldering firebrand in her hand and shouted, "I release this energy! Let it be as I will it!" The flames transformed into a white bird, which flew straight into the air and swooped away.

"How dare you—"

"I can and I dare!" Helen said. "You cannot hurt me anymore. My power has returned. Air and wind and spirit live in me! The breath of life! You cannot fight against that!"

Mrs. Hartle screamed as Helen raised her hand and summoned a hurricane blast that threw her mother deeper into the stone's cold heart.

"No!" she gasped. "I forbid you—I am the Priestess—"

"And I am a queen," I said. The air was filled with the sound of drums, and I welcomed their ancient, triumphant music. "I am a queen and I bind you in earth's kingdom." The two halves of the rock snapped shut like a trap, and Mrs. Hartle's screams were silenced, as though she had never been.

Thirty

It was finished.

The day was dawning, pale and silver, and the Dark Sisters had abandoned the fight. They pulled their hoods down over their eyes and tried to hide their faces from us, as the Kinsfolk rounded them up with their spears. Then Miss Scratton went to speak to the shivering women.

"Do you see now that your quest is hopeless? Celia Hartle is mortal, although she evades death, and every mortal being must face the Great Truth in the end, whether they hide from it or seek it. Don't pin your hopes for eternal life, or great power, or wisdom, on such a wretched being."

"She is our Priestess and Mistress still!" hissed one of them. I recognized Miss Dalrymple's mottled face under her robes. "Do not speak ill of her! She will return.

Nothing can keep her prisoner for long, not even death."

Miss Scratton sighed. "You are right, she will return one day. Only the Great Creator can remove her from this earth. But she will not trouble us for a while."

"We will wait for her."

"And then what? When she returns, you will fight for her again and you will lose again, and with every fight your spirits will grow more corrupt and bitter and the way back to the light will be harder for you. Don't do this to yourselves. Return to the life you have, the life you could enjoy."

But the women huddled together and chanted defiantly, "We are the Priestess. We are the Priestess. Long live the Priestess."

Miss Scratton bowed her head and sighed again. "I have tried, but you have chosen your path. There is nothing more we can do for you. We cannot force you to see as we see. We will not punish you, or kill you. That is not our way. Your punishment is the choice you have made." She nodded at Kundar. "Let them go."

He and his men stood aside to let the women shuffle away. Miss Scratton watched them pass, but as they did so, something bright flashed out in the pale morning sun. There was a cry and a sudden scuffle as Miss Dalrymple flung herself onto Miss Scratton and stabbed her in the side.

Evie screamed, and we all ran to Miss Scratton as she collapsed, her face twisting in pain. Miss Dalrymple darted away and the rest of the women ran helter-skelter after her down the hillside. Kundar and his men gave a great roar and set off in pursuit, but Miss Scratton waved for them to stop.

"Don't follow them—let them—let them go—" Her face was white, and every word seemed an effort.

"Kundar," I called. "Come back!" Reluctantly he and his people slowed down and shook their spears and jeered as the women disappeared from view. "The day is coming," I said. "You must go back to the cavern and sleep. You mustn't be seen, not now anyway."

"The Spirit Woman is dead?" asked Kundar.

"She is not dead, but she is a prisoner, for now."

"Your friend is hurt. Her life bleeds into the ground. We will avenge her."

"No!" gasped Miss Scratton. "I don't want revenge. Return to your caves. Do as your queen says."

Kundar touched his chest and his forehead and bowed to me. The others did the same. "Farewell, great queen. Your people will come if you call." They stole away like the shadow of a dream. I watched them go, then knelt next to Miss Scratton.

"We must get you back to the school and get a doctor—"

"There is no doctor who can cure me," she said. "My time has come." Then she smiled faintly. "You did well, Sarah. Maria did not encounter the Kinsfolk in vain. I knew when she came to me so many years ago that all things would one day connect." She winced in pain and murmured, "I am proud of all of you, and sorry to leave . . . there was so much I wanted to tell you—"

"But I thought you weren't like us," I protested. "I thought you could live always."

"My spirit . . . is eternal," she said. Her eyes seemed to grow dim, and she forced herself to speak. "But the body I inhabit on earth can be harmed, even killed. It has served me well and all through the long years I have walked in Wyldcliffe's valley, coming and going—from one generation to another. I have had many names, and been to many places, but Wyldcliffe is where I belong. But that time is over. All things come to an end, even death." She gasped in pain once more, and I couldn't stop myself from crying.

"I'll never forgive that woman," I said. "Never!"

"It is not Rowena's dagger that has brought this about.

Do not blame her. Remember—forgiveness is stronger than hatred. I knew I would not be allowed to stay. I just did not see the way it would end. When I am gone, it will be as though the car accident was real. Only you will know the truth." She coughed weakly, then struggled to sit up. Cal and I lifted her head and supported her in our arms. Evie was huddled close to Josh, but Helen stood apart, very pale and still.

Miss Scratton looked up at her. "Helen—I need to tell you—"

"Why were you working against me?" said Helen abruptly. "It was you all the time, wasn't it, holding me back?"

"I had to." Miss Scratton sighed. "It wasn't your time. I had to hold you back to protect you from your mother. She was calling you—and other powers too. We have fought over you—I had to make sure Celia Hartle didn't find you on the secret ways through the air—she was searching for you and could have trapped you there and captured you. She was once like you, and she knows those paths well. But she rejected the secrets—the secrets . . . of pure air . . . the light . . ." Miss Scratton's voice faded, and we strained to listen to her words. "It's you she really fears, Helen. In some part of her sad heart she still loves you, which makes her hate and fear and anger even more terrible."

"You're wrong about that. She never loved me. Her love has become corrupt. It fuels her hatred now. The Priestess will try to destroy you—the whole of Wyldcliffe, in order to tear the last trace of love from her soul."

"Helen—I'm so sorry, I should have done more for you." Miss Scratton beckoned Helen to come closer to her as her voice grew weaker. "I thought—I thought there would be more time. I didn't tell you the whole truth about the brooch. I didn't find it in the High Mistress's study, though the coven was searching for it there. I had it, all these years. I was there in the home—I was your nurse, I kept the token—your mother's seal. I kept it for you. Later I made sure that you could come to Wyldcliffe, and I watched over you. I found your father. But in all this I knew that you were unhappy. I would have liked . . . I would have liked you to have been my daughter." Miss Scratton coughed again, struggling to breathe, and tears poured down Helen's face. I let her take my place at our Guardian's side, and she buried her fair head against Miss Scratton's shoulder.

"This was Sarah's time," Miss Scratton whispered, clutching Helen's hand. "But someone is coming—your destiny is near—yours is the greatest gift of all. You have been marked with the sign—the sign of the great seal." She whispered something privately in Helen's ear, her voice slurred and indistinct; then she turned to the rest of us and tried to speak aloud.

"You are all part of an eternal dance, good and evil, day and night, hope and despair. They will try to destroy you—destroy Wyldcliffe. But the secret . . . the secret of the keys is coming . . . be ready . . . be ready when he comes . . . the dance . . . I will find you . . ."

Then her eyes closed, and she fell back against Cal. A light seemed to radiate from her. And then the life left her body and the light was extinguished. Helen turned away and hid her face as Evie wept, clinging to Josh. Everything felt so still, as though the world had stopped turning.

The sleeve of Miss Scratton's robe was crumpled awkwardly. I reached out to smooth it into place and noticed that there was a curious mark on her arm. It was a circle, cut across by a shape like a bird, or a pair of wings. Or even, perhaps, the crossed blades of two sharp daggers. The sign of the great seal. I pulled the sleeve down to cover it and said nothing. All explanations would have to wait. This was the time to mourn.

We waited until the sun had climbed into the pale, clear sky and then stood up. Enough tears had been shed, but our hearts were still heavy. As the light grew stronger, Miss Scratton's body dissolved into a golden mist. She was gone.

Slowly and reluctantly, we left the stone circle and started to make our way down the Ridge. A veiled figure crouching in the grass ahead of us stood up and began to run in the direction of the school.

"Who was that?" asked Evie.

"I don't know," said Cal, standing next to me protectively. "One of the coven women, I guess, eavesdropping. Anyway, she's gone. There's nothing we can do about her."

But I had seen those eyes. It hadn't been a Dark Sister spying on us. It had been something more unpredictable—a Touchstone. Velvet Romaine. I hadn't been expecting that. Not here. Not now.

"I hope it wasn't Miss Dalrymple," Evie said with a shudder.

"Don't worry," Helen said to Evie. "There are four of us, and only one of her."

"Four?" said Josh.

"Evie, Sarah, me, and Agnes, of course," replied Helen.

"Don't you mean six of us?" he said softly. "There's Cal, and me too." Josh turned to Evie. "That's if you still want us to stick around and be part of this. Do you want that?"

His eyes were asking her more than his words.

"I want you to stay, Josh," Evie replied. "You know I do."

He looked at her gratefully, and slipped his arm around her shoulders. They walked ahead of us down the hill as the sun shone golden and warm.

"'All shall be well, and all manner of things shall be well,'" Helen murmured. Then she looked up at me and Cal.

"Don't forget," she said. "Hang on to what's real, like a stone in your pocket."

"For all eternity," I answered, and she nodded and followed Evie and Josh down the slope, leaving me with Cal. I took one last glimpse at the circle of stones, stark against the bright morning sky. One day, I promised myself, I would know Miss Scratton's true name. And one day, I would see her again.

Thirty-one

"It's a shame about Miss Scratton," sighed Sophie. "I know she was really strict, but she was always fair, wasn't she? And she taught my mom when she was at Wyldcliffe, years ago. It's a real shame."

I glanced down at the headline of the newspaper that Sophie was holding. She appeared to have recovered from her upset over Helen's accident, and Velvet's dubious friendship. I had done what I could to be kind to Sophie in the past few troubling days since the news had broken of Miss Scratton's death after her "accident." Good old Sarah, looking after everyone, always looking out for the underdog.

No, that wasn't fair, or true anymore. I was kind to Sophie because I liked her, not because I felt I had to be some sort of mother hen to everybody. I had changed. I had learned that I didn't always have to be strong for everyone else. Sometimes, I could be strong just for me. Sometimes, I could lean on other people's strength, like a rose twining around a pillar and blossoming in the sun. It was my choice, my decision. I had learned so much, but even so, the scars of this term would take a long time to heal. Without Miss Scratton, Wyldcliffe was a far bleaker, more dangerous place.

"I said Miss Scratton was quite nice really, wasn't she? Honestly, Sarah," Sophie complained. "Aren't you listening at all?"

"What? Oh . . . um . . . no," I said. "She wasn't bad."

Sophie shook the paper importantly and started to read the article aloud.

"'*SCHOOL PRINCIPAL IN FATAL CRASH. The High Mistress of Wyldcliffe Abbey School for Young Ladies has been killed in a road accident involving the school minibus and a deer. The animal leaped out in front of the vehicle, causing it to swerve off the road. The students and the driver suffered only minor injuries. They had been visiting the exclusive boys' school St. Martin's Academy to arrange a social event.*'

"'*This is not the first setback for Wyldcliffe Abbey in the last few months. The previous High Mistress, Celia Hartle, was found* dead on the moors near the school. The coroner recorded an open verdict on Mrs. Hartle's death. The incident caused some parents to withdraw their daughters from the school, which attracts the country's wealthiest families. Recently appointed Miss Miriam Scratton—'" Sophie pulled a face. "I didn't know she was called that."

"That wasn't her real name," I said softly. "No one knew her real name."

"Whatever . . . 'Miss Miriam Scratton had announced a program of modernization at the highly traditional institution. A teacher at the school, who did not want to be named, said, "I hope her plans are still carried out. We needed her to bring the school into the modern age. It's a great loss." But others were not so happy with Miss Scratton's plans, and critics of her scheme will be secretly relieved that Wyldcliffe and its traditions may now remain untouched.'

"'Wyldcliffe Abbey has had a colorful history, with many legends, including the story of the ghost of Lady Agnes Templeton, who it is said will come back to Wyldcliffe one day to save it from great peril. . . .' Ooh, do you think that's true?"

"Don't be silly, Sophie," I said. "How can anyone possibly come back from the dead?"

"I suppose so. Oh, and look, it mentions Velvet. It says, 'Velvet Romaine is the newest student to join the school. . . .' And there's a photo of her—Sarah? Where are you going?"

I couldn't trust myself to stay and listen without giving myself away. My Wyldcliffe was different from Sophie's, and I didn't ever want her to know the truth. "Just remembered something," I said quickly. "I've got to go, see you later. . . ."

I walked out of the room and into the red corridor. It was Sunday afternoon, and the school had a sleepy air. Evie was out riding with Josh, and Helen had taken herself off to the library to write to her father. In a few minutes I would be heading down to the stables to meet Cal. And out on Blackdown Ridge, a bitter spirit was trapped in an ancient monument to the forgotten gods. Mrs. Hartle's wasted soul was gnawing away in captivity, fretting and plotting and waiting to return with her army of Bondsouls and destroy us all. But we had one another, and we had the memory of "Miriam Scratton," and we had hope. We would never lose that.

Two sulky-looking girls trailed down the corridor in tennis clothes, heading for the common room.

"It's so unfair," one of them was complaining. "I'm sorry for Miss Scratton and all that, but everyone's saying that we won't even get our dance now."

"And those St. Martin's boys are so *hot*. . . ."

They passed on. Disappointment about a canceled dance was the greatest tragedy they could imagine. They were on the other side of the glass, like all the other Wyldcliffe students, remote from me and my life. I needed to be alone, just for a little while.

Instead of heading the way that would lead me to the stables and to Cal, I walked to the very end of the crimson-lined passage to where the old ballroom was kept locked. Miss Scratton had intended to open it up at Christmas and allow some warmth and laughter into this gloomy, haunted house. I supposed the gossiping girls were right and that all her plans would now be squashed by Miss Dalrymple and the rest of them.

The entrance to the ballroom was screened by a moth-eaten silk drape. I pulled it to one side to reveal high double doors, carved all over with fruit and flowers. I placed my hands on the door and spoke silently to the trees they had come from, descendants of the one great Tree. I touched the lock and saw the metal as it had once been, a streak of ore in the deep earth. "Let me pass," I asked. The locks clicked and the doors swung open. I slipped inside, pulling the drape back over the doorway so that no one would know that I was trespassing there.

It was a cold, high, beautiful space, like a sleeping palace waiting to be brought back to life. The walls were lined with pale gray silk decorated with white rosettes, and silver framed mirrors reflected my image on every side until it disappeared into infinity. Long white blinds covered the French windows, and the chandeliers were swathed in protective dust sheets. I seemed to catch an echo of Miss Scratton's voice—*Ladies, we must let the light into Wyldcliffe.* I crossed the polished dance floor to the nearest window and opened the blind. The warm May sunshine poured in. Outside, the Abbey's gardens and the ruins and the lake lay innocent and quiet.

I loved this place, despite all its stupid snobberies. I loved its history, and its secrets, and the wild hills whose roots went so deep. But Wyldcliffe's secrets were dangerous, too. So many of us had been hurt. Laura was still hurting. The Priestess was still out there. Velvet was torn between friendship and enmity, wondering where she fitted into this strange tale. This wasn't over yet.

Do not be afraid.

For the moment, I had played my part. It had been my time. I had stepped into the spotlight and I hadn't failed after all. I had kept my promises.

I heard the sound of music and laughter, quick and bright and far away, like the voices of ghostly children.